For months she'd searched for h.... ....w that he was here, she didn't know what to do...

W9-BSN-187

For several seconds Nikki simply sat there, unable to believe she'd heard Michael's voice. Unwilling to turn around and perhaps discover a stranger.

"In very many ways I am a stranger," he said softly. "We had less than a week together."

His breath washed warmth across the back of her neck. She shivered and rubbed her arms. Why hadn't she felt him enter? Why did she feel nothing in the link between them but an odd sort of grey, when once it had been so full of color and emotion that she had feared its brightness? Now, of all times, when he was standing so close that the heat of his body caressed her skin, she should have felt the rainbow of his thoughts.

That she didn't scared the hell out of her.

"Nothing has happened to the link, Nikki. It is still there."

His soft tones wrapped around her, warm and yet somehow wary. She closed her eyes and took a deep, shuddering breath. Six months she'd waited to hear his voice. Six long months. Now he stood behind her, and she wasn't entirely sure what she should do or say.

"I used to know when you walked into the room, used to be able to feel you," she said softly. "Even before the link became strong between us."

"Many things have changed."

"And some things haven't." He was still talking in riddles, still not coming out with the entire truth. Last time it had led to death. She had a horrible feeling it just might again.

To Gabrielle, for her support and friendship.

OTHER BOOKS BY KERI ARTHUR

Dancing with the Devil
Circle of Fire
Circle of Death (Coming in 2002)

Hearts in Darkness

***

Keri Arthur

ImaJinn
Books

The sale of this book without its cover is unauthorized. If you purchased this book without a cover, you should be aware that it was reported to the publisher as "unsold and destroyed." Neither the author nor the publisher has received payment for the sale of this "stripped book."

HEARTS IN DARKNESS
Published by ImaJinn Books, a division of ImaJinn

Copyright ©2001 by Keri Arthur
Printed and bound in the United States of America. All rights reserved. No part of this book may be reproduced in any form or by any means (electronic, mechanical, photocopying, recording, or otherwise) without prior written permission of both the copyright holder and the above publisher of this book, except by a reviewer, who may quote brief passages in a review. For information, address: ImaJinn Books, a division of ImaJinn, P.O. Box 162, Hickory Corners, MI 49060-0162; or call toll free 1-877-625-3592.

ISBN: 1-893896-71-4

10 9 8 7 6 5 4 3 2 1

PUBLISHER'S NOTE:
This book is a work of fiction. Names, characters, places and incidents are products of the author's imagination or are used fictitiously. Any resemblance to actual events or locales or persons, living or dead, is entirely coincidental.

Books are available at quantity discounts when used to promote products or services. For information please write to: Marketing Division, ImaJinn Books, P.O. Box 162, Hickory Corners, MI 49060-0162, or call toll free 1-877-625-3592.

Cover design by Patricia Lazarus

ImaJinn Books, a division of ImaJinn
P.O. Box 162, Hickory Corners, MI 49060-0162
Toll Free: 1-877-625-3592
http://www.imajinnbooks.com

One

The breeze whispered around her, its touch furnace hot. Sweat beaded her skin, staining her T-shirt black and dripping from her ponytail.

Around her the night pulsed, a bass-heavy rhythm that made her want to dance. The air was rich with the scent of sweat, alcohol and chlorine.

Nikki stood in the shadows of an oak and sipped a lukewarm soda. Below her, on the main pool deck, bodies writhed in time to the music, unmindful of the heat or the closeness of others.

They had to be mad. If *she'd* had any choice, she would have been in the pool, allowing the cool water to wash the heat and sweat from her skin.

Instead, she was stuck here in the shadows with a lukewarm cola, awaiting the next move of a wayward teenager.

It was an all too familiar feeling. Six months before, she'd followed another teenager through the night, and had found herself caught in the middle of a war between two vampires.

Pain rose like a ghost, stifling her. She bit her lip, blinking away the sting of tears.

It was her own stupidity that had driven Michael away. Her refusal to trust, to admit what she'd felt, had worn him down as surely as the sea wears down a rock.

But what hurt the most, perhaps, was the fact that he'd left without saying good-bye.

She crossed her arms and stared moodily at the star-drenched sky. She'd looked for him, of course. She'd spent the first two months after she'd awakened in the hospital doing little else. But America was a big country, with lots of places to hide. And when the man she was hunting was one with the shadows, what hope did she really have of finding him?

None. Not that it really mattered. She'd keep looking until she found him—though what happened then would very much depend on how he reacted.

The two-way clipped to her lapel squawked. "Nik, you there?"

It was Jake—her boss and her best friend. He sounded as bored as she was. Nikki pressed the button. "No, I'm at home enjoying a nice, cool bath."

"Forget the bath. A cold beer would go down real well right now. The kid still in your area?"

She scanned the crowd. Matthew Kincaid, a redheaded, flap-eared teenager, stood out from the mob like a wart on a thumb. But it wasn't so much his looks as the fact that he towered a good foot or more over his peers. Basketball material for sure, if someone could teach him to catch a ball.

"Yeah. He's hovering near the bar, trying to convince some of the adults to buy him a drink." She hesitated and took a sip of her cola. The warm liquid slid like raw sugar down her throat. She shuddered and upended the rest into the garden bed. "He's not acting like a kid on the verge of running away from home, you know."

"No. But his mom's paying us to watch him, so watch him we will. Besides, we need the money."

"When don't we?" she said dryly. They'd been working together for close to ten years now, and she couldn't remember a time when the business hadn't been strapped for cash. Private investigators didn't make a lot of money—not in Lyndhurst, anyway. "Why is Mrs. Kincaid so convinced he's going to disappear tonight?"

"A conversation she overheard when passing his bedroom last week. Apparently, he's been chatting to this girl over the Internet and has formed quite a relationship with her. He's arranged to meet her during the party."

She frowned. "That doesn't explain why she thinks he's going to run away."

"The kid's unhappy at home. Hates his dad, who's an alcoholic and hardly ever home, and argues constantly with his mom."

"Sounds like your average teenager to me."

Jake laughed softly. "Yeah, I guess it does. But lately, the kid's apparently been saying that he doesn't need them any more, that he's found someone who understands him."

Nikki raised her eyebrows. "The Internet friend?"

"Maybe."

"Has Mrs. Kincaid asked Matthew about the friend?"

"Yeah," Jake said, voice dry. "And the reply is one I'm not about to use over the two-way."

She grinned. "Has she tried going into his computer when he's at school?"

"You need a password to get into his E-mail and chat logs."

"Clever kid."

"Too clever, apparently. That's why he's something of an outcast at school."

She snorted. "I think the ears and the height might have something to do with that."

"On the Internet, looks don't matter."

"They do if you intend to meet the person."

"Yeah, but there's no indication Matthew's lied about his looks."

There was no indication that he hadn't either, and she had a bad feeling the teenager had lied through his teeth while on-line. Given his height, his coloring, and those ears, he would surely have been the butt of many harsh jokes at school. The Internet would have given him not only anonymity but also the ability to reinvent himself.

So why would he risk all that to meet his friend and reveal the truth? And why did she have a feeling that it could all go horribly wrong?

She glanced at her watch. "It's close to eleven-thirty now. Does his mother have any idea when the meet was going to happen?"

"Midnight, apparently."

Witching hour. The time when all things dark and deadly came out to play. Things like Michael. Or Jasper.

She shuddered and lightly rubbed her wrist. In the worst of her dreams, she could still feel Jasper's touch—in her thoughts, and on her skin. But Jasper was dead, burned to ashes by the sun's heat. His evil could never touch her again.

Could never feed off her again.

A chill ran through her. Jasper wasn't the only malevolent being in this world. She couldn't shake the certainty that evil of another kind was on the move in Lyndhurst tonight. And that it was after Matthew Kincaid.

The bass-heavy pounding faded, replaced by a gentler, more romantic song. On the pool deck, teenagers drew close. There was probably more kissing going on than dancing.

She looked across to the bar. Matthew was staring at the crowd, his expression a mix of envy and anger. He slammed his drink onto the counter then walked away.

"Heads up. He's on the move."

"Where?" Jake sounded relieved.

Matthew disappeared behind the tent that housed the bar. Nikki broke into a run, keeping to the shadows as she skirted the sweating mass of slow-dancing teenagers. The teenager came into sight, arms swinging as fast as his legs as he strode along the path.

She slowed, not wanting to get too close and attract his attention. "He's heading for the back gate."

"Anyone else in sight?"

"Not unless you want to count the teenagers getting passionate under the trees."

Jake snorted softly. "I'll bring my car around. Keep me posted."

"Will do."

Matthew reached the gate and stopped to unlock it. She stepped behind a tree. The kid threw the gate open, then glanced over his shoulder. His look was petulant, like a child who sees candy he knows he can't have.

It wasn't his family making him run, she thought with a grin. It was his hormones.

He headed out and turned right. She pressed the two-way, telling Jake, then followed the teenager out the gate.

Matthew's long strides had taken him a good way down the street. She crossed to the other side then broke into a run, closing the distance between them. The slow beat of the music began to fade, and silence closed in, broken only by the occasional roar of a car engine or the blast of a horn.

The teenager strode on, looking neither right nor left. She swiped at the sweat dripping from her chin and studied the street ahead. They were in the Heights—a ritzy and very expensive section of Lyndhurst nestled into the western edge of the mountains that ringed the town. Below them, lights blazed, a neon sea of brightness that outshone the stars. Matthew could have been heading toward any one of those lights, but her gaze stopped at the docks. Ocean Road led down to there. *And that's where he's going,* she thought.

The two-way buzzed softly. "Nik, I'm in the car. Where are you?"

She pressed the receiver. "Ocean Road, just past Second."

"I'm parallel on West. Let me know if he changes direction or meets a car."

"Will do."

They continued on—Matthew striding out, her half running to keep up with him. Boxlike shapes began to loom up around them as houses gave way to factories and warehouses. The faint wash of traffic noise seemed to die completely, and in the silence, her breathing seemed sharp and harsh.

Ahead, Matthew stopped in the puddle of an overhead light and glanced at his watch. He looked briefly to his right, then turned left, heading into a small side street.

She pressed the two-way. "He's just turned into an alley. He's heading your way."

"Last cross street?"

She frowned, thinking back. "Sixth."

"Just passed it. I'll park and wait."

She stopped near the street entrance and peered around the corner. Matthew was nowhere in sight.

Swearing softly, she hurried down the street, keeping an eye on the fences lining either side of the road, looking for gaps or gateways the teenager could have gone through. Nothing. But halfway down on the right she came across a small street. The teenager was a dark shadow moving quickly away.

She sighed in relief. "He's turned off again," she told Jake. She glanced up, studying the unlit street sign. "Heading down Baker's Lane toward the docks."

"That street comes to a dead end."

She hoped it was just a figure of speech and not a reality.

"It's a rather odd place to meet an Internet friend, don't you think?"

"If it is a friend he's meeting, then yes. But all sorts of perverts go trawling the chat rooms looking for innocents like Matthew."

She kept close to the fence on the off chance that Matthew turned around. At least in the darker shadows lining the fence she'd be harder to spot. "Problem is, I've got a feeling it's not your average pervert we're looking at here."

Jake groaned. "That's all we need. I'm heading in—and bringing a gun."

"Be careful, Jake. I really don't like the feel of this."

"Oh, great. Maybe I'll call the cops, just to be safe."

"And tell them what? I've a got feeling?" When it came to her psychic abilities, skepticism ran high within the police department. It was doubtful if a statement like that would get anything other than laughter.

Jake grunted. "Don't do anything stupid until I get there."

Meaning she could do something stupid after he got there? She grinned, though it didn't ease the tension knotting her stomach.

The street narrowed, and the warehouses on either side seemed to loom in on her. She skirted several Dumpsters and screwed up her nose. From the amount of rubbish overflowing onto the street, they hadn't been emptied for several weeks. Combine that with the heat of the last few days, and the result was stomach turning.

Matthew stopped. She ducked behind a stinking Dumpster and held her nose as she peered around the side. He was studying the buildings on either side, but after a few seconds he turned and ran at the fence on the left. She waited until he'd disappeared over the top and moved after him.

"He's just climbed a fence. Third warehouse from the end."

"Wait for me."

"I might lose him if I do."

Jake swore. "Damn it, be careful."

"You be careful. I'm not the one who can die here."

"But you're not immortal either, and I'm more than a little

certain Michael didn't tell you everything about his gift of life everlasting."

She smiled grimly. Michael had never told her more than what he thought she needed to know. Bare facts, nothing more—especially when it came to anything concerning his past or what he did for a living.

"I'm heading over."

She grabbed the chain link and pulled herself over the fence. Dropping to the ground on the other side, she crouched, her gaze sweeping the darkness. It had to be some sort of produce warehouse—packing crates were lined in neat rows, those closest containing limp remnants of lettuce leaves.

Matthew could have gone anywhere. She stayed where she was, listening intently. The wind moaned through the silence, raising the hairs on the back of her neck. She rubbed her arms, then reached down, withdrawing a knife from her right boot. Made of the purest silver, it was one of two she'd had specially designed after her little dance with Jasper. If an old kitchen knife with only the smallest amount of silver in it could stop *him*, her new knives should stop just about anything. That's what she was hoping, anyway.

From the right came a soft, metallic squeal. She rose, padding quickly through the rows of crates. An old brick building loomed through the darkness. She stopped at the end of the row and peered out. To her left were several large entrances, all shuttered. To the right, nothing but brick wall. The sound had come from around the corner.

She ran to the wall, then edged forward and looked around the corner. Matthew's sandals were disappearing through a window.

"Jake, Matthew has just entered the warehouse through a window on the right side of the building. I'm just about to follow."

"I'm almost with you, Nik."

Almost wasn't good enough. She couldn't afford to wait. The sensation of danger had risen tenfold and was threatening to stifle her.

She edged around the corner and made her way to the window. It was a foot or so above her reach, but there were several packing crates stacked close enough to use as a ladder. She climbed them carefully and peered through the window.

There was no sound, no light. Just a darkness thick enough to carve. Yet the warehouse was far from empty. Somewhere in the blackness, evil waited.

Fear rose, squeezing her throat tight. Nikki closed her eyes and took a deep breath. If she didn't go into the warehouse after Matthew, Jake would. Though he was armed, they both knew from experience that guns weren't much of a threat to a vampire.

Why she thought it was a vampire who waited inside, Nikki couldn't say. Evil came in many forms—some of them human, some of them not. Maybe it was just Jasper's memory rising like a ghost to tease her fears to life.

But she'd let those fears get the better of her once—and had lost Michael because of them. They would never get the better of her again.

She pulled herself through the window then hunkered down, listening for any hint of sound. Beyond the harsh note of her breathing the silence was absolute—as absolute as the darkness. If Matthew was moving around in this, he had to have the eyes of a cat.

Keeping one hand against the outer wall for guidance and the other in front of her, she slowly moved forward. Five steps in she hit another wall and followed it out into the warehouse.

A sound broke the silence—something heavy clattering across the concrete. A soft curse followed.

"Lizzie? You in here?" Matthew's voice held a combination of petulance, bravado and fear. "Why don't you stop playing games and come out?"

"You lied to me, Matthew."

Though the words were soft, there was something in them that spoke of death. Ice crawled across Nikki's skin.

"Only about my age." The whine in Matthew's voice was more evident this time. "Only by a few years."

"Years matter, especially to someone like me."

The husky voice was drawing closer to Matthew. So was the sense of death. A chill chased its way across Nikki's overheated skin. She closed her eyes briefly, restraining the urge to scream for help. If she did, Matthew would die.

"So what if I lied about my age. It doesn't change who I am or what I feel."

He was close, maybe only a few steps away. Nikki edged to her left, the knife grasped tightly in one hand, the other outstretched. She'd probably scare the life out of him if she touched him, but at least it was a touch he'd survive. He wouldn't be so lucky if his husky-voiced girlfriend got to him first.

"It changes everything. Your age means people will worry about you. Your age means people will follow you and attempt to protect you."

Nikki froze. The woman knew she was there. Knew she was following Matthew.

Air stirred sluggishly, whispering past her cheek. Someone was moving. Someone she couldn't see or hear. Someone other than the woman Matthew had come here to meet.

Sweat trickled down the side of her face. She ignored it, not daring to move, her breath lodged somewhere in her throat.

The sense of impending doom was so thick her skin crawled with it. Kinetic energy crackled across her fingertips. She clenched her hand, searching the cover of night, looking for the source of the movement.

The air stirred again, and with it came the sound of a soft step behind her.

Nikki spun, and hell broke loose.

Two

Michael, are you listening to me?

The voice edged through his consciousness, as sharp as fingernails down a blackboard. He opened his eyes, watching the flames dance in the hearth. Despite the fire, the chill of night sat heavily in the cabin. But outside the howling wind no longer rattled the windows, and the smell of rain was in the air.

From down the valley came the soft calls of the cattle that were his main source of sustenance. Hunger stirred in his belly. He glanced at the clock on the mantle. It was just past six in the evening. He'd been asleep for close to nine hours and hadn't eaten in at least two days.

It was a good sign that his demon was finally on the retreat.

Michael, I know you can hear me. If you don't start answering, I'm going to raid that damn cabin of yours and slap some sense into you.

He smiled reluctantly. Over the last six months, Seline had been a constant, if distant, companion. She badgered him endlessly, never letting his resolve slip, never letting him give up hope. She'd been his strength in the early days of darkness, when the demon was close to winning control, and he'd just wanted to give up the fight permanently.

He owed her his life, but she still managed to annoy the hell out of him.

A man would be hard-pressed to sleep with you around, Seline.

If a man wants to sleep when I'm around, he needs to be certified.

The gentle lilt of her mind-voice deepened provocatively. He snorted softly. Seline was a thin, frail-looking woman, but she certainly didn't look the one hundred and eighty years he knew her to be. And she certainly didn't act it—as her many lovers would no doubt attest.

Bit early for your nightly check-in, isn't it?

We have a problem, Michael. I think we're going to need your help.

He rubbed a hand across his eyes. Seline's type of problem was the one thing he could live without right now. He'd spent too long battling the need to kill, struggling against the urge to taste the sweet strength of human blood. To confront such desires in another might be too much of a test for his newly found resolve.

Yet if he stayed locked up here in his retreat, he would never really know if the battle had been won.

What type of problem?

Disappearances.

He frowned. People disappeared every day in the U.S.— some intentional, some not. It was something Seline didn't usually involve the Circle in—unless there were dark forces at play.

What type of disappearances are we talking about?

Her confusion swept down the mental link between them. It was an odd enough occurrence to make him sit up straight and start paying more attention.

We're not really sure. For almost a week now, I've had a feeling that something was wrong. But it wasn't until I picked up the paper this evening and read about the disappearance of Vance Hutton that the feeling crystallized into certainty.

Michael frowned. *We're talking about Vance Hutton, the actor? Didn't he just get married?*

Yeah—to that scrawny English actress.

Scorn overlaid her thoughts, and he smiled. The old witch had been rather keen on Hutton. *She beat you to the punch, huh?*

She chuckled. *I wasn't planning to marry the boy—just bed him.*

Had she really set her mind to it, she would no doubt have succeeded. It was amazing what makeup and a little magic could hide. *How did he disappear?*

He was apparently honeymooning in Wyoming—some exclusive resort in Jackson Hole.

He frowned. Jackson Hole was primarily a ski area, although with the abundant wildlife and its proximity to Yellowstone and several other national parks, it had a good run with summer tourists as well.

So what happened to him?

Her shrug shimmered down the mental line. *That's the problem—no one knows. That skinny woman he married woke up one morning to find him gone. He apparently left everything behind—wallet, money and most of his clothes. There was no note, and no indication that he was feeling suicidal or depressed.*

Have the police been called in?

Naturally. They're as clueless as the wife.

Michael scratched his chin, then rose from the sofa and crossed to the window. Night had closed in, but the moon was bright, silvering the aspens lining his driveway. Jackson Hole wasn't that far away—a couple hours' drive at the most.

A fact Seline was well aware of.

Yet he held back the offer to go investigate. Past experience warned it was wise to wait when it came to Seline and her visions. Jump too soon, and you didn't get the entire story. Not that she ever sent her investigators into situations blind—far from it. But she often had information on the emotional impact of certain situations that she didn't impart unless pushed.

It had happened to him. She'd sent him to Lyndhurst to catch the man who'd murdered his brother. He'd not only succeeded in killing Jasper, but had lost his heart in the process.

He closed his eyes, fighting the desire to reach out through the link forged between him and Nikki. Six months without contact seemed like an eternity, and he wasn't entirely sure how he was going to survive the years ahead without her. Yet some days it seemed all he had to do was close his eyes and he could feel the caress of her fingers against his skin. Could feel the warmth of her smile in his mind.

Neither of which he would ever actually feel again.

He had no intention of contacting her after all this time. It wasn't fair to give her hope when his work made even the possibility of a life together an impossible dream.

He caressed the silver cross he wore around his neck and stared moodily at the star-drenched sky. *What makes you think this is a case for the Circle to get involved in?*

Instinct, Michael. There's more to this case than meets the eye. I checked back through the papers. It seems people have a habit of disappearing from this particular resort— fifteen in the last year, in fact.

How could fifteen people disappear without someone— particularly the press—getting wind of the fact and raising a commotion? *Have any of the missing turned up again?*

All but three. I did some checking, though, and it appears they have become somewhat reclusive, only seen at night, never in daylight.

They're vampires. Hence Seline's desire for him to investigate. Sometimes the only way to track down a killer was to send another after them.

Yet they do not exhibit the classic feeding-frenzy symptoms of a newly turned vampire. From all accounts, they're still working, still living with their families, still eating normally.

Then what are they? There was no way around the feeding frenzy stage—no magic that could cure the insatiable hunger of the newly turned. It was something you had to work through and survive. Not many did, and certainly not in a matter of weeks.

I'm not sure, and at this stage, it's not them I'm worried about. It's the resort. Whenever I try to do a reading on the place, all I get is darkness. Something evil resides there, Michael, and its influence grows by the day. We have to stop it.

But why me? If it wasn't a vampire they were dealing with, just about any of the Circle's other investigators were currently better equipped to investigate.

Seline was silent for a second. Michael crossed his arms and leaned a shoulder against the window frame. She was trying to decide just how much to tell him. If he played hard to get, she'd eventually open up and explain why she wanted him on this mission rather than the others.

There are two reasons it must be you.

Her mind-voice was hesitant. He raised an eyebrow in

surprise. In the century he'd known the old witch, indecision was something he'd rarely heard in her.

And they are? he prompted, when she showed no immediate signs of continuing.

The darkness is linked with your past, Michael. I don't know how, and I don't know why, but it is something you must deal with.

I have over three hundred and sixty years behind me, Seline. Don't suppose you'd like to be a little more specific?

I'm sorry, but no, I can't. My visions are limited in many respects, unfortunately. I just know that it's vital you go to this resort, or more people will disappear.

He sighed softly. It looked like he had very little choice in the matter. *And the second reason?*

The silence stretched between them once more. He frowned. This time worry, and perhaps even a little fear, mingled with the hesitation coming down the mental line.

It was the fear that concerned him, more than anything else.

Eventually, she sighed. *You're not going to like this.*

Just cut the dramatics and tell me what the problem is, Seline.

His irritation tingled down the line, and he felt her frown. *You must take Nikki with you.*

"No!"

His reply was abrupt. Instinctive. Angry. There had been more than enough darkness in Nikki's life already—and he'd caused her more than enough pain in the brief time they'd been together. He wouldn't drag her into a similar situation.

Michael, she's already involved. She walks the path to the resort as we speak. If she is not accompanied by you, she will die.

Fear slammed through his heart. *We share a life force, Seline. She cannot die as long as I live.*

But the image of her dead, her head torn from her neck, went through his mind. Bile rose, swift and sharp. He pushed the vision away and swallowed heavily.

But she is not immortal, as you are not immortal. Seline's mind voice held an edge of sharpness. *Your actions have marked her for others of your kind to see. They will know what she is. Know how to get rid of her.*

Only the very old vampires have any knowledge of thralls, Seline. And the term can only be used loosely when it comes to Nikki.

Perhaps. You have yet to test the limits of what you have done, so who can say what control you have over her?

Michael rubbed his eyes. It wasn't control he wanted. It was her heart. But she wasn't willing to risk that again—and certainly not with someone like him.

I have no wish to test the limits. No wish to even see her again.

Do not lie to me, my friend. I can see the truth in your heart.

Then you can also see the resolve.

She sighed. *Yes. But the only true option you have right now is whether she lives or dies.*

Then there was no choice. *Where is she now?*

Seline's smile shimmered down the link. *Where she always has been—Lyndhurst. The company helicopter is on the way to pick you up as we speak. The files will be on it, and I've made arrangements for a room at Jackson Hole.*

So she'd been certain of his response all along. He clenched his fists and somehow managed to keep his mind voice even. *Tell me one thing, Seline. Can you see the ending to all this?*

All I can see is danger, and much pain. The road you walk will not be easy—for either of you.

He smiled grimly. Danger and pain had been his close companions over the century he'd been a part of the Circle, and were a major part of the reason he could not allow Nikki into his life.

I'll keep in contact, Seline.

Do that. And watch out for the past, Michael. Remember, the memory of love can be potent, but it is nowhere near as satisfying as the reality.

He frowned. What in the hell was *that* supposed to mean? The mental line went down before he could ask. He punched the window frame in frustration.

It looked like Jake had been right after all. Fate would not let him walk away from Nikki without a damned good fight.

Three

Matthew's scream ripped across the silence, as sharp as the gunshot that followed—a gunshot that had come from outside the warehouse.

Fear squeezed Nikki's heart, and for a moment she found it difficult to breathe. Jake was in trouble. Every instinct she had said she should go help him. Yet if she did, she'd face his wrath. *The client is all that matters.* How often had he told her that? Her priority had to be Matthew, no matter how much the decision tore at her.

The air stirred then fell still again. Someone was standing in front her, someone whose very presence made her skin crawl.

It was a taste of evil that reminded her of Jasper.

She shivered and backed away, her fingers aching from the fierceness of her grip on the knife.

From the corner of her eye, she glimpsed movement to her left. Something snarled, and canines gleamed briefly against the cloak of night. It wasn't a dog but a vampire, moving in fast. She flung out her free hand, thrusting him away kinetically. He hit the back wall with enough force to shatter a nearby window and fell heavily to the concrete floor.

Moonlight filtered into the warehouse, filling the night with yellow softness. The vampire didn't move, his head bent at an odd angle to his body. *Broken neck,* Nikki thought with a chill. She'd killed him without really meaning to.

She spun and ran towards Matthew. The teenager was wrestling with two smaller men. Blood glistened on his skin, mingling with sweat as it ran down his arms and face. She raised her hand, lashing energy at one of the vampires. He yelped and disappeared through the darkness. The second vampire launched himself at her. She slid to a stop and thrust the knife at him. The blade punched into the his stomach a second before his weight hit her. She was slammed backwards, hitting the concrete hard, the vampire pinning her down.

Gasping for breath and blinking back the sting of tears, she heard the vampire snarl. His wild blue eyes were inches from hers, his canines extending and dripping blood onto her cheeks. *Getting ready to feed,* she thought. Bile rose swiftly. Swallowing heavily and fighting memories of Jasper, she thrust a hand into his face. The teeth aimed at her neck sank into her palm instead. Agony ran like fire down her arm. She yelled, thrusting him away kinetically, and scrambled up. The vampire was on his feet, a feral look on his face. Silver gleamed in the middle of his stomach—her knife, still lodged in his flesh. Sound whispered behind her. A chill chased its way across her skin, and the hairs at the back of her neck rose. Evil was on the move.

She reached again for energy. Pain slivered though her mind, a warning that she was beginning to push her psychic strength too far. Ignoring it, she focused on the blade, ripping it from the vampire's body and aiming it at the darkness to her right.

It sliced through the air and thudded hilt-deep into the side of a packing crate. Silence washed across the warehouse, chilling in its intensity.

Matthew no longer screamed. Was no longer anywhere to be seen.

The vampire watched her, blood oozing from the wound in his stomach, his expression furious and fists clenched. But he didn't move. She wondered why.

Laughter flowed across the silence. Laughter that was throaty, rich and very feminine. Nikki shivered. The underlying edge of depravity in the sound chilled her soul.

"You are very good."

The whisper flowed from the darkness to her left. Nikki clenched her fists. Blood oozed between her fingers, splattering against the concrete. Though there was no one to be seen beyond the bleeding vampire, the air stirred.

Evil, slowly circling.

She licked her lips. "What have you done with Matthew?"

"I have done nothing with him. The young fool ran into a packing crate and knocked himself out."

The woman was behind her now. Nikki fought the need to turn around. The real threats were the vampires who'd accompanied this woman. She wouldn't attack herself. Why Nikki was so sure of this, she couldn't say, especially when she was almost choking on the corruption that was this woman's soul.

"Let him go," she said softly. Her voice sounded calm despite the fear squeezing her throat. "You said yourself he was too young."

"He is younger than I had expected, true. But I'm afraid it is a decision that is not really mine."

Which suggested the woman was not in charge—something Nikki found hard to believe. "Then whose decision is it? These clowns you've bought with you?"

Perhaps it wasn't the thing to say, but she had a feeling that if she showed anything less than bravado, the woman would unleash her companions.

More laughter washed across the night. "They are only young, and would have been more than a match for any human."

Alarm slithered into her heart. "I'm human."

"No, my dear, you are not. As you know well enough."

Nikki clenched her fists, holding back fear, holding back anger. "What do you mean?"

"You have the taste of a vampire on you. I have no wish to upset your master, whoever he may be."

Nikki snorted softly. "What planet are you from? I have no master—whatever you mean by that."

"They all say that, in the beginning."

"I'll be saying it until the end."

"Perhaps you will. There is an unusual strength in you."

The softly spoken words came from the left again. The woman had stopped moving. Nikki wished she knew where Matthew was—wished he'd move, or groan or do something to help her locate him. Until he did, she didn't dare attack the woman or her vampire companion.

Another gunshot ripped across the silence. Relief and worry surged through her. Jake was alive, but for how much longer? A vampire could move with the speed of the wind. How long would Jake be able withstand such an attack?

She thrust out a hand as the knife-wounded vampire stepped forward. He stopped, but not, Nikki guessed, because of the threat of another kinetic lance. The woman was still holding him in check.

But why?

"It appears your companion still lives. You're both more resourceful than I'd imagined."

"Never underestimate us humans," Nikki commented. "We

get pretty clever when we're scared."

The woman's smile flashed briefly, canines bright in the darkness. "So I see. It does present me with a few problems, however."

"Let Matthew go. He's too young to be a part of whatever deviancy you have planned."

"He was more than old enough to contact me. More than old enough to engage in cyber-sex with me."

No wonder Matthew was a little less than careful in getting to this meeting. He'd hoped the written word would become reality and wasn't particular about where. "But he's not old enough to die. That's what you intended, wasn't it?"

"Perhaps. It depends on whether he can live up to his claims."

Nikki had a feeling she wasn't talking about sexual prowess. "Tell me, why is a vampire trawling the Net for victims?"

"Why does any predator hunt? When you get as old as I am, it becomes such a tedious affair. Cyberspace is filled with lonely hearts desperate to find a mate, and it provides a whole new field in which to play." The woman smiled again. It washed across the moonlit darkness like a wave of ice. "I have become quite addicted to the test of luring quarry to my bait and slowly reeling them in. "

Well, it certainly put a new spin on the term cyber-menace, if nothing else. Nikki rubbed her arms. "But why?"

"Ah, well, that is something I cannot tell you."

From the darkness just beyond the unseen woman came a slight groan. Matthew, regaining consciousness. Nikki clenched her fists. If she was going to save the teenager—and herself— she was going to have to be damn fast.

Faster than the wind. Faster than a vampire.

She licked her lips. *I can't do this.* She may have beaten Jasper, but only because Michael had been there to help— giving her strength. Giving her courage. If she'd been left to cope alone, she would have been dead—or worse.

For an instant, she was tempted to reach for the link— reach for him. But the link between them had been dead ever since she'd awakened in the hospital, and she doubted it would come to life now simply because she needed it.

From behind her came the sound of a cautious step. Nikki

tensed, muscles beginning to ache. Her neck tingled a familiar warning. It was Jake. He'd only fired two shots. He still had four left in the gun.

More than enough to blow a vampire's brains out.

The thought turned her stomach. She ignored it. There was no time for squeamishness—not if they were all going to survive this mess.

"Why can't you tell me your plans?" she said to the woman. "You intend killing us all anyway, don't you?"

Again the smile shimmered coldly across the darkness. "Oh yes. But as you said, it pays to never underestimate humans— or the not-so-human."

"Then I'm afraid I'm just going to have to spoil your party."

Nikki thrust kinetic energy at the bleeding vampire, lifting him up into the air and propelling him toward the window. "Jake, incoming at four o'clock!"

Gunshots reverberated through the silence, and pain ripped through her brain. Nikki gasped, tears stinging her eyes. She was pushing the limits of her abilities. Too much further, and she'd hit the wall.

But she had no choice. She slid the last knife from her boot and ran to her left, straight at the darkness that hid the woman. She stabbed wildly, felt the knife strike something solid and slice deep. Heard a gasp of pain a second before a fist hit her chin and flung her backwards.

She crashed against a packing crate and air whooshed from her lungs. She slumped to the ground, gasping for breath and seeing stars. Groaning, she felt the back of her head. Her fingers came away bloody. The night around her stirred, and the air was so thick with the sense of evil it felt as if she was sucking in liquid.

Move, move, she thought. On hands and knees, she scrambled away. Another shot roared across the silence. The woman cursed. She was close, so close.

Nikki flung energy in the woman's direction, heard a slight grunt before the red hot knives hit her brain. She gasped, holding her stomach, rocking back and forth. Tears mingled with sweat on her cheeks. This couldn't happen. Not yet! She hadn't rescued Matthew.

"Nikki? You okay?"

Jake's voice came from her right. Another warning prickled across the back of Nikki's neck. The woman was on the move, circling. Heading for Jake.

"Behind you," Nikki gasped.

Something glittered in the darkness, and the smell of burning flesh stung the air. Moonlight glinted off silver as a knife arced through the air. *Her* knife, the one she'd used against the male vampire, now in the woman's hands.

A gunshot reverberated. Jake grunted, then something heavy hit the concrete. Silence returned. *Oh God no...*

She pushed upright, ignoring the pain, barely able to see as she staggered forward. Her feet hit something solid. She bent, reaching out, touching jeans, shirt, and then unshaven face.

"Jake," she said, her voice harsh, her throat constricted with fear. "Don't you dare die on me."

He didn't respond. She felt for his neck. His pulse was weak, thready. *Jake, you can't leave me. You're all I have...*

Air stirred, brushing coldly across her back. Nikki thrust through the pain barrier, reaching deep. Energy burned through her body, fuelled by anger—fuelled by grief. She twisted and flung a bolt of energy toward the woman.

There was a thump, then silence. Nikki waited, fists clenched, kinetic energy dancing like fireflies across the tips of her fingers.

The sense of evil slowly dissipated, and the darkness became benign once more. Nikki pulled the cell phone from her jeans' pocket and called 911. Then she rose and walked to the crates where she'd last heard Matthew.

He was nowhere to be found.

Four

Nikki winced as the paramedic pulled the bandage tight. He glanced up. "Too tight?"

"Depends," she muttered. "Are my fingertips supposed to be blue?"

A smile crinkled the corners of the medic's kind blue eyes. "No, but you have to admit, it is a pretty shade."

"Yeah, but it's not a good look on fingers."

She glanced past the doctor and watched Detective Col MacEwan approach. They'd obviously dragged him out of bed. His normally neat brown hair was everywhere, and he wore a striped pajama top half-tucked into his jeans. "Any news on Jake?" she asked.

"Yeah. He's in surgery now, with wounds to his stomach and chest. The doctors are hopeful." MacEwan planted his feet behind the doctor and crossed his arms. "Now, you want to tell me about your little fight here?"

Nikki scrubbed her good hand across her eyes. She was hot and tired, and her head still pounded something fierce. All she could smell was sweat and blood and fear. She just wanted to go home and stand under a hot shower to wash it all away. The last thing she needed was MacEwan and his questions.

"It didn't start out as a fight, you know."

MacEwan snorted. "Never does with you. But it always ends the same, doesn't it?"

With people dead or missing, Jake in the hospital and her getting patched up. The unspoken words hung like a sword in the air. She glanced down at her newly bandaged hand and muttered a thank-you to the medic.

"Don't use that hand too much, or the clips won't hold," he warned. "And if you start getting a headache, I want you to come straight to the hospital."

She snorted softly. She already had a headache, and its source certainly *wasn't* the knock on the head. But she nodded and waited until he'd gathered his bags and left before she looked back to MacEwan. "The woman wasn't human. Neither were the men who'd accompanied her." He studied her for a minute, then dug a packet of cigarettes from his pocket. He lit one and took several long drags, blowing the smoke toward the starlit sky. "I suppose you expect me to believe that."

"You're the only one who will—and the only one I'll say it to. My official statement is that we were attacked by five unknown assailants—one woman and four men."

MacEwan's brown-eyed gaze was shrewd. "That doesn't jell with the number of corpses I have in that warehouse."

"There should be at least three—one with a broken neck, two with gunshot wounds."

"We've got two. And no sign of the kid you were following."

So one of the vamps hadn't been killed. She wondered if the woman had rescued him, or whether he'd simply slid away before the cops had arrived. "If you don't believe we were here following Matthew, check with his mother." She rolled her neck, trying to ease the ache.

"Oh, I did."

She snorted. Why was she not surprised? She and MacEwan might have come to a better understanding of each other during that whole Jasper mess, but that didn't mean friendship had blossomed as a result.

"And?"

"And it's the only reason your ass is not currently parked in a cell."

"For what? Having the audacity to defend myself?"

MacEwan smiled grimly. "Blowing someone's brains out is manslaughter, regardless of whether it's done in self-defense or not."

"I didn't blow anyone's brains out—a fact I think you'll discover once you run prints on the gun."

They wouldn't find Jake's prints, either, as he'd been wearing gloves—gloves that were now sitting in her jacket pocket. She'd taken them off him before the cops arrived.

MacEwan snorted. "Like I can take that at face value. The gun's registered in Jake's name, isn't it?"

It was, but they still had to prove Jake had pulled the trigger. Which would be rather hard, seeing she and the vampires were the only witnesses. "If the case is so clear-cut, why haven't you charged us?"

"Not saying I won't. I was just stating that Mrs. Kincaid backed part of your story, and it's the only reason you're still sitting here."

Great. Now she was going to spend the next twenty-four hours wondering when MacEwan was going to bust her butt and throw her in jail. Just what she needed on top of everything else.

She ran a hand through her sweat-heavy hair. "Don't suppose you saw anything in the warehouse that would give us some clue as to where Matthew might have gone?"

She hadn't had the chance to look herself. She'd stayed with Jake until the ambulance arrived, and the cops had pretty much followed the paramedics in.

MacEwan blew a smoke ring skyward. "Nothing that I can see on first glance. We do have witness reports of a car speeding down Ocean Road away from here at approximately the time you gave us."

She raised an eyebrow. "Don't suppose these witnesses saw how many people were inside?"

"Three. One woman, two men."

"Your witnesses had rather good eyesight, didn't they?"

MacEwan gave her a smile that was all teeth and no warmth. "It was a patrol car that spotted them. They gave chase, but the perps managed to lose them."

"Back to driving school for them," she muttered. "What about the plate number?"

"Wyoming plates. We're checking it out."

She crossed her arms and frowned at MacEwan. He was being just a little too helpful. Usually he only provided information in small dollops—if that. "What are you after?"

He crushed his cigarette under his heel and gave her another wintry smile. "Help. Jake told me some time ago about an ability of yours...physiometry?"

Nikki's smile was tense. "Psychometry. The ability to touch objects and get some sense of the owner."

He nodded. "He said you can use it to trace people—that

that was how you kept finding Monica Trevgard."

She rubbed her arms. They'd been nowhere near quick enough to save Monica, and she hoped the same wouldn't be said about Matthew. The woman in the warehouse had given her the impression that Matthew's death wasn't a first option, so maybe she had some time to find him yet.

"It's a talent that's a little shaky. It doesn't always work."

He shrugged. "At this stage, I'm willing to give anything a try."

The edge in his voice suggested this was something personal. Her frown deepened. "What do you want me to do?"

He raked a hand through his dark hair then glanced around. "My niece was abducted three months ago. We've tried everything we can think of to find her—gone through every official channel. There's no sign of her. My sister's going crazy. I thought that maybe..." He shrugged. "You help me, and I'll help you."

She frowned. "Why are you so convinced she's still alive?" He'd been a cop long enough to know the chances of that were remote—especially given the fact it obviously wasn't a ransom-induced kidnapping.

"She *is* alive." His voice was flat, but there was desperation in his eyes.

Clutching at straws. "I can't guarantee anything." After three months, whatever psychic resonances his niece might have left on her personal items would probably be fading.

"Just try."

She nodded. MacEwan had to be frantic if he was coming to her for help. In the past, he'd been the biggest denouncer of her gifts. Yet he hadn't mocked her months ago when she'd called him for help with Jasper and his zombies, nor had he mocked when she'd mentioned that the bodies in the warehouse were vampires. MacEwan wasn't a man easily figured out, that was for sure.

He took a business card from his jacket and handed it to her. On the back was a handwritten address.

"I should be finished here by six," he said. "You can reach me at home anytime after seven."

She nodded and tucked the card in the pocket of her jeans. It looked like she wasn't going to head home and grab that shower after all. She'd barely even have enough time to go see Jake at the hospital. "I'll need something of your niece's—something she wore all the time."

MacEwan frowned. "Like what? Jewelry? Clothes?"

She shrugged. "Jewelry works best—metal seems to hold the resonance of its owner longer. But I can sometimes get quite good readings from a bra."

"I'll talk to Sondra, see what she can come up with." He half turned away, then stopped, looking back. "I know you'll want to see Jake once you leave here, but don't screw me around on this."

Nikki snorted. As if she would. She knew better than anyone how stupid that would be. Though she'd never felt MacEwan's wrath herself, she'd seen it fall on others. Fair cop or not, he had a mean streak wider than the Mississippi when pushed too far.

"Just don't expect me to perform miracles."

He nodded and reached for another cigarette. "I won't. I just have a feeling time is running out for her. If we don't find her soon, we won't find her alive."

"I'll be there as soon as I check on Jake." Hopefully, he was fine. Hopefully, the wound wasn't as bad as it had looked. "Don't suppose you could talk to Matthew's mother and see if you can convince her to part with something of Matthew's?"

The chances of Mrs. Kincaid being willing to see her, let alone touch something of Matthew's, weren't likely to be high right now. Hell, they'd be lucky if she even bothered paying them—not that Nikki could really blame her.

MacEwan nodded. "I'll talk to her." He took a drag on the cigarette, then crushed it under his heel and walked away.

She wondered why he bothered smoking. In all the years she'd known him, she'd never actually seen him finish a cigarette.

She pushed off the crate she'd been sitting on and headed for the street. Jake had given her a spare set of car keys for use in emergencies like this—when he was stuck somewhere and his much-loved Mercedes was parked in a dubious area. He'd kill her if she left it there.

The car was parked under a streetlight about a block down from the warehouse. She climbed in and sped over to the hospital.

Mary, Jake's wife of twenty years, was pacing the confines of the hospital's waiting room. Her long gray hair had been pulled back into a tight bun, giving her lined features a severe, almost gaunt, look.

"How is he?" Nikki stopped a couple of feet away from the older woman.

Although she'd known them both for a long time now, she still found it easier to talk to Jake rather than Mary. Maybe because Mary always looked so perfect, so polished, and talked about art and literature and other things that went way over Nikki's head. Things that made her aware of her years on the streets and her lack of schooling.

Not that there was anything resembling malice on Mary's part. After all, she'd welcomed a grubby sixteen-year-old into her home some ten years ago and had become, in many ways, a surrogate mother. But she was a mother Nikki couldn't easily talk to.

"He's still in surgery. He's lost a lot of blood. They don't know..." Mary faltered, tears spilling down her cheeks. "...don't know if his heart will take the strain of two major operations so close together."

A chill slithered through Nikki. Jake hadn't mentioned anything about heart problems. She hesitated, then stepped forward and drew Mary into her arms, offering the comfort words couldn't. A shudder ran through the older woman's slender frame, and hot tears fell on Nikki's arm.

"This has to stop. *He* has to stop."

The chill increased. "He'll be fine, Mary." Yet even as she said it, Nikki tasted the lie. Would this be a case of third time unlucky?

Maybe Mary was right. Maybe it was time for him to stop. To walk away while he still could. Though what she would do—where she would go—if he did was something she didn't want to think about.

Mary sniffed and pulled away. "The police told me he was attacked—and that he'd possibly killed his attacker. Do you think they'll charge him?"

"I don't know." As MacEwan had said, manslaughter was manslaughter, regardless of the circumstances. And the gun was registered to Jake, even if his prints weren't on it.

Mary's gaze searched hers. "What happened out there? I thought you were only following a teenager?"

"We were. The people he met with weren't all that happy about our presence. There were at least five of them. We're lucky to be alive." Lucky the woman had run, rather than attacking a final time.

A doctor wearing blue surgical scrubs came into the waiting room. Mary spun around. His gaze briefly met Nikki's, and her stomach clenched. The operation hadn't gone well—she could see it in his eyes.

"We've removed the bullet from his stomach, but the knife punctured his lung. He made it out of surgery okay, but the next twenty-four hours are vital."

Meaning there'd been complications, Nikki thought, and rubbed her arms.

Mary went white. Nikki gently cupped the older woman's elbow, ready to catch her should she faint.

Mary didn't seem to notice. "But he'll be all right, won't he?"

There was a tremulous note to the older woman's voice. The doctor hesitated. "I can't promise anything."

"Can I see him?"

"Not for the next couple of hours. Why don't you go home and get some sleep? We'll call if anything happens."

Mary snorted softly. "Would you do that if it was your wife in there?"

The doctor smiled. "No. I don't suppose I would." He hesitated again. "I'll keep you posted."

Mary sank down onto the chair once the doctor left. "He has to live, Nikki. He has to."

"He will." Jake was tough. If he'd lived through Jasper's attack, surely he could live through this. She glanced at her watch.

Mary caught the movement. "You have to go?"

She nodded. "MacEwan wants to see me."

"Then go." She reached out, gripping Nikki's arm tightly. "Just don't you go after the madmen who did this. Jake wouldn't want that. He never did believe in revenge."

Neither did she. Jasper had taught her the folly of seeking retribution, if nothing else. "I have to find Matthew. He'd want me to do that."

Mary nodded. "Be careful."

"Always am." She took the car keys and parking ticket out of her pocket. "Tell him his car is safe. It's on level three, to the right of the stairs."

Mary accepted the keys with a nod. "I'll let you know if anything..." Her voice trailed off, and she blinked several times.

"Do that," Nikki said, her throat restricted and aching. Turning away sharply, she swiped the tears from her eyes and went in search of a cab.

***

MacEwan opened the door at the second knock. He'd obviously just come out of the shower—his hair still dripped, and he wasn't wearing a shirt. Not that it mattered. A thick brown mat covered much of his skin. Nikki smiled slightly. He seemed to have more hair on his chest than he did on his head.

"Come in," he said. "The living room is the second door on your left. I'll just go get some clothes on."

She nodded and headed down the hallway. MacEwan's house was something of a revelation. She expected spartan— white walls and minimal furniture. The reality was rich claret walls, cream ceilings and lots of antiques. The house exuded warmth and friendliness—totally the opposite of the man himself.

She entered the living room and stopped. A woman rose from an overstuffed chair, a look of expectancy in her brown eyes. MacEwan's sister, obviously. Nikki hoped he hadn't raised her hopes too much.

"You must be Nikki James," the woman said, her large hands clasped tightly together, knuckles almost white.

Nikki offered a hand. "Yes, I am. You're Sondra, I gather?"

Sondra nodded. Her handshake was firm, her skin slightly clammy. "Thank you for agreeing to help us."

She hadn't exactly agreed, but there was no point saying that. "No problem."

Sondra perched on the chair again. "What happened to your hand?"

Nikki glanced down. The white bandages really stood out against all the claret and browns that filled the living room. "Stabbed myself with a knife. Apples are tougher than they look these days." Why she lied, she wasn't entirely sure. Maybe because the other woman, despite her size, looked as fragile as glass—and any reminder, no matter how distant, of what might have happened to her daughter might just break her.

A smile touched Sondra's pale lips. "Rachel was always doing that..." She looked away quickly.

Nikki shifted her weight from one foot to the other and wished MacEwan would hurry up. She'd never been comfortable attempting small talk—especially with desperate strangers.

Sondra blew her nose, the sound strident against the silence. She tucked the handkerchief back into her purse and glanced at Nikki. "Col said you needed something of Rachel's."

She nodded. "I can sometimes use personal items to get impressions of the owner."

Hope flared in Sondra's brown eyes. "And find them?"

She shifted uncomfortably. The last thing she wanted was to build up this woman's hopes. "Not always."

"Oh." Sondra blinked several times, then reached into her purse and took out two plastic bags.

Nikki raised an eyebrow in surprise. MacEwan had obviously been doing a little research on psychic abilities if he knew wrapping items in plastic was the best way to prevent outside influences interfering with the resonance of an item.

"I brought over a necklace she wore a lot, and a favorite bra."

She accepted both and looked around as MacEwan entered the room. "Just remember, there's no guarantee this will work.

Not three months down the road."

Sondra gave a slight sob. MacEwan's look was severe. "Try."

Nikki sat on an overstuffed sofa. Taking a deep breath, she tore open the bag containing the necklace and let it drop into her hand. The gold chain felt cool against her skin. She wrapped her fingers around it, pressing it into her palm. Then she closed her eyes and reached for the place in her mind that could call forth the images locked within the bracelet.

It felt like she was drilling for oil in a barren desert. Sweat trickled down her cheek, splashing against her fist. She frowned, reaching deeper. Gradually, an image formed. *A man, in his mid twenties. Blond hair, green eyes.* Her mind seized the pictures, storing them for later. If she stopped now, if she even spoke, she feared she might lose the fragile impressions forever.

A white convertible with Wyoming plates. Money, lots of it, splashed about almost carelessly. Laughter and love in the darkness...

The images slipped away, dissipating like ghosts. Nikki swore softly and ran a hand through her hair. There'd been no sign of trouble in any of those images, and no telling if they had anything to do with the niece's disappearance.

"Anything?" MacEwan asked, voice tight.

"Just wait." She ripped open the bag containing the bra.

This time, the images came thick and fast. *Green eyes shining bright. White candles, flickering in the darkness. Gold-rimmed china on a red tablecloth. A glass filled with wine as thick as blood. Warmth and desire intermingled. A four-poster bed covered in gold...*

Given the strength of the images, it was obvious the niece had been seduced the last time she'd worn the bra. Nikki reached a little deeper to find out what had happened afterward. Rachel must have at least gone home, otherwise they wouldn't have had this bra.

Fear. Deep fear, blossoming in the midst of passion. Struggling, fighting, unable to breathe...

Nikki's breath caught in her throat, and her heart pounded so fast she feared it was going to gallop out of her chest. The images flowing from the bra faltered. She tried to calm down. This fear was not hers. She had to remain apart from it. Only then would she see what had happened.

Pain, flaring bright. A flicker of white, stabbing through the darkness. Fire on her neck, burning deep. Lethargy... darkness...darkness...the sensation of floating... waiting...just waiting...

Nikki dropped the bra into her lap and rubbed her temples wearily. MacEwan's niece wasn't dead, but she wasn't exactly alive, either.

She opened her eyes. Sondra was still sitting on the edge of the chair, her hands locked together, expression a mix of anxiousness and hope. MacEwan stood behind her, his hands shoved deep in his pockets.

"Anything?" His voice was deadpan, as lifeless as his expression.

She realized then he hadn't really expected this to work. Like Sondra, he was grasping at straws and hoping for a miracle. She tucked her hair behind her ears. "I can't tell you whether she's alive or dead, I'm afraid."

MacEwan's gaze narrowed. He obviously sensed the lie but made no mention of it. Maybe he didn't want to upset his sister any more than she already was.

Sondra made a choking sound and put a hand to her mouth. Tears spilled past her fingers and splashed onto her knees.

MacEwan placed a hand on his sister's shoulder, squeezing lightly. "What *can* you tell us?"

"I saw a room. It had a four-poster bed and seemed covered in gold."

Sondra looked quickly at MacEwan. "That's Rachel's bedroom."

MacEwan nodded, his gaze not wavering from Nikki's. There was a warning in his brown eyes—don't say anything to upset his sister any further. "What else?"

"She was there with a green-eyed, blond-haired man. They were lovers. He drove a white convertible with Wyoming plates, and he had lots of money."

Sondra frowned. "I never saw anyone fitting that

description."

"He only visited at night," Nikki said softly.

MacEwan continued to stare. Whether he'd caught the implication or not, she couldn't say. She'd always found him a little hard to read.

"But I would have seen him if he'd come to our house. Rachel lived with me, you see. She couldn't have gotten anyone in without—"

MacEwan lightly squeezed his sister's shoulder again, silencing her. "Did you see him well enough to work up a sketch?"

Nikki nodded. Not that it would do much good—not if Rachel's lover had been a vampire. "I can come done to the station later today, if you like."

MacEwan nodded and glanced at his watch. "I'm back on shift at five. Anything else?"

Nothing she could mention with Sondra in the room. Nikki shook her head. "Did you manage to get anything from Mrs. Kincaid?"

MacEwan nodded. "A watch. You want to do the reading now?"

"Yes." She hesitated and glanced at Sondra. "But I need a drink first, if you don't mind."

"Sondra, why don't you go and get us all something cool?"

The other woman nodded and left the room.

"What aren't you telling me?" MacEwan said immediately, his voice soft but fierce.

Nikki rubbed her eyes. She didn't need this, not on top of Jake getting hurt—and losing Michael. "There was a struggle in her bedroom. She was hurt, but I don't know how badly." She hesitated, not sure if she should go on.

"And?" MacEwan's voice was clipped, harsh.

She licked her lips. "Her lover was a vampire. He turned her."

He stared at her for several seconds. "But if she's like Monica was, there would have been mass killings reported, and there hasn't been anything like that. There's only been a couple of shootings."

One of which was Jake, she thought, and swallowed heavily. "It might only mean she's no longer in Lyndhurst." She hesitated, frowning. "Ask your sister if she's missing anything—something personal but old, that has perhaps been in your family for years."

Michael had once told her a fledging vampire had to return to home ground and find something of the past to carry with them through eternity—a reminder of everything they once were, and everything they had lost. If Rachel were alive, then some family heirloom of her mother's would be missing.

MacEwan frowned. "Why?"

"Because it'll mean she survived the turning process and is out there somewhere."

MacEwan scrubbed a hand across his jaw. "There was no sign of a struggle in her bedroom, you know. No blood."

Which might only mean the vampire who'd turned Rachel had cleaned up after himself.

"You're wrong," he continued. "You have to be."

Though his voice was harsh, Nikki saw the anguish in his brown eyes. Despite his words, MacEwan believed her. He'd seen Monica rise from the dead and had battled against the zombies. He knew what Rachel's turning meant. Knew what he would eventually have to do.

"For Sondra's sake, I hope I am," she said softly. It wouldn't be the first time, and it was always possible she'd somehow read the images wrong. Though her gut feeling was that this time she hadn't.

Sondra returned, carrying three glasses. Nikki accepted her drink with a smile, but the cool lemonade did little to ease the dryness in her throat.

MacEwan took a plastic bag from his pocket and tossed it to her. Her fingers tingled as she caught it, and wisps of color danced before her eyes, images that were unfocused but strong, even through the plastic. *This one could be bad*, she thought, but she really had no other choice. Not if she wanted to find Matthew alive.

She opened the bag. Sensations flooded her. Heat and color and sound became thick threads she could reach out and touch. They flowed like music around her, and every fiber of her being thrummed to their tune. The watch burned into her skin, and her senses leapt away, following the rainbow-colored trail back to Matthew.

But she didn't just see the resonances of past events. This time, she could feel his thoughts, see what he saw.

This time, she became one with him.

Five

The room was black. He couldn't see anything, not even a small crack of light. Matthew scrubbed his nose with the back of his hand. For the moment, he didn't mind the darkness. It meant no one could see he'd been crying.

He hadn't seen Lizzie since they'd dragged him from the trunk of the car and down a long series of steps to this room. He'd been hot and sweaty and thirsty, but he hadn't said anything. Just curled up in one corner of the bed like a scared animal.

Matthew sniffed. No wonder the guys at school hated him. They must have known what a coward he was.

Beyond the darkness of his room, he heard footsteps. He hugged his knees tighter and wished he'd listened to his mom. At least then he'd be home—though if his dad was there, drunk and beating up on her again, he was probably better off here.

The footsteps stopped. He stared into the darkness, his heart pounding in his ears. A door opened, and light flooded the room. He threw up a hand to protect his eyes.

"Matthew Kincaid, I gather."

He swallowed. He didn't like the sound of that voice. It was low pitched and hollow, as if the stranger spoke from the bottom of a deep well.

"Yes?" he said, his own voice high and shaky. He squinted but couldn't see anything more than a shadow. A big shadow—with wheels.

"You made several claims to Elizabeth. I hope they are true."

Elizabeth? Did he mean Lizzie? Matthew edged further into the corner. "Who are you?"

"No one you should fear if you told the truth."

"I did, I really did. Except for my age."

"For your sake, I hope so. Elizabeth? Make our young friend a little more...comfortable, will you?"

The door closed, leaving him in blackness again. He wiped his nose with the back of his hand and wished he'd had the courage to ask for a drink.

"How are you feeling, Matthew?"

He yelped and scrambled down to the far end of the bed, hands shaking as he stared into the darkness. The voice had come from right beside his bed, yet he couldn't see anyone.

"Relax. I mean you no harm."

He edged further away. "I don't believe you."

"You wanted to come here. You wanted to see Yellowstone with me, remember?"

"This isn't Yellowstone."

"No. But we're close. We could go there soon—tomorrow perhaps."

"I want to go home," he muttered sullenly. "This isn't fun."

"Reality never is," Lizzie agreed. "Look at me, Matthew."

"I can't see..." His voice faded. Gold fire flickered to life in the darkness. He stared. The flame grew brighter, transforming itself into a pair of dark amber eyes.

Something touched his hand. He tried to pull away, but couldn't. The eyes drew closer until they filled his sight. The touch moved to his neck. Pain hit him, filling his body. He tried to scream but no sound came out...

***

...Nikki jerked upright, the scream dying on her lips. MacEwan and Sondra were staring at her, their expressions alarmed and confused.

"Christ Almighty, what was that all about?" MacEwan reached for the pack of cigarettes on the side table.

"That was something I really hadn't expected." How in the hell had she joined minds with Matthew? It was something she'd only ever done once, when Michael had telepathically channeled her psychometry abilities in an effort to find and save Jake from Jasper's clutches.

"That doesn't really explain what just happened. You were scampering across the floor like some frightened animal."

It was only then that she realized she was no longer sitting on the sofa but on the floor, close to the fireplace. Heat crept across her cheeks. She must have been acting out what was happening to Matthew.

She rose and walked back to the sofa, grabbing her drink

from the side table. The ice had melted, making her wonder just how long she'd been in Matthew's thoughts.

She sat down. Sondra's face was ghostly, and there was fear in her eyes. Nikki wondered if it was fear of what had just happened—or maybe fear of *her.*

"Answer the damn question," MacEwan growled. "What in the hell just happened?"

She sighed and rubbed her eyes. It was a good question and not one she was entirely sure she could answer. "Instead of seeing images like I usually do, I somehow joined Matthew's mind. Became him, if you like."

MacEwan frowned. "So what you were doing was what Matthew was doing?"

For someone who supposedly didn't believe in psychic talents, he caught on pretty fast. "Yes."

"Then he's alive?"

"Yes." Though given the woman was apparently feeding off him, she wasn't about to take bets on how long he would remain that way.

MacEwan took several puffs on his cigarette and blew the smoke toward the ceiling. "Any idea where?"

Nikki shrugged. "The woman mentioned Yellowstone National Park, but that doesn't mean he's anywhere near there."

"Well, if it's Yellowstone, that pins it down to either Wyoming, Montana or Idaho," MacEwan said dryly. "Don't suppose you care to be a little more specific?"

She glanced at the watch still clenched in her hand. "Wyoming. He's in Wyoming." The images reached for her again—images filled with lust and wanting. She shuddered and thrust the watch back in the bag.

MacEwan sniffed. "Jackson is the biggest town near Yellowstone. I'll send a report to the sheriff's department, get them to keep an eye open."

"He's not in Jackson." She frowned, concentrating on the ghostly images still flitting past the protection of the bag. "But some place called Jackson Hole."

"Ski resort area," MacEwan muttered. "I'll see what I can do."

Nikki nodded and gulped down the rest of her drink. "You mind if I keep the watch for a while?"

MacEwan's look was shrewd. "You intending to track down Kincaid?"

She nodded. Just because they were near Yellowstone now didn't mean they would stay there, and Wyoming was a big place. She'd need something to help pin down his exact location.

"You said the man who took my niece had Wyoming plates," MacEwan continued, his voice flat once again. "Don't suppose you'd want to take something of hers along and see if you can find anything once you're there?"

She had a feeling saying no wasn't an option. "I'll take the bra. Just don't expect miracles."

He nodded. "And don't go anywhere before you give me that description."

"I won't." She rose and offered her hand to Sondra. "Sorry I couldn't be of more help."

Sondra's grip was wet. "Thank you for trying."

The dam in her brown eyes was threatening to overflow again. Nikki quickly followed MacEwan out of the room.

He opened the front door then scowled down at her. "If you find anything on Rachel, no matter how small, I want to be told."

Or there would be serious consequences, she thought. "I'll see you this afternoon."

The door slammed shut behind her. She stopped, studying the traffic flowing past. Despite the early hour, the air was already uncomfortably hot. She shaded her eyes and glanced up at the sky. Not a cloud in sight, despite the weathermen promising relief in the form of severe thunderstorms. In this day and age, how could they get it so wrong so often?

It was useless going home. Though she was dog-tired, she wouldn't sleep. Not in this heat, and not until she knew how Jake was.

She glanced back at MacEwan's house. Maybe she should use his phone and call a cab. But that would mean facing Sondra again. Nikki grimaced. She'd never been comfortable with overt displays of emotion—which, she thought bitterly, was part of the reason Michael had left. Besides, she doubted if she actually had enough cash on her to pay for a cab.

Taking a bus was definitely out as an option. Given it was nearly eight-thirty, the buses would be overflowing with the day's workers. She'd probably end up crammed nose first in someone's armpit. *No thanks.* But she'd left her car at the office, so her only other option was walking. She resolutely walked toward the business district.

It took nearly an hour to reach the single story office block that was the agency's home. She leaned her forehead against the door for several minutes, not having the energy to reach into her pocket and get the keys. Sweat dripped off her chin, splattering to the pavement, only to dry almost instantly. If you listened hard enough, she thought, you'd probably hear it sizzling.

Above the noise of the morning traffic came the soft whump-whump of rotor blades—a helicopter, flying low. She glanced up. A sleek black and silver machine swept from behind the buildings at the end of the street and flew towards her. It was low—too low really, unless they were intending to land. Trouble was, none of the nearby buildings had helipads big enough to handle a helicopter of that size. The nearest was down near the docks.

It swept over her building, the noise almost deafening, then did a sharp left and disappeared. The noise faded. Probably one of those traffic reporters checking the roads for the local radio station—though if that were the case, why had the windows been so darkly tinted? Shrugging, she entered the office, dumping the two plastic bags on her desk before walking across to the counter that held the coffeepot. Jake had left it on earlier, presuming they'd only be gone a few hours. She bit her lip, blinking back the sting of tears. Jake would be all right. He'd survived Jasper. Surely he could survive this.

She grabbed a cup and filled it with coffee. It looked strong enough to hold a stick upright, but she didn't care. The coffee was hot and, more importantly, full of caffeine. Just the sort of energy boost she needed.

She headed back to her desk. Lights flashed madly on the phone, indicating several people had tried to call. She ignored them and picked up the phone book, sipping her coffee as she searched for the airline numbers.

It would probably cost a damn fortune to fly to Wyoming. But if she wanted to find Matthew fast, then flying was her only real option. Her car barely made it across town these days—driving to Wyoming was out of the question. She just had to hope the agency's credit card had enough left on it to cover the cost of the trip, because she certainly didn't have all that much left in the bank.

Suddenly, the back of her neck tingled a warning, and she froze. Though she hadn't heard the door open, someone had come into the office...

"Hello Nikki," Michael said softly behind her.

Six

For several seconds she simply sat there, unable to believe she'd heard his voice. Unwilling to turn around and perhaps discover a stranger.

"In very many ways I am a stranger," he said softly. "We had less than a week together."

His breath washed warmth across the back of her neck. She shivered and rubbed her arms. Why hadn't she felt him enter? Why did she feel nothing in the link between them but an odd sort of grey, when once it had been so full of color and emotion that she had feared its brightness? Now, of all times, when he was standing so close that the heat of his body caressed her skin, she should have felt the rainbow of his thoughts.

That she didn't scared the hell out of her.

"Nothing has happened to the link, Nikki. It is still there."

His soft tones wrapped around her, warm and yet somehow wary. She closed her eyes and took a deep, shuddering breath. Six months she'd waited to hear his voice. Six long months. Now he stood behind her, and she wasn't entirely sure what she should do or say.

"I used to know when you walked into the room, used to be able to feel you," she said softly. "Even before the link became strong between us."

"Many things have changed."

"And some things haven't." He was still talking in riddles, still not coming out with the entire truth. Last time it had led to death. She had a horrible feeling it just might again.

He sighed. "Will you at least face me?"

She bit her lip and slowly turned. He stood at the end of her desk, a briefcase clutched in one hand, his knuckles almost white. His dark hair was longer than she remembered, and the finely chiselled planes of his cheeks sharper. *He's lost weight*, she thought. The arms that had once held her so tenderly seemed leaner, as if what little fat there was had been burned off, leaving only muscle. Her gaze dropped. His jeans were tight enough to show the sinewy strength of his legs...legs that had once locked her close, as if he never meant to let her go.

But he had let her go. He'd walked away when she was in the hospital, not even waiting until she was conscious to say his good-byes.

As if she'd meant nothing to him.

"Why won't you look at me, Nikki?"

"Because I don't want to see the truth in your eyes," she said quietly. A truth told by the silence in the link and the lack of emotion in his words and actions. A truth that knifed through her hopes and turned them to ashes.

He hadn't come back for her.

"I almost killed you six months ago. I'll not take the chance of it happening again."

The edge of pain in his soft voice cut through her. He still cared, no matter how controlled, how distant, he seemed.

She lifted her gaze, finally meeting his.

His eyes were endless pools of ebony in which she'd once so gladly lost her heart. "I thought you said I couldn't die as long as you lived."

"You are not immortal, Nikki, as I am not immortal." He hesitated. "And because it is my psyche you share, I can kill you more easily than other vampires could."

You have the taste of another vampire on you, the woman in the warehouse had said. Did that mean she'd sensed the life force Michael had shared with her? Or did it mean Jasper had left an imprint when he'd dined on her blood?

She shivered. She had to hope it was the former. The thought that a small part of Jasper might linger within her chilled her soul.

"And that's why you walked away?" Jake had said as much in the hospital, but she hadn't been willing to believe Michael would walk away over something so trivial. Besides, if he'd had the strength to stop drinking her blood when he was basically unconscious, what made him think he wouldn't when he was fully aware of what he was doing?

He met her gaze. There was no emotion in his eyes, no emotion in his expression. Nothing that would give her some clue to what he was thinking and feeling.

But perhaps she was looking for something that had never really been there in the first place. He'd once suggested that theirs was a love destined to burn brightly but die quickly.

He might still care, but caring wasn't the same as loving. Damn it, why wasn't the link active between them? If ever there was a time she needed to read the color of his thoughts, it was now.

"It is for the best," he said flatly.

Her smile felt as brittle as her heart. "You once asked me if I had the courage to look beyond the gift you gave me. Perhaps it is a question you should also ask yourself."

A gentle, almost wistful, smile touched his lips. "Nikki, I have had six months to think about nothing else." He raised a hand, pushing a wisp of limp hair away from her eyes. His fingers trailed heat against her skin. "There has been enough darkness in your life. I cannot change what I am or what I do, and I will not bring you into the darkness of my world any more than I already have."

She raised an eyebrow. "Don't you think that's a decision I should at least have a say in?"

His fingers drifted down her cheek. She clenched her hands, resisting the temptation to step into his arms. To hold him and never let him go.

"No." His voice was distant, distracted. His fingertips fell to her neck and brushed back her hair.

Though his touch was gentle, it burned deep. She wanted, needed, this man in her life.

"Jasper was but a taste of the things I hunt, Nikki. Do you really think you could walk in that darkness all the time?"

Did he really think she could walk through the years ahead without him? Damn it, she loved him. If he could read her thoughts so clearly, surely he could see the three words she feared to say out loud.

"I don't know." She hesitated, staring at him. Just for an instant, something glimmered in his dark eyes—an echo of depravity that reminded her of Jasper.

He snatched his hand away from her neck, then spun and walked away. Fear stepped further into her heart as she watched his retreat.

Instinct suggested she'd come close to death. Suggested that Michael's vampire instincts had almost overridden his control.

And it was her fault. In saving his life by feeding him her blood, she'd destroyed the control it had taken him three hundred years to achieve.

"Oh, God, Michael, I'm so sorry," she whispered.

"Don't."

He'd stopped near Jake's desk. She stared at his back, saw the tension in the set of his shoulders and arms. Could feel his anger and frustration, a wave of heat that boiled across her skin.

"You did what you thought was best," he continued.

Yes, she had, but what good had it done? In some respects, she'd still lost him. She rubbed her eyes wearily. "Why are you here?"

He glanced around. The wisp of depravity had left his eyes, but the anger still burned. "You are working on a case at the moment, are you not?"

"I'm a private investigator," she reminded him blandly. "That's what I do."

Two could play word games. If he wouldn't come straight out and tell her why he was here, why should she offer anything more than what he'd actually asked?

He sat on the edge of Jake's desk and slowly swung one leg. He looked casual, unconcerned, yet she knew the appearance was a lie. Tension and worry were emanating from him in waves thick enough to touch.

"This is a case that has gone wrong," he said.

"Lots of cases go wrong, Michael. Take Monica Trevgard's case. It certainly didn't end the way I wanted it to."

If her words had any impact, it certainly didn't show. His face remained as impassive as ever. "Stop playing games, Nikki. You need to go to Jackson Hole, Wyoming, and I need your help."

"I'm not the one playing games. Nor am I the one skirting the real issue here." She stared at him for several seconds.

When he didn't respond, she sighed and wrapped her hands around her coffee cup, studying the dark liquid intently. "Why me? Why now? Don't you belong to some organization full of psychics and vampires and God knows what else?"

His reply was terse. "Yes. And it is the lady in charge of that organization who insists I accompany you."

Obviously, given the choice, he'd rather be anywhere else than here. She closed her eyes, fighting the sting of tears. "That still doesn't answer the question of why it has to be me."

He hesitated. "Seline did a reading. If you go there alone, you will die."

Fear rose. Yet death, in one form or another, had been a constant shadow in her life. She glanced up sharply. "Why was she doing a reading on me?"

"She wasn't. She was trying to discover more information about Vance Hutton."

Nikki frowned. "The actor? Why?"

"He's disappeared from an exclusive resort in Jackson Hole, and apparently he's not the first."

"So why are you getting involved?"

"The resort is the base for some form of dark force. Whether it is a vampire or something worse, Seline can't say. So she sends a killer to hunt a killer."

A chill raced across her flesh. What in the hell could be worse than a vampire like Jasper? "So how did my name get involved?"

He shrugged gracefully. "Seline's visions sometimes have a will of their own."

"And you believe her?"

His dark gaze met hers. "I would not be here otherwise."

Though she'd known this all along, having it said out loud seemed to make it final. Unchangeable. Like he'd taken the knife from her boot and sliced open her heart.

She looked down at her coffee. A tear ran down her cheek and splashed against the back of her hand. She ignored it. "What happens if the kid I'm looking for isn't in Jackson Hole?" Even though it felt as if someone were squeezing her throat tight, her voice came out even, as devoid of emotion as his.

"If it comes to that, you can search nearby areas during the day."

She frowned. It was tempting, if only because she'd be close to Michael. Yet she couldn't escape the feeling that he wasn't telling her everything. "How expensive is this place?"

"The Circle will pay for everything."

"And in return?"

He hesitated. "You are to be my cover. The resort is geared towards couples."

A couple? How could that work when he couldn't even touch her? And even if he could, could she survive touching and kissing and loving him, knowing all along it was nothing more than a lie? That after the mission was over he'd simply leave? "If you think you can share my bed and just walk away again, I've got news for you—I'm not that easy."

"I never thought you were." He sighed and looked away. "Believe me, this is as hard for me as it is for you. But we have no other choice."

"Bullshit, Michael. We have plenty of other choices. You're just afraid to try." As she'd been, not so long ago. Yet even then, even as he'd tried to make her admit her feelings, he'd warned he would never stay. That she could never share his world.

She hadn't believed it then, and she didn't believe it now.

"I have watched the passing of three centuries," he said softly. "I have buried those that I cared about more times than I want to remember. I do not want to have to bury you as well."

"And I have lived just over a quarter of a century, but I've watched my mother, father and lover die brutal deaths. What makes us so different?"

"The fact that I must drink blood to survive." His voice was as hard as his expression.

"A fact I'm well aware of, believe me."

He made a chopping motion with his hand. "Enough, Nikki. This is strictly a business proposition, nothing more."

After what they'd been through? After what they'd shared? Not likely.

"Okay then," she said, her voice sharp. "When do we leave?"

He raised an eyebrow in surprise. "No further arguments? Questions?"

"Nope. You can brief me on the details during the flight there."

"Okay." He hesitated, his expression a little confused. "We have seats booked on the eight-thirty flight."

She glanced at her watch. If she went home now, she'd have plenty of time to catch a shower and rest before she had to get ready. She gulped down the last of her coffee and rose.

"Since it's nearly ten and the sun plays havoc with your health, do you want to stay here? The sofa's still in the storeroom if you want to lie down."

"If that is all right by you." He was regarding her warily, as if expecting a violent explosion at any second.

"I have to see MacEwan at five, so I'll come by and pick you up after that."

"Fine." He frowned. "Are you okay?"

"Yes." She picked up her keys and headed for the door, then hesitated, looking back. "The last time you were in Lyndhurst, you taught me a very important lesson. Life is for living. You cannot fear it. You cannot retreat from it. I'm not retreating, Michael, and I'm sure as hell not giving up. I never will."

She walked out, slamming the door shut behind her.

Seven

The aircraft engines' droning was the only sound that broke the silence. Night filled the cabin, and around him, people slept and dreamed.

Michael stretched out his legs, grateful that Seline had booked first-class seats. He wasn't sure he could have handled anything else right now—he hated flying at the best of times, especially in economy, with its cramped seats and lack of elbow room. Conditions that would have been made all the more unbearable with Nikki wedged beside him.

He'd known his blood lust might pose a threat to her, especially since she'd been the first human he'd tasted in well over three hundred years. Yet the urge to feed off her had been surprisingly easy to control.

What he hadn't expected was the fierce and utter joy of simply seeing her again. The need to touch her, kiss her, had been so strong that he'd walked across the office to her desk before he'd managed to restrain himself.

But like his lust for blood, his desire for her was something he could not afford. He rubbed a hand across his eyes, then looked at her. She was asleep, curled up in the seat next to him, her dark chestnut hair falling across her delicate features like a veil. She smelled of cinnamon and vanilla, of life and love and everything he wanted and couldn't have.

He reached out, gently tucking behind her ear the silken wisps of hair. She stirred at his touch, murmuring something he didn't catch. He trailed his fingers down to her mouth, remembering the last time they'd kissed, and the warmth of her lips against his. Remembered their mind's fiery dance that had made them one in a way the mere joining of their bodies never could.

Memories that were dangerously seductive when she was so close.

He dropped his hand and stared out the window again. The plane was beginning its descent. Lights twinkled starlike in the darkness beyond the window. The resort was sending a limousine to pick them up from the airport—an extravagant service that wasn't really surprising, given the sort of money they were paying.

"Just how expensive is this place?" Nikki said softly.

He glanced at her. Her smoky amber eyes regarded him steadily. Had his touch woken her, or had she been feigning sleep? "I thought you said you couldn't read my thoughts?"

She frowned. "I get a whisper every now and then. Most of the time, it feels like there's interference on the line. All I get is a dead sort of silence."

He had to hope so, given the psychic strength he was expending trying to keep the link closed between them—something that wouldn't have been possible before he'd shared his life force and made them one. The joining had given him that much control, at least. "Give it time, Nikki."

She raised an eyebrow, her gaze clearly skeptical. "Will time make any real difference?"

It wouldn't, and they both knew it. He could see the understanding, the hurt, deep in the amber depths of her eyes. "Have you got a photo of the child you're looking for?"

She regarded him a minute longer, then shrugged and dug into her purse. "Matthew Kincaid," she said, handing him a photo of a red-haired, gangly-looking youth. "Sixteen years old and has an I.Q. rated in the genius class. Few friends in or out of school, but plenty on the Net, according to his mother."

"And it was one of those friends who abducted him?"

She nodded. "Only the friend was a very old vamp with lots of vamp buddies."

He raised an eyebrow in surprise. "Why do you think it was a very old vampire he met?"

She frowned slightly. "Just a feeling I got. She felt evil, like Jasper—only different."

"Different how?" And what was it about Lyndhurst that seemed to attract vampires like Jasper—and now this woman?

Her frown deepened, and worry etched deep lines across her forehead. He clenched his hand against the sudden desire to smooth them away.

"I don't know how to explain it," she said softly. "It's just a feeling I get—a taste, if you like." She hesitated, her gaze searching his. "Remember when you were following me through that park, before we actually met? I knew then what you were capable of. I knew you'd come to Lyndhurst to kill. But you didn't feel evil, and I never really feared you. Not like Jasper—or this woman."

The fear she refused to show now ran wild in her thoughts. He touched her hand, gently entwining his fingers with hers. The warmth of her skin cut through him, as sharp as any knife. "Can you describe her?"

She looked down, a small smile touching her lips. "No. She kept to the shadows. I only saw her assistants clearly."

"How many did she have?"

"Four or five. Which was odd, really, considering their quarry was only a gawky teenager."

He frowned. If the vampire were as old as Nikki seemed to think, she certainly wouldn't have any need for one assistant, let alone five. "Did she say anything?"

Nikki's shoulders tensed, and her heart rate jumped several notches. Hunger stirred to sluggish life deep in his gut. He frowned and untwined his fingers from hers. Too much too soon, he thought, and knew he was going to have to tread carefully around her. The hunger for her blood might be under control, but it hadn't yet abated.

She crossed her arms and leaned back in her seat, a distancing that was as much mental as it was physical. Yet in her eyes he saw understanding. She knew what was happening to him.

"Actually, for a vampire she was a damn chatterbox. I don't think she intends to kill Matthew right away. She said they have other plans for him."

"I guess she didn't say what?"

"No vampire is *that* chatty." Her voice held a slight edge of sarcasm. "Not the ones I've met, anyway."

He smiled slightly. "Did she say anything else?"

She hesitated. "Yeah. She said I had the taste of a vampire on me, and that she didn't want to upset my master." Her expression was curious and more than a touch afraid. "What did she mean by that?"

"It means she could sense my life force in you." And meant this woman was old—older than he, even. Only the very old vampires knew about thralls—and only they could sense them.

Could this woman be the darkness Seline had sensed at the resort?

"But what did she mean by my master?" She hesitated again, glancing around at the other passengers.

"Don't worry," he said. "They're all asleep." He'd touched their thoughts and made sure of that a few hours ago.

Her quick frown made him wonder if she'd realized what he'd done. She hated any sort of psychic intrusion, even when it was attempted on other people. And her first lover, Tommy, and to some extent Jasper, had certainly insured that she feared it.

"And why did she say I'm not human? If I'm not, then what the hell am I?"

"You are still human, Nikki, as I am still human."

She snorted. "Oh, *that's* so very comforting. You have a serious aversion to sunlight and drink blood to survive."

"And you do not."

"No. But there are drawbacks you haven't told me about, aren't there?"

"No," he said, even though there were. Lots of them. Like being an easy target for those vampires old enough to know what she was—and how to use her to get to him and destroy him. If the vampire who'd taken Matthew was also involved in the resort kidnappings, they were both in serious danger.

But he also knew he didn't have a hope in Hades of getting her to turn around and go home. As she'd warned, she didn't give up and she didn't give in. He'd just have to find some way to keep her out of trouble.

"Why can't you just be honest with me, Michael? Even on something as simple as this?"

He looked away from the accusation in her eyes. "I can not change three hundred years of habit in a matter of months."

"Can't, or won't?" she muttered.

"Both." Because honesty was a dangerous weapon when you held as many secrets as he did.

She pulled her gaze from his, but not before he'd seen the glitter of tears. He rubbed a hand across his eyes and silently cursed the capriciousness of fate. Why couldn't it have just left well enough alone? He didn't want to hurt her, but he had no doubt that he would, and more than once—until she accepted they were something that could never be.

And what is she supposed to do in the long years that

lie ahead? He shoved the thought aside and reached for the briefcase near his feet. "You should read this," he said, handing her a manila folder.

"What is it?" She accepted the folder without looking at him.

"Background info. How we met, when we were married."

"I see we're on our honeymoon." She snorted softly and glanced up. "That'll be a hard act to pull off when you won't even touch me."

"As you can see," he said, ignoring the tartness in her words, "Seline kept as close to the truth as she could. Less room for mistakes that way."

"Are you rich? This implies you're a multimillionaire." She raised an eyebrow and studied him warily.

Why? What was it about wealth that worried her? "You cannot live for as long as I have without collecting a certain amount of financial independence."

"Which is a roundabout way of saying you're swimming in it." She shook her head, then added in a voice that was little more than a murmur, "I really don't know anything about you, do I?"

And that was the way he intended to keep it. He pointed to the ring taped to the top of the folder. "Your wedding ring."

"Not what I would have chosen," she muttered. She slipped it on her finger, then held out her hand, studying it. The diamond crusted ring looked huge on her. "Ugly. I hope you didn't choose this monstrosity."

"No, that's Seline's doing, and part of the cover." If he ever gave Nikki a ring, it certainly wouldn't be made of diamonds or gold. It would be simple, carved from the stone of his birthplace, Eire. Like the ring he wore on his right hand—the ring his grandfather had made. A ring made from the heart.

She glanced back to the folder. "Oh great," she continued after a few moments. "I not only have bad taste in rings, but I'm a gold-digger as well."

"Nine of the fifteen people who have disappeared from the resort had marriages that could be classified as dubious—huge age discrepancies or vastly different socioeconomic backgrounds."

"So? Old rich guys marry dumb, busty women all the time.

If you ask me, it's a fair swap. She gets his money, and he gets a pretty body to play with until he dies." She closed the folder and handed it back. "Besides, Vance Hutton hardly falls into that category."

"No, he doesn't. But what is even odder is the fact that his wife is the only one who's actually raised a fuss."

Nikki raised her eyebrows. "You mean, fifteen mega-wealthy men have disappeared and no one's noticed? That's not possible."

"You would have thought so. Mind you, all but three have reappeared."

"Unharmed?"

"Apparently. Reports are that they only seem to go out at night, but otherwise, it's life as normal."

"Are they vampires?"

"No."

"Weird."

It was weird all right, and he couldn't help thinking the answers might be in the same league.

The 'seat belts' light pinged on, and a flight attendant announced they were getting ready to land. Michael clipped his in, then helped Nikki with hers. But in leaning over, their bodies brushed, and her scent ambushed him. For several heartbeats all he could do was stare into the dark amber eyes that had haunted his dreams and wish he was free to touch her, hold her.

She cupped her palm against his cheek. Heat splintered through him, sharpened by longing.

"What lies between us will not go away," she said softly. "You can deny it all you want, push it away and ignore it, but it will still be there. And so will I."

He pulled away from her touch. It was probably the hardest thing he'd ever had to do. "My world is darkness, Nikki. Yours is light. We cannot be."

She raised an eyebrow and didn't reply. He met her gaze steadily, undeterred by her determined expression or the edge of hurt in her eyes. After several seconds, she looked away.

Leaving him feeling like a bastard.

The plane taxied to a stop, and the crew cheerfully ushered them from it. He guided Nikki through the crowd, one hand held lightly against her back as they headed to the baggage area. "The limo driver should be waiting near the carousel."

She nodded. Under the harsh light of the terminal, the dark circles shadowing her eyes looked like bruises. "I have to call the hospital when we get to the resort. I want to find out how Jake is."

"He's tough, Nikki. He'll be okay."

"I hope you're right," she murmured. "Because he's all the family I have left."

And I'm not sure what I'll do without him. The thought skimmed through the link, sharp with pain. "I have never met a human with a will to live as strong as Jake's. He'll be okay." Meaningless words when it wasn't the will but the heart that was apparently the problem.

She smiled slightly. "Thank you for saying that."

He nodded, hoping he was right. He liked Jake. He touched her back again, guiding her to the right, towards the carousel.

Several uniformed men and woman stood close by, each holding up different name cards. Surprisingly, his name wasn't among the cards.

Nikki stopped suddenly, and fear surged like fire through the link.

"What's wrong," he said, glancing around quickly. He couldn't see or feel any threat, but he'd learned to trust her senses when it came to situations slightly out of kilter.

"See that guy dressed in the blue and red uniform with the resort's gold logo on the pocket? The one holding the sign with the name Rodeman on it?"

He looked, and saw what she saw.

The chauffeur was a vampire.

Eight

"But not just one of your plain old, garden variety vampires," Nikki said softly. "He's one of the vamps who attacked us in the warehouse."

And judging from the way he was bent over slightly, as if he had stomach cramps, he was the vamp she'd stabbed with the knife. He looked different under the harsh lights—scrawnier, somehow.

Michael took the bags from the carousel and dropped them onto a cart. "It can't be a trap of any kind. The booking's been made under my name, not an alias, and Seline would have contacted me had there been any inquiries."

"But if he sees me, he'll know who I am." She met Michael's dark gaze. "Is this what Seline meant when she said if I came here alone I would die?"

"I doubt if a lone vampire intent on vengeance would pose much of a threat to you these days." He touched her shoulder lightly, his fingers burning heat through her soul. "Stay here. I'll just go and have a nice little chat with him."

"Why do men always say 'stay here'?" Irritation bit through her words, despite her best efforts to remain calm. "Don't you know by now it's only an open invitation to do the exact opposite?"

He placed a finger against her lips. "Will you please be quiet and just wait? I'll be right back."

His eyes were filled with the promise of death. She shivered and crossed her arms, watching him walk away. The other vampire chose that moment to turn around. Recognition widened his gaze for a second, then he looked from her to Michael. How he knew they were together she wasn't sure, but the sudden fear in his eyes was visible even from where she stood.

He ran for the main entrance and out into the night. Michael ran after him. Nikki cursed under her breath. Damn it, she wasn't going to be left behind like some good little wife...even if that was exactly what she was supposed to be.

She grabbed the cart with their luggage and ran after them.

The night air was cool and the wind held only the faintest memory of the day's heat. She stopped and looked around. People pushed past her, heading for the waiting cabs and buses. Headlights spotlighted the night as other passengers climbed into cars and drove away. She couldn't see Michael or the other vampire, but she didn't really need to. Not when the presence of the younger vampire itched at her skin.

She wheeled the cart toward the parking garage. Darkness soon engulfed her, broken intermittently by the wash of brightness from the overhead lights. The noise and bustle of the airport faded, and the silence became blanket heavy.

Her gaze swept the silent rows of cars. Someone was close, even if she couldn't see them. Her skin was itching so fiercely it felt like it was burning. Noise scuffed to her left. She jumped slightly, half turning, then a prickle of awareness ran across the back of her neck. He was behind her.

She swung, seeing only darkness, yet knowing the night lied. Air stirred, flushed with heat and anger, rushing toward her. Fear squeezed her throat tight. She jumped back, but before she could lash the night-cloaked vampire with energy, Michael dove in from the left. He hit the unseen vampire hard, driving him to the ground with a thump that made her wince.

The shadows abandoned the vampire almost immediately, revealing a gaunt, pain-ravaged face and wild blue eyes. He reminded Nikki of the feral kids she'd met so often in the days when she'd lived on the streets herself. He even fought like them, spindly arms and legs going everywhere but with little effect. There was no real strength or method in his movements, just desperation to get what he wanted—which in this case was her.

Michael sat on the vampire's chest, then grabbed his arms, crossing and pushing them toward the ground. The vampire had no choice but to stop fighting or risk breaking both his shoulders.

"Why are you here?" Though Michael's voice was soft, there was a deadliness to it that chilled her. There was no compassion in his words, no life.

"I'm a chauffeur, man." Sweat was beginning to bead the

vampire's forehead. "What do you think I'm here for?"

"And does the resort often send vampires to greet their guests?"

"No."

"Then tell me why you are here." Michael punctuated his soft words by pushing a little harder on the vampire's crossed arms.

The vampire yelped. "To meet with a guest and his wife and take them to the resort. I swear, that's all."

Sweat was trickling faster down his face now, and his cheeks were beginning to glow with heat. She rubbed her arms. There was something more than fear happening here.

"And the name of this guest?"

The trickle had become a stream. Water dripped from the young vampire's face, pooling near the back of his neck. Dark stains were appearing under his arms and across his stomach.

"Rodeman," he said, voice high and cracked with pain. "Some old dude and his new wife."

She met Michael's glance and smiled grimly. "Want to bet that this Rodeman is number sixteen on the disappearing list?"

"Too much of a chance, given the publicity caused by Hutton's recent disappearance."

The vampire's eyes widened even further at the mention of the actor's name. He looked like an owl—all white face and huge eyes. He also looked gaunter than he had in the terminal—almost skeletal.

"You some kind of cop?" he asked.

"Some kind," Michael agreed. "Would you like to tell me what you intended to do with Rodeman once you'd picked him up?"

The vampire licked his lips—lips that were so dry they were beginning to crack and bleed. "Drive him to the resort. That's all, really."

"No stopping for midnight snacks along the way?" Michael said, his voice deepening sharply.

"No. I swear..."

Smoke was beginning to curl from the vampire's shoes, and the pungent aroma of roasting meat fouled the night air.

Her stomach began to churn. Jasper had smelled that way the day the sun had burned him out of existence. A chill raced across her skin.

"Michael, get off him."

"I'm in control, Nikki." Though his voice was even, his anger ran sharply through the link.

Smoky tendrils had crept up to the young vampire's ankles and were creeping towards his knees. "That's not what I meant. Get off him, *now!*"

He glanced at her, then released the vampire's arms and climbed quickly to his feet. She grabbed his arm, pulling him away. The vampire didn't move. Couldn't move. His eyes were wide and glassy, bloody mouth open, as if he were screaming. Water was pooled under his entire body, and the steam was rising from both legs.

She held a hand to her mouth. "It's like he's melting," she said, swallowing heavily. "Like he's wasting away from the inside."

"I think he is."

Michael clasped her hand, but the warmth of his touch did little to ease the coldness creeping through her. "How is something like that possible? He's a vampire—I thought you guys were impervious to just about everything."

"We normally are, but I think we can safely say this goes beyond the realms of what can be considered normal."

The vampire's body was closing in on itself, collapsing as quickly as a tent. Steam was rising from most of his body, and the stench of burning flesh was thick enough to carve. Though his face was little more than a skeleton, his eyes were alive with horror.

Whoever or whatever was doing this to him hadn't had the decency to take that awareness away. He was little more than a puddle, and yet he could still think. Could still feel.

Bile rose in her throat. She wrenched her hand from Michael's and stumbled away, losing behind the nearest car what she'd eaten on the aircraft. He touched her back, holding her gently until the shudders had passed, then offered her a handkerchief.

"You should have stayed in the terminal, like I asked," he chided softly.

She straightened and wiped her mouth. What she needed now was a drink and an explanation, not an I-told-you-so. "Did you honestly expect me to wait?" she muttered.

He smiled, a warmth she felt deep inside, and tucked a wisp of hair behind her ear. His fingers trailed heat across her chilled skin. "I guess I didn't."

"What just happened? How can someone simply melt away like that?"

Though his dark gaze was emotionless, his unease surged briefly down the link between them. "They say the human body is ninety-percent water. I guess melting is not beyond the realms of possibility."

"Obviously, seeing it just happened." Sarcasm bit through her words. She crossed her arms and glared at him. "But my real question is *how*? Melting is not something often attached to the human condition, you know."

He shrugged, studying the empty uniform and puddled water, all that remained of the younger vampire. "I think we're dealing with some form of black magic."

She blinked. "Magic?"

He nodded. "I'll have to talk to Seline, since she's the expert in that field. But it really happened too quickly for it to be anything else."

"*Magic?*" she repeated dumbly.

He glanced at her, amusement flitting through his eyes. "It's as real as vampires, and just as dangerous."

Fear rose, squeezing her throat tight. "Then whoever's behind all this knows we're here. They killed him to stop him talking."

"I doubt it. Even in the terminal, he didn't look well. Whatever happened to him was happening then, I think."

"But why send a vampire—and a sick one at that—to greet guests? That doesn't make any sense."

"And probably won't until we discover exactly what is happening at the resort."

She thrust a hand through her hair. "I don't like the feel of this, Michael."

"Then go home."

She snorted softly. "Go home. Keep safe. Is that your answer to everything?"

"It's only sensible. You're out of your league on this one."

Yeah, right. And wouldn't sending her home suit him right down to the ground—at least then he wouldn't have to worry about her hanging around upsetting his precious resolves. "And you're not? You've already admitted black magic is not a field you're familiar with. Besides, I made a commitment to find Matthew Kincaid, and I have no intention of going anywhere until I do." And no intention of going anywhere *once* she did.

Annoyance stirred around her. She frowned, wondering why the link surged to life only when his emotions got the better of his control.

"Matthew may not even be at the resort," he said steadily.

"Then I'll use his watch to discover his exact position and rescue him." She raised an eyebrow. "You're not going to get rid of me that easily, you know."

"So you keep saying." He sighed and gestured toward the airport terminal. "We'd better get back and see if we can find our chauffeur."

"And what about him?" she said, pointing to the wet remains.

"Let his employers worry about him." He grabbed the cart then lightly touched her arm. "Let's go."

They walked back to the terminal. There were fewer people around this time. Most of their fellow passengers had obviously found transportation to whisk them from the airport. Michael grabbed a soda from a dispensing machine and handed it across to her. She sipped it warily, not wanting to upset her stomach but needing to get rid of the bitter taste in her mouth.

Just inside the main doors, a chauffeur dressed in blue and red waited, holding a sign with the name Kelly marked on it. With him was another couple—a man in his mid-sixties and his much younger, very busty, blonde wife.

"I'm Kelly," Michael said. "Sorry we're late. My wife was feeling sick and had to get some fresh air."

The driver nodded. He looked to be in his mid-thirties, his plain face suntanned and bored looking. "Would you mind if we take Mr. and Mrs. Rodeman with us? It appears their chauffeur has disappeared."

"Really? Well, sure, that's no problem." He held out his hand to the older man. "Michael Kelly."

"Lucas Rodeman and my wife, Ginger."

There was more than a hint of pride in the old man's voice. He touched his wife's arm, patting her gently. It reminded Nikki of the time Jake had won the amateur's trophy at the local golf club. He'd caressed the trophy in much the same manner—as if he couldn't quite believe his luck and just had to keep touching it to ensure it was real.

"Hello," Ginger said, her voice throaty and mellow.

She held out a limp-looking hand. Michael shook it quickly, then touched Nikki's back, his hand sliding a little, as if wiping away the feel of the woman's fingers.

She held out her hand. "Nikki." She shook Lucas's hand and moved on to Ginger's.

The blonde's fingers wrapped around hers—cold, clammy, and holding little strength. Yet heat rushed up Nikki's arm at her touch, burning through her body, her mind. She stared at the blonde's vacant blue eyes and saw only fire. Fingers of red heat reached out, flooding her mind with images. *A figure in black, chanting words that compelled. Ghostly forms that were nothing more than flame rising from the rocks, bending before the will of the words. Anger and humiliation and a hurt so deep it burned the air around it...*

The blonde's eyes widened slightly. Under the harsh brightness of the terminal lights, a myriad of scars seemed to cobweb the left side of her face and neck. Nikki wrenched her hand away, her legs suddenly weak.

Michael's hands went around her waist, steadying her. "Are you okay?"

Concern filled the air, and his voice seemed to be a million miles away. She didn't answer. Couldn't answer. Her throat was so dry it felt like it had been burned. Darkness whirled through her mind, and her whole body was trembling as if her strength had been sucked away by heat.

As consciousness slipped, she stared into the blonde's eyes and knew one thing.

Ginger Rodeman wasn't human.

Nine

Michael held onto Nikki tightly as she collapsed. She was limp and shivering, yet her skin burned so fiercely he could feel the heat though her clothes.

He gathered her in his arms and glanced at the chauffeur. "Would you mind grabbing the bags for me?"

"Is she going to be okay?" Concern flitted across Rodeman's pudgy features. "She doesn't have anything contagious, does she?"

"No, I just think she's eaten something that disagreed with her on the plane," Michael said, though he knew it was anything but.

Rodeman seemed placated by his comment. Michael touched the old man's thoughts—he wasn't thinking of anything more than getting his wife to the hotel—and bed. Ginger was a different matter entirely. Her thoughts were a vast well of emptiness. It was almost as if there was nothing there.

He frowned. What in the hell had gone on? He'd felt the surge of electricity through the link. For a second, it had felt as bright as flames. Then it had died, and Nikki collapsed. Was the blonde at fault, or had something else happened?

He wouldn't know until Nikki woke, and until then Rodeman and his wife weren't going to get beyond his sight. No matter what it took or what he had to do.

He followed the chauffeur out to the limousine. Nikki was featherlight in his arms. She certainly hadn't gained any weight in the six months he'd been away, and he wasn't surprised. She'd barely eaten enough to keep a gnat alive back then, and he doubted if his walking out on her would have improved her appetite any.

The chauffeur opened the rear door. Michael placed Nikki on the seat then climbed in beside her. He pillowed her head on his thigh and carefully brushed the hair from her closed eyes. Her skin still burned but, thankfully, the heat was at least abating. He reached down the link between them. Her thoughts were beginning to stir. Confusion and fear were uppermost in her mind, fogging the lingering images. But the reflection of flames came through clear and strong. Why? What was it about the blonde's touch that conjured so much heat in her mind and body?

Rodeman and his wife climbed into the limousine and made themselves comfortable on the opposite seat. The chauffeur leaned in the doorway. "There's some ice water in the refrigerator. And there are linen cloths beside the fruit platter. Might help if you cool her down a little."

"Let me," Ginger said.

Her mellow tones set his teeth on edge. She took a small bottle of water from the refrigerator and carefully wet the cloth before holding it out.

"Thanks," he said, managing to keep his voice neutral despite the anger surging through him—an anger that was born not only from worry, but his own inability to protect her. Damn it, this was the *precise* reason he couldn't afford to have her in his life.

He touched the cloth to Nikki's forehead. She sighed, and awareness surged through the link. He only partially raised his barriers. He needed to know what had happened, and the only way to do that immediately was to use the link.

Michael?

Her mind voice was full of uncertainty, as if she feared that by simply acknowledging it the link would disappear again. As it would once he knew what had happened to her.

Are you okay? He wiped her cheeks and neck, then placed the cloth back on her forehead.

Her sigh shimmered through him. *Yes. I just wasn't expecting that to happen.*

What exactly did happen?

Confusion surged, touched by fear. *I'm not sure. But my psychometry ability has been taking some strange turns lately. First I go so deep into Matthew's mind that I actually start acting out what he's doing, and now this. When I touched Ginger's hand, I was hit by images. Weird images, filled with flames and chanting and emotions.*

He frowned slightly. Going deep into Matthew's mind didn't

really surprise him. She'd had the psychic strength and the
capability to do it all along, but she hadn't realized it until he'd
merged their minds with Jake in an effort to find where Jasper
had him hidden. But touching the blonde's hand and seeing
images was something she should not have been able to do.
That was a form of clairvoyance, and as she said, her gift was
seeing the past from inanimate objects, not humans.

*What do you think these images were? Nightmares
lingering on the surface of her thoughts, perhaps?*

*No. They were memories. Ginger isn't human. I'm not
sure what in hell she is.*

Michael glanced out the window for several seconds,
watching the dark landscape go by. Four hearts beat steadily
into the silence—Nikki's, the chauffeurs, Rodeman and his wife.
Ginger looked, sounded, and smelled human. If she wasn't,
then she was the best damn imitation he'd ever seen.

What exactly did you see?

The images didn't make any sense.

*Tell me. Whether they make sense or not doesn't matter
right now.* Seline might see their meaning, even if he couldn't.
He had to contact the old witch before the morning, anyway, to
let her know they'd arrived safely.

Okay. She hesitated. Heat whispered across the link,
embers of memories stirred briefly to life. *There was a man
dressed in black, chanting. His words seemed to compel
flames from the rock. I could feel anger, humiliation and
hurt. Whether it belonged to the figure or the flames I'm
not sure.*

Is Ginger evil?

Confusion washed through the line, a timorous wave of
yellow. Michael frowned, wondering why her emotions seemed
to come through as colors. Odd, to say the least.

She's not evil—she's not anything. She just is.

His frown deepened. How could someone not be *anything*?
It didn't make any sense.

Her sigh shimmered. *I told you it didn't make any sense.*

She was reading his thoughts again. The link had to be
more open than he'd thought. *I told them you'd eaten*

something on the plane that disagreed with you.

Okay. She hesitated. Just for an instant, her spirit reached out to his, entwining them in a dance that was gentle and yet shocking in intensity. Then she was gone, from his thoughts and his soul, leaving him aching for more.

"Shouldn't have eaten that chicken," she murmured aloud.

He touched her face, his fingers still trembling from the power of the dance. "I did warn you about airline food," he said softly. "You feeling any better?"

She looked up at him, her dark amber eyes filled with laughter and longing. At that moment he knew she was going to make it as hard as she possibly could for him to walk away a second time.

But walk he would.

Because he'd rather see her lonely than dead. Because he didn't want to see her used in some madman's sick plot of revenge against him. Jasper had tried and failed, but others might succeed.

"A little," she said, then glanced across at Rodeman and his wife. "Sorry about fainting on you. I think it was a combination of bad food and the heat."

"Don't you worry about it, little lady. Why, Ginger here, she faints all the time."

Ginger smiled and patted her husband's hand. "I have only fainted once in the time we have been together. That, too, was caused by something I ate."

Her voice still grated against his nerves. Why? It wasn't exactly harsh on the ears. "How long have you two been married?"

"Three moons," she said. Heat crept across her pale cheeks. "Three months, I mean."

Michael raised an eyebrow. Moons was an interesting phrase to use.

"Moons, months, who cares, huh?" Rodeman chuckled and clasped wife's hand. His touch seemed more possessive than gentle. "As long as we're happy, time don't mean a damn."

Michael had a feeling it was an expression often repeated. Maybe he was trying to convince himself as much as everyone else. "So this is not your honeymoon?"

"Hell, no. But Ginger was feeling poorly, and I thought a holiday might do her some good."

"What made you come here?" Nikki said softly. She wasn't looking at Ginger or Rodeman, but at some point in between them. Perhaps she was trying to get a reading on the blonde.

"I asked to come." Ginger shrugged. "I have never been here before, and I have heard much about it."

"Did you hear about Vance Hutton's disappearance?" Michael asked casually.

Ginger didn't react. Didn't blink. Rodeman almost slipped off the seat. "Hutton disappeared? When? How?"

"Walked out on his wife a few days ago and hasn't been seen since."

"Well, I'll be damned," Rodeman muttered. "Didn't they just get married?"

"A week ago. They were on their honeymoon."

"Just as well we're not then, huh doll?"

Ginger's smile was ghostly. Sadness crept into her eyes, only to disappear when she blinked.

"What about you folks?" Rodeman continued. "You honeymooners?"

Michael smiled and glanced down at Nikki. Her gaze was still caught by some point between the Rodemans. Worry snaked through him. What was she seeing? "Married two days ago."

"I guess that means we won't be seeing much of you in the next few days then." Rodeman's laugh was like the man, big and affable.

"Probably not." He shrugged. Unless the Rodemans' were night owls, it was doubtful whether they'd see them at all.

The limousine pulled to a gentle stop. The driver climbed out and opened the doors. Rodeman edged forward on the seat. "Been nice meeting you folks. Come and have a drink with us sometime in the next couple of days."

"We will. Thank you." Relief surged through Michael as the two of them left.

He glanced down at Nikki again, removing the damp cloth from her forehead. "Are you okay?"

She met his gaze, her dark amber eyes glinting with gold in the car light. "Ginger was lying through her teeth. She's not only been here before, but she *is* here. She's a part of this land, a part of this place."

He raised his eyebrows. "Do you mean spiritually connected or physically connected?" The two had far different implications.

She frowned. "Both."

"You folks need help getting out?" the chauffeur said, poking his face in the doorway.

"No. We're fine," Michael said, and could have killed the driver when Nikki sat up. He hadn't wanted to lose the moment of closeness so soon.

"Let's get this show on the road," she murmured, tucking her hair back behind her ears. She flashed him a grin that was pure cheek. "Ready, dear husband?"

So the battle lines had been drawn. Michael smiled slightly. He'd had over three hundred years of practice resisting temptation and the needs of his heart, but in all that time, he'd never met anyone like Nikki.

And even though this was one battle he couldn't afford to lose, he had a sudden feeling that he just might.

Ten

Nikki climbed out of the limousine and breathed deep. The night air was crisp, laced with balsam and other scents she couldn't quite define. Lights blazed in the resort's lobby, a warmth that was beckoning, inviting. The hotel seemed to rise out of the land itself, the lobby a mix of stone and wood that flowed from a natural outcropping of rock and became a building.

Michael touched her back, and warmth crept down her spine.

"Ready?" he said, his gaze meeting hers.

Wariness warred with amusement in the dark depths of his eyes. She wondered why. "As I'll ever be."

She slipped her arm through his and felt tension slither through his muscles. He wasn't as relaxed with this situation as he liked to appear. And *she* was going to make sure he got a damn sight more uncomfortable, unless he came to his senses.

A porter collected their bags and led them toward the main entrance. Twenty steps swept them down into a lobby area that simply took her breath away. The walls were made of redwood, as was the ceiling, which seemed to soar far above her. Sandstone pillars supported it yet in no way dominated the room. Directly opposite the stairs, a two-story high wall of windows stared out over the dark plains. By day, she had no doubt that they'd provide amazing views over the nearby ring of mountains. Even though it was the middle of summer, flames danced in the sandstone fireplaces to the left and right of the entrance, lending the room a welcoming amber glow.

"I'm glad I'm not paying for this," she muttered. It was doubtful if even the agency's travel account would offer enough to stay here more than a couple of nights.

"Nothing but the best for you, my love," he said and squeezed her hand.

Surprised more by the warmth in his voice than the words themselves, she looked up. His gaze flickered to the right in warning. Ginger was standing near one of the pillars, watching them.

She looked...different, somehow. A little taller, a little fuller, and a lot more color in her skin.

Definitely someone to keep an eye on, Nikki thought. As was Rodeman. She had a suspicion he was slated to be the next ultra-rich guy to go missing. But just how deeply was Ginger involved in the scheme? Was she merely bait, or something more?

Michael signed the register, then took her arm again as the porter led them through the lounge and up another set of stairs. She could feel the weight of Ginger's stare long after they'd left the area.

Their room was another revelation. Her whole damn apartment wasn't as big as their suite appeared to be. The soaring ceiling and wall of windows were again a feature, but this time the wood on the walls was cedar, and the fireplace looked like it was built out of river rock rather than sandstone.

The bed was a platform affair and big enough to fit ten people in. She touched it, her fingers sinking into the silk-covered comforter. The mattress was firm, but not overly so. Just the way she liked it. The bathroom, to the right of the bed, had a spa big enough to hold a party in.

The porter placed their bags on the redwood-framed day bed that sat near the glass doors leading out onto the balcony, then collected his tip and left.

She sat down, grinning and patting the bed beside her. "Care to take it for a test run?"

"We are here to work and save lives, not play." He walked across to the windows and clasped his hands behind his back, staring into the darkness.

She hadn't really expected him to say anything else. No doubt he'd already worked out a roster system to share the sleeping between the bed and the day bed.

"What's first then?"

"For you? Sleep." His voice was remote. "I have to contact Seline and tell her I arrived safely. I'll also get her to check on Rodeman and his wife, see what she can find."

Power surged through the room, tingling across her skin and standing the hairs on end. Perhaps he was already attempting to connect telepathically with his boss.

"Which reminds me," she said, rising from the bed. "I'm supposed to call Mary."

"Don't use the room phone," he warned. "Just in case it's bugged. Use your cell phone."

She raised an eyebrow. "Why would they bug our phone? We only just got here—why would they even suspect us?"

"I have not lived as long as I have without being cautious, Nikki. Just do as I ask."

She frowned at his back and half wished she had something to throw at him. Being cautious was the reason she'd spent the last six months alone—and the reason she'd spend the future alone if she couldn't convince him otherwise. She walked over to her bag and retrieved her cell phone. Mary answered on the second ring.

"Nikki—where are you?" Her voice was edged with tiredness and pain.

Fear constricted Nikki's throat, and her question came out a hoarse whisper. "How's Jake?"

"Still hanging in there, but it was touch and go an hour ago..." Mary hesitated, and her sob echoed down the line. "Oh God, I don't know what I'll do if I lose him."

How often had she said the same thing? Nikki closed her eyes, but tears squeezed past anyway. She couldn't do this. She couldn't stay here chasing after some errant teenager when two of the three people she loved most in the world were in such trouble.

"I'm coming home-"

"No! You can't. Promise me you won't, Nikki. You know how Jake is with the damn agency—the client is all-important. He wouldn't want you here. You know that."

She knew. But if he died while she was stuck here, and she didn't get the chance to say good-bye...

"Promise me you'll stay. Promise me you'll find the teenager for him."

"If you'll promise me you'll call if his condition worsens again. I need to be there if...if..."

"I will. Take care."

"You too."

She hung up then dropped the phone into her bag. She couldn't lose Jake...couldn't...and yet the thought that she might lodged somewhere in her throat and made breathing almost impossible. Tears coursed warmth down her cheeks and splashed onto the carpet near her feet. She wrapped her arms around her body and tried to stop the shaking.

Hands touched her arms, turning her. She buried her face in Michael's chest and gave free rein to the anguish squeezing her heart so tight. He held her gently, his arms a safe harbor in which her tremors slowly eased.

"It'll be all right," he said softly, his breath caressing warmth past her ear.

"No, it won't. It'll never be all right."

Because she still might be left alone even if he did survive. Mary had often talked about going back to San Francisco, the city where she and Jake had met, and the place where her family still ran a successful hotel business. This time, she might just convince him to make the move. Leaving *her* alone. Something she'd feared most of her life.

She bit her lip. *I'm being selfish.* As long as Jake survived, it didn't really matter where he lived. It wasn't as if she couldn't hop on a plane and visit him.

"Being alone is something we all fear, Nikki."

She pulled back and looked him in the eye. "Do you?"

His smile made her heart do odd things in her chest. He touched her face, his thumb trailing heat down her cheek as he wiped away her tears. "I fear it as much as anyone else, and for good reason. I have lived three hundred years alone. I know its taste and do not like it."

"Then why continue to push me away?"

"Because I fear seeing you dead more."

Anger surged. She wedged her arms between them and thrust him away. "So you'd rather see me miserable than dead? Great. Just great."

He sighed and thrust a hand through his hair. "We barely even know each other. We may share thoughts and we may share passion, but we have never once shared our dreams or our desires for the future. I do not know your favorite movie or color or food, or even what you like to read. And you know as little about me. How can you trust what you feel when we do not even know if what lies between us will last?"

What she felt had been strong enough to survive six months of not seeing him. Six months in which she'd swung between anger and aching loneliness. "But you won't even give us the chance to find any of those things out."

"No."

"You're a coward, you know that?"

His smile held a touch of sadness. "You will not change my mind, no matter what you do or say."

She glared at him for several minutes, then shook her head and swept up a room key from the coffee table. "I'm going for a walk."

"It's after midnight. You need to rest."

"I need fresh air more." She stalked from the room and slammed the door behind her.

The sound echoed through the silence and, no doubt, woke the other guests. Michael took a step after her, then cursed and swung back to the window. She needed time alone, time to cool down...and so did he. Time to forget the warmth of her touch, the smell of her hair. Time to forget his need to hold her and love her and never let her go.

He crossed his arms and leaned a shoulder against the window frame. In the darkness beyond the window, light flickered, distant flames of civilization. They looked lonely, those lights, lost in the darkness. He knew exactly how they felt.

But he shouldn't be thinking about Nikki or loneliness or anything else except what they were here to do. He took a deep breath and closed his eyes. Contact was instant.

Michael? Seline's mind voice seemed almost hesitant. *You okay?*

Fine. We've just arrived at the resort.

No problems?

A couple. One of the young vamps who attacked Nikki at the warehouse turned up at the airport, but he melted away before we could question him much.

You're slipping, Michael. You don't usually let fledglings get the better of you.

He snorted softly. Jasper had gotten the best of him for more years than he cared to remember. But he couldn't really regret that because if it hadn't been for Jasper he wouldn't have met Nikki. *He didn't get away, Seline. He melted, literally.*

Surprise rippled down the telepathic line. *That's not possible.*

Well, apparently it is.

Her amusement shimmered. *My, don't we sound a little testy tonight. What's wrong—have a lover's tiff, did we?*

Irritation swept through him. The last thing he needed right now was Seline dissecting his love life—not that he *had* one to dissect.

Ever heard of anything like that happening before?

Spontaneous melting? No, but I'll do a search through the files, see what I come up with. Anything else happen?

She was referring to events with Nikki, even if she didn't come out and say it. But that was something he had no intention of discussing. The old witch thought him a coward, too—something else she hadn't yet come out and said.

Yes. We came in with a couple who might just be our next victims. I want you to do a search on Lucas Rodeman—and pay particular attention to his wife, Ginger. He didn't bother describing them. Seline would see their images in his mind.

You suspect her?

Yes, and for two reasons. I couldn't touch her thoughts—or rather, there was nothing there to touch.

You're the strongest telepath I've ever met, Michael. That shouldn't be possible.

Shouldn't be, but it was. Up until now, Nikki had been the only other person he'd never been able to fully read.

There's more. Nikki did a reading on her and saw images of a man calling forth fire from rocks. She says Ginger isn't human, that she's a part of this place, neither good nor bad.

Is Nikki clairvoyant? I know you said she has psychic abilities.

Yes, but her fields are psychometry and telekinesis. And the fact that she *had* read Ginger had him worried. Developing a new psychic ability at her age was almost unheard of.

Keep an eye on her, Michael. It's unusual for something like that to be suddenly happening. Seline hesitated slightly. *How much do you really know about thralls? Could it have something to do with that?*

I don't think so. The original intent of a thrall was a servant, and only eternal life is given. Besides, I'm not clairvoyant, so it's hardly something she'd pick up in the transfer.

No, but you didn't make Nikki a thrall to make her a servant. You did it to save her life. Perhaps that is the difference.

That still doesn't explain why she's suddenly developed this extra ability.

No. Seline's unease sang down the line, and only succeeded in increasing his own. *It may only be a singular event. It may not be a new talent emerging.*

Her tone told him she didn't really think this was the case, and neither did he.

I'll do a search on thralls, see what I can find, she continued. *And I'll check what entities we might have living in that area.*

He glanced at his watch. It was nearing one. Nikki had been gone ten minutes. *Good. I'll contact you tonight.*

Do that. And remember what I said earlier. Her heart lies wrapped in darkness, Michael. Don't trust her.

He frowned. *Trust who? Nikki?*

But once again, the old witch cut the connection before he could finish his thoughts. He thumped the window frame. Damn, she could be annoying.

He glanced at his watch again. If Nikki didn't come back within the next five minutes, he was going after her—no matter how mad that might make her.

He couldn't let her wander around alone at night in a place

where people had a habit of disappearing.

***

Nikki stopped beside the pool and stared into the crystal water. The lights had switched off as she'd come down the stairs, and only moonlight played on the gently rippling water. She glanced at her watch. It was close to one, so maybe the lights were on a timer. Most normal people were asleep at this hour, anyway, not wandering the night as furious as hell.

But then, most normal people weren't in love with a vampire who had the mindset of a brick wall.

For half a minute she thought about jumping in the pool, clothes and all, simply to cool down. Only the fact she'd have to walk dripping wet through the hotel stopped her.

Yet she was more annoyed at herself than she was at Michael. He'd warned her from the very beginning that he couldn't share his life with her. Warned her that no matter what, he would walk away. It shouldn't come as any surprise that he was fighting his feelings, fighting *her*, every step of the way.

She scrubbed a hand through her hair. She didn't know if she had the strength for the battle that lay ahead. But what other choice did she have? She couldn't just walk away, as much as he wished her to. She'd sworn not so long ago to stop running, to start fighting for what she wanted—and what she wanted was to be a part of Michael's life, now and forever. Sighing softly, she stared into the darkness.

In the distant ink of the night, lights moved. Pearls of orange, red and gold danced and swayed, as if in rhythm to some unheard beat.

A warning tingled across her skin. They weren't lights. Weren't flame, either. Curiosity piqued, she walked around the pool and down the rough stone steps leading to the tennis courts.

She continued on, her footsteps sure despite the darkness. Oddly enough, she could see quite clearly. Everything seemed bright, like frost shining on grass in the first rays of sunlight.

Her night vision had always been good, but never like this. What in the hell was happening to her? First Ginger, now this. She hesitated, glancing over her shoulder. Perhaps she should go back to the room and talk to Michael. But then, would he really help her? Or would he tell her only what he thought she needed to know?

She bit her lip. Ahead, the pearls of light continued their dance, swaying back and forth like autumn leaves tossed in the wind. She had to see what they were.

Manicured lawn gave way to meadow grass. Trees loomed—rich scented cottonwoods and ghostly aspens—casting threatening shadows through the ice-bright darkness.

The closer she got to the pearls, the more obvious it became that they had a life of their own. They reminded her of miniature comets, their incandescent tails trailing sparks through the night.

She stopped behind the deep-grooved trunks of some aspens. Half a dozen flames danced in the clearing, all circling an outcropping of rock. There was no wind, no sound, yet the hairs on her arms stood on end, and cold fingers of air crept across her skin. Evil was gathering out there in the darkness beyond the flames.

They danced on regardless, shivering and twirling to some tune of their own. They were too ethereal in form to be some sort of bird or animal, and their movements too controlled for them to be any sort of weather phenomenon.

The sense of evil grew closer, chilling in its intensity. She rubbed her arms and glanced at the flames. They seem oblivious to everything but their dance. Should she somehow warn them? Whatever the flames were, they were doing no harm, simply enjoying the night and their dance. But whatever approached out there in the darkness was coming for them.

But how did you warn flames that danger was headed their way? She bit her lip, then stepped forward. Only to stop as a warning tingled across the back of her neck. Someone was behind her.

Fear surged. She spun, but far too late. Something hit the side of her head, and the darkness claimed her.

***

Michael opened the patio door and stepped into the crisp night. The silence was intense, almost stifling. To his left and right he could hear steady heartbeats—couples sleeping the night away. Like Nikki should be.

His gaze swept the darkness. Where in the hell had she got to? He made for the steps leading down to the pool, half expecting her to be swimming in the dark, clothes and all. But the clear water lay undisturbed.

He braced his hands on his hips, studying the night uneasily. Nikki could take care of herself, and had for many years before he'd come onto the scene. But there was a feel to this place he just didn't like. There was more than disappearances happening here, of that he was sure.

She could be anywhere. He opened the link and searched the darkness for the flame of her thoughts. After several minutes he found her. If the distance of her thoughts was anything to go by, she was a good quarter mile away from the hotel. Why? Didn't she know it wasn't wise to wander around in the dark out here? Besides all the grizzly and brown bears, there was also the suspected vampire element living here.

He headed quickly down the steps and past the tennis courts, only running once he hit the meadow grass. The night became a blur around him. In the space of a heartbeat, he was with her.

She was sitting on a rock, her hands covering her face. She wasn't crying and her thoughts were free of hurt. But they were also indistinct. It was almost as if he were viewing them through some sort of haze. He frowned.

Then he smelled the blood. Hunger surged, along with anger—at the person who'd touched her, at himself for letting her walk out that door alone.

"Nikki?" He knelt in front of her. Blood smeared her fingers and glistened in her hair. Hunger clenched his gut. He needed to feed or his demon-half might wrest control again. "Are you all right?"

"Yes." She sighed and pulled her hands away from her face. A cut on her forehead disappeared into her hairline. Blood smeared the left side of her face. He gently probed the wound. She winced, but remained silent. Thankfully, the cut wasn't deep. She'd probably have one hell of a bruise in the morning, though.

"What happened?" he asked. He could smell her blood on

his hand and clenched his fingers against the sudden urge to taste it.

"Something attacked me."

Why would someone attack her out here in the middle of nowhere? It didn't make any sense. "What were you doing?"

She shrugged. "Nothing much."

Her gaze flickered away from his, studying the night behind him. Why was she lying? "Did you sense something out here?"

She frowned. "I was standing near that grove of aspens when I sensed evil approaching. Not exactly vampire-type evil but something else—something more sinister. Then someone hit me, and I blacked out."

Which didn't tell him why she was out here in the first place. "And you didn't feel or hear the approach of the person who attacked you?"

"No."

The vagueness behind her words and her thoughts worried him. Maybe the bump on the head had given her a concussion. He'd better call the resort's doctor when they got back to their room.

"Are you up to walking back to the hotel?"

"I'm fine."

No reaction to his question, no flash of annoyance in her thoughts. Worry bit through him. "Can you stand?"

"Yes."

He touched her arm, and she rose. There was no life in her eyes, no rainbow splash of color through the link. It was almost as if she was on automatic pilot. What in the hell had happened out here?

She began walking—away from the hotel, not towards it. He cursed and picked her up. She didn't struggle, didn't react in any way. The night blurred as he raced back to the hotel room.

He placed her on the bed, then washed the blood from his hands before wetting a cloth. He sat beside her and carefully cleaned her face.

"I'm okay. Stop worrying."

She still sounded out of it. "I'm calling a doctor just to be sure."

"No."

She touched his arm, her fingers pressing heat into his skin. Too much heat, in fact. He jerked his arm away from her touch. His flesh was red and beginning to blister. The sliver of worry became a knife.

"Really, I'll be fine," she continued softly. "I just need to sleep a while."

He had a feeling that whatever was wrong with her wasn't going to be cured by a conventional doctor. Something had happened out there in the field, something beyond the norm.

Besides, if it *were* just a concussion, she should be okay. She was a thrall. She shared his life force and could recover from just about any wound, given time.

"Please," she murmured, closing her eyes.

He frowned, but the plea in her voice was one he could not ignore. He rose from the bed. She sighed and snuggled down into the thick comforter. Almost instantly, she was asleep. He pulled up a chair and rested his feet on the end of the bed. For the next three hours, he watched her. She barely stirred, but her dreams were filled with flame and sorrow. Worry continued to eat at him.

Dawn was spreading golden fingers across the cover of night when he finally rose. His need for blood was an ache that thrummed through his body. He had to hunt, and he had to do so before the day dawned fully or the other guests woke. He doubted if his control would last another twelve hours. It had taken several years to fully control his demon the first time. He couldn't expect miracles in a mere six months.

He bent and brushed a kiss across Nikki's forehead. Her heartbeat was strong and steady, a siren's song that called to the darkness in him. His canines extended, anxious to taste the sweet offering of life. Cursing, he swung away and walked quickly from the room.

When he came back an hour later, his thirst finally slaked, Nikki was gone.

And the link was dead.

Eleven

Nikki jerked awake. For several seconds she lay in the darkness, wondering where in the world she was. The stars had disappeared from overhead, as had the dancing pearls of light. She frowned and glanced around. So had the trees.

She sat upright. Hot lances of fire shot through her skull like some madman with a jackhammer was loose in her head. Her stomach turned, threatening to leap into her throat. She took a deep breath and gently massaged her temples.

Only to discover *that* hurt almost as much. She touched her left temple gently. Her head had been cut, and her hair was matted with blood. She must have done it when she'd fallen. Warmth began dribbling down her cheek.

The headache eased slightly but not the sick churning in her stomach. What had happened?

The last thing she could remember was something smashing into her head, but she had an odd feeling a fair amount of time had passed. She reached out for Michael, but the link was dead. And she wasn't sure if that deadness was due to the wall he had raised between them since his return, or something else entirely.

She swept a hand cautiously through the darkness. Stone met her touch, not grass. She licked her lips. She wasn't in the meadow. Someone had moved her.

Light gleamed briefly in the darkness to her left. It reappeared minutes later, closer than before. Whatever it was, it was moving toward her. She inched away, but her back hit something solid. She swallowed her gasp and carefully felt behind her. It was a wall of some kind. The stone was as smooth as ice, yet felt almost furnace hot. It burned into her back, easing the chill of her fear.

The light grew closer still. Energy crackled across her fingertips, firefly bright in the darkness. She clenched her fist and waited. There was no sound, no whisper of breathing, nothing to indicate that whatever approached was anything remotely human.

More importantly, though, there was no whisper of evil, no taste of death. Whatever that light represented, it wasn't a vampire.

Another light appeared to her right, dancing brightness through the cover of night. This time she recognized it. The lights she'd seen in the meadow. More appeared, until a semicircular ring of warmth surround her.

Through this warmth walked Ginger.

Surprise rippled through Nikki. There was an ethereal glow to the redhead's skin, and a light in her eye that recalled the heat of flames. She looked very much at home with the stale-smelling darkness and the dancing pearls of light.

She stopped several feet away, regarding Nikki steadily, her head tilted slightly to one side. "You are all right?"

Nikki nodded. There was something not quite right about the way Ginger moved and spoke. In some ways it reminded her of a newborn—or maybe someone just recovering from a major accident who had to learn to control her body all over again. "Why am I here?"

"You saved our lives." Ginger waved a hand around the darkness. The lights shivered in response, their brightness muting and casting shadows the color of rich amber through the night. "We are sorry if we hurt you. We did not mean to."

Nikki waved the apology away. For now, the wound on her head was the least of her worries. "How did I save you when I didn't do anything?"

Ginger smiled. "You felt him coming."

She must mean the evil Nikki had felt approaching before something smacked into her head and the lights went out. "Yeah, so?"

"We felt your fear. It warned us. We hid in your unconscious form, and he did not find us."

Nikki scrubbed a hand across her eyes. This was making less and less sense. "Ginger, what the hell are you talking about?"

"He binds us," she continued. "He captures us, forces us into human form. You must stop him."

The lights behind her shivered and swayed, as if emphasizing her words. *I've stepped into wonderland*, she thought, and felt the lump on the side of her head. Maybe this was all just some weird dream. Maybe she was still unconscious in the meadow.

"Who binds you?" she asked eventually.

Her question sparked feverish activity in the lights. Rainbows splashed across the darkness, reflecting brightly off the black stone walls that surrounded them.

"He does," Ginger said.

Nikki snorted softly. "Yeah, but who is he?"

"He who is accompanied by she."

This was not making a whole lot of sense. It had to be a dream, surely. "And she is?"

"She has the darkness in her. Like the man who accompanies you."

A chill ran through her. She swallowed to ease the sudden dryness in her throat. "What do you mean?"

"She feeds off life. She walks in darkness and knows no light."

Vampire, Nikki thought, rubbing her arms. Perhaps the same vampire that had attacked her in the warehouse. "But what did you mean about Michael?"

Ginger shrugged. It seemed an awkward movement. "He walks the line between light and dark. He has the taste of the woman on him."

Her words made no sense. In three hundred years, Michael had only tasted one human—her. Or was that a lie, too? The chill biting through her limbs increased. "Meaning?"

"We can not trust him. Only you. You must help us."

"How can I help you when I don't understand what it is you want?"

"You must stop him," Ginger repeated, as if talking to a child.

Back to square one, Nikki thought wearily. Maybe she should try a different tack. "What are you, Ginger? What are the lights?"

"We are flame imps. We are of this land."

As explanations went, it didn't help much. But perhaps Michael would know. "And you can take human form?" It seemed an obvious question, yet the awkwardness of Ginger's movements suggested she was unfamiliar with this particular body.

"Only when the new cycle begins. He has forced this form upon us."

Nikki had a feeling that if she asked what 'new cycle' meant, the answer would only leave her more confused. She eyed the lights for a minute. They seemed agitated by Ginger's words. "And he wants to do the same to your friends?"

Ginger shook her head. "Only some. Others he uses in his magic. We die."

The lights muted, becoming gray. Sadness seemed to hang in the air.

"What about Rodeman. Why marry him? What was the purpose behind that?"

"He makes us marry."

"But why?"

"To bring them here."

"Do you know why?" She felt like a CD that had become irreparably stuck on one line.

Ginger shook her head. "We only bring them here."

"So where is Rodeman now?"

"He is with him. In the darkness."

Alarm spread through her. Sparks leapt across her fingers. "This darkness?"

The lights shivered, their glow darkening to purple. "No," Ginger said. "This is our last home. The last place of safety we have."

Nikki didn't ask where exactly that was. Given the heat in the rocks, the deadness in the air and the night's utter pitch, she had a feeling the answer was one she wouldn't like. "Then where has he taken Rodeman?"

"To the spaces underneath the hotel."

Caverns, she probably meant, though this didn't seem the sort of area that would have much in the way of underground caves. Nikki again scrubbed a hand across her eyes. "What about you, Ginger? What happens to you now?"

"We will die, as others have died. This body will not contain me. It will burn, and we will go with it. No longer will we dance under the orb of life."

The cavern went dark, and sadness washed in waves over her. Tears stung her eyes. "And nothing can stop this?"

"He must die for us to survive."

Then somehow, some way, she had to help make that happen. Not only for the sake of these strange lights, but for people like Rodeman and Matthew—lonely people who were only after company or for someone to understand them. Easy prey for the likes of that woman in the warehouse or the man killing the flame imps. "How many of you does this creep have under his control?"

"Four. Eight will no longer dance in the orb's light."

She meant the moon, Nikki realized suddenly. That's what they had been doing tonight—dancing under the light of the moon. "And you can tell me nothing about the man who binds you?"

"No. We hear his words, but we cannot see him."

Ginger obviously didn't mean he was invisible. He'd had a shape in the images she'd received when she'd touched Ginger's hand—though his form *had* been little more than a shadow. "Does he wear a mask or something?"

"No. He is not of our world."

Nikki snorted softly. "I'm not of your damn world, but I can see you."

"You have the fire in you. It dances across your fingers as we speak. You can see us. Others, like the one who binds, only feel what we are."

So Michael wouldn't see them, even if they were to appear before him. That wasn't going to make an explanation any easier.

"Will you help us?" Ginger asked. The lights thrummed behind her, pulsing yellow across the walls.

"I'll do what I can." But she wasn't about to make promises. Not when she had no real idea what she was going up against.

The lights danced in brightness. Nikki couldn't help smiling.

"We will return you to the surface now," Ginger said.

Nikki barely had time to nod before the darkness hit her

again.

***

Awareness surged through the link, followed quickly by a flash of red pain. Michael raced onto the patio, wincing at the sun's brightness. It was nine-thirty, and here in the mountains where there were no smog nor high rise buildings to block the sun's heat, he was really pushing his limits.

He didn't care. He headed past the pool and tennis courts and out into the meadow. He found her sitting on the same rock as last night.

She looked up when he appeared, her expression troubled. "What are you doing here? Shouldn't you be inside, out of the sun?"

"What in the hell do you think I'm doing out here?" He squatted in front of her. The wound on her temple was bleeding again, and there was black dirt on her shirt and jeans. The soil around here was a reddish brown. "You've been missing for four damn hours."

Four hours in which he'd gone quietly crazy, imagining the worst. He'd not only searched the grounds thoroughly but had touched the thoughts of every man, woman, and child currently staying at the hotel—whether they were guests or workers. No one had seen her, not even in passing.

"I'm okay," she said softly. She touched his face, her fingers trailing warmth down his cheek to his lips. But it was a gentle warmth, not the blistering heat of before.

He captured her hand, brushing a kiss across her fingers before rising. "Let's get back to our room, and you can tell me what happened."

She rose, but again was unsteady on her feet. He picked her up and raced back to their room. He set her on the bed then drew the curtains closed. He could feel the heat tingling across his skin. No sense pushing it to extremes.

"So what happened?" He rinsed the washcloth again and began cleaning her wound.

She sighed and pushed his hand away. "I feel like Alice."

He sat back on his heels, wondering if the knock on her head had addled her brains a little. "Alice?"

She smiled slightly. "Yeah. I've just been to Wonderland."

"Oh, *that* Alice." He could vaguely remember reading the tale a hundred years or so ago. He handed her the cloth, then rose and walked to the bar. "What hole did you fall into?" he said, pouring them both a drink.

"A big black one." She accepted her drink with a smile and gave him a quick rundown of the events in the cavern. "Have you ever heard of these flame imps?"

He shook his head. "But as Seline often says, fantasy is a reality we walk every day." And they had sure as hell seen more than their fair share of the fantastical, be it good or bad. "Seline's doing a check on what entities are known to be in the area. She may come up with them—if not, I'll get her to do another check."

"What about these caverns?" She hesitated and yawned. "Shouldn't we be looking for them?"

"Not until you get some sleep," he said, rising. "I'll head down to the library and see what I can find about the history of this hotel and the geography of the area."

She raised an eyebrow, a teasing light suddenly in her eyes. "I promise not to make unwelcome advances if you want to lay down with me."

He smiled slightly. *That* was a situation he had no intention of getting into—simply because her advances would be welcome. *Very* welcome.

"You need to rest," he said, unsure who he was trying to convince.

"I need you more," she murmured.

She rose and wrapped her hands around his neck, her lips brushing heat across his. He groaned and pulled her close, claiming her mouth. She tasted as warm as sunshine, as rich as honey. Heat flared in the link, a caress that stole past his heart and wrapped around his soul. She was everything he had ever longed for and everything he dared not take.

Her heartbeat pulsed through the silence, an unsteady rhythm that matched his own. His need for her was an ache that sang though his entire being. But deep down, the demon stirred. He dare not embrace what he might just destroy. Until his control was absolute, he would not take the risk of losing himself in her touch.

Even then, it might not be wise. He doubted if he could make love to her and have the strength to walk away from her again.

He pulled back, his breathing a little ragged. "Bedroom tactics will not win the day."

Her expression was a picture of mischief. "We'll just have to see, won't we?"

"I'm going," he said, not trusting her—or himself.

"Like that?" Her gaze scooted down his body, and she grinned. "The staff's female members will be impressed."

He tugged his shirt out of the waistband of his jeans to hide his erection. "Just go to sleep. And don't go anywhere until I get back."

"Only if you promise not to be long."

The low pitch of her voice sent heat racing to his loins and almost shot his control to hell.

He scrubbed a hand through his hair and got out of the room.

Twelve

It was close to four by the time she woke. Nikki yawned and stretched, then felt across the bed with one hand. She'd spent the day alone.

Sighing, she got up and grabbed fresh clothes, then headed into the bathroom. The cut on her hand was little more than a pink scar. Even the cut on her head looked half-healed, though the bruise around it was awful—a big, blackish-purple mass stretching from her temple to just above her eye. Not good, when Michael and she were supposed to be honeymooners. Biting her lip, she studied her reflection for several minutes. It wasn't natural to heal so fast—wasn't human. Ignoring the chill that raced across her skin, she turned on the taps and stepped into the shower.

Once she'd dressed, she walked over to her suitcase and pulled out the two plastic-wrapped items MacEwan had given her. Even through the plastic, Matthew's watch sent images scattering through her mind. If the strength of these were anything to go by, he was close. She shoved the watch into her shorts pocket, then opened the second bag. The bra belonging to MacEwan's niece felt dead when compared to Matthew's watch. She sat down and closed her eyes, reaching for whatever images the bra might give her. Gradually, they came.

Darkness. Fear. Hunger so fierce it burned through every fiber of her being. Words softly spoken, spinning through the darkness, surrounding her with power, locking her in chains. Heat burning through her body, through her soul. Sadness that rose in a wave, consuming her consciousness...

Nikki dropped the bra into her lap and rubbed her eyes. She had no idea what was happening to Rachel, but one thing was certain—it wasn't good. The voice that had flowed so powerfully through the darkness was the same voice evident in the images she'd received when she'd touched Ginger's hand. But how were MacEwan's niece and the flame imps connected?

She put the bra back into the plastic and returned it to her suitcase. She couldn't exactly run around the resort holding a bra, so finding Rachel would have to wait until the other guests were asleep.

She grabbed a room key and headed down to the library. Probably a dozen or so people were in the airy room, browsing the shelves or sitting in the overstuffed armchairs reading newspapers. Michael was close to the ceiling-high windows, nose deep in a book. Given it was well after three, the fading rays of sunlight did little more than glimmer off his damp, dark hair.

She knelt next to him, resting her elbows on one arm of the chair. "You've changed."

The black shirt he now wore clung to his body and seemed to emphasize the lean strength of his shoulders and forearms. She resisted the urge to touch him then remembered they were supposed to be honeymooners. She ran her fingers up his forearm and played with his ear.

He pulled her hand away, brushing a kiss across her fingers before releasing them. Amusement touched the corners of his eyes.

"And you're awake." He dropped the book onto the nearby coffee table. "You were snoring last time I saw you."

"I don't snore!" She slapped his leg. "Why didn't you wake me?"

"Because you needed sleep." He touched her face, his fingers warm and oh-so-gentle. "People are going to think I hit you."

She placed her hand over his, pressing his palm against her cheek. Heat slithered through her body, and deep inside the trembling began. Lord, she craved this man's touch so much it was beginning to hurt. "Let them. You and I know the truth, and that's all that matters. Did you find anything here?"

He withdrew his hand, but the heat of his touch still lingered on her skin. "Nothing much. A few vague mentions of underground caverns in the area's history, but nothing concrete. They haven't anything official on the area's geology."

"Really? That's odd, isn't it? From the quick look I had

coming in, they seem pretty well-stocked on books about the area's history and stuff."

He shrugged. "Maybe someone removed them. I checked the computer records, though, and there's no mention there, either."

"Computer records can be altered easily enough." Especially when you had a computer nerd like Matthew on hand. Though admittedly, he'd probably been kidnapped for projects loftier than hacking into a library cataloguing system.

She looked around. The old couple sitting close by weren't paying them any attention, but she lowered her voice anyway, just to be safe. "You feel like going for a walk? I've got Matthew's watch in my pocket."

Michael raised his eyebrows. "He's here? In the resort?"

She nodded. "Somewhere."

He glanced at his watch. "Most people will be heading to the restaurant for dinner soon. It's either now, or later tonight."

"Now. And we'd better start hunting around for Rodeman, as well. Ginger said the man who binds them had him in the darkness."

"Whatever that means." He rose and caught her hand, entwining his fingers through hers. "Shall we go for a walk, my love?"

Though she knew he spoke for the benefit of the nearby couple, the endearment still warmed her heart. They strolled into the lobby. She put her free hand into her pocket, wrapping her fingers around the watch. Images skated through her mind. She only had to focus slightly, and she would be with Matthew. A tremor ran through her. Why was this happening? What was it about Matthew that linked her so strongly?

Michael squeezed her fingers. "Where to?" he murmured.

"Left," she said. "Down toward the Health Center."

A young woman glanced up as they entered. Her welcoming smile faded almost immediately, and her brown eyes narrowed slightly. "How may I help you?" The look she gave Michael was cold, almost hostile.

He was right. People did think he'd hit her. "Just thought we'd look around, if that's okay?"

"Sure. Feel free to use any of the facilities, although private gym sessions, massages and facials do have to be booked. We're open until midnight every night."

Michael accepted the woman's brochures with a smile. The ice, Nikki noted wryly, began to thaw at that precise moment. She wondered if he'd touched the woman's thoughts and erased her suspicions.

The throbbing in the watch became stronger as they headed toward the treatment rooms. There were few people around, and little noise. Unease began to creep up her spine. Something didn't feel right.

Michael stopped at a tee in the corridor. "Which way?"

She looked left and right. Both corridors lay in semidarkness. There were four doors to their right, two to the left, and not a sound to be heard from either direction. Even the air seemed still, as if the air-conditioning wasn't working in this section of the center. She closed her eyes, briefly clenching the watch. "Right," she said after a moment. "End room."

Though they walked on carpet, her footsteps seemed to echo across the hush surrounding them. Michael made no sound, as silent as a ghost. Goose bumps crawled across her skin, and the sensation of danger churned her stomach. Or maybe it was just nerves.

They stopped in front of the last door. Michael twisted the handle. "Locked," he said, then smiled. "Not that it has much hope against you."

"Haven't met a lock yet I can't master," she said lightly and directed a bolt of kinetic energy at the handle.

The door clicked open. The room beyond was empty and dark, and the air even mustier than the corridor. Obviously, this particular treatment room hadn't seen a lot of action recently. He ushered her through the door, then closed it behind them. The darkness was blanketing, and yet the chairs and tables in the room seemed to glow almost luminously. What in the hell was going on with her sight? Why could she see them so clearly?

"Where now?" His voice, though soft, seemed harsh against the sudden edginess that seemed to fill the unlit room.

She frowned. "Straight ahead." Which didn't make much

sense. The only thing straight ahead was a concrete wall.

"It's not solid, though." He brushed past her and ran a hand down the blocks.

She touched it. It sure felt solid. Her frown deepened. "Why do you say that?"

"Because I can see the space beyond it." His reply was absent, his concentration focused on the wall.

She raised her eyebrows. "You can? How?"

"Vampire sight is somewhat similar to infra red. It allows me to see through most walls."

"Really? Bet that was handy in your youthful, wild days."

He glanced at her, smiling again. "I can't see flesh, as such. Just the heat of blood. Here we go," he added, pressing his palm against the wall.

For a second, nothing happened. Then a crack appeared in one section of the wall, accompanied by a sound that could almost have been a scream. It snaked along until it formed the shape of a door, then slowly opened.

"It is a door," he said. "Only it's been disguised by magic."

The magic was obviously active, because it still looked like a concrete wall. She reached out again. This time rough timber met her fingertips. The wood felt warm and somehow oily. She shivered and jerked her hand away.

"Can you see anything beyond the doorway?"

He shook his head. "Just a set of stairs, leading down." He hesitated and raised an eyebrow. "You want to stay here while I investigate?"

She snorted softly. "I think you can guess the answer to that question."

He grinned and held out a hand. "Shall we go as one?"

If only, she thought, and placed her hand in the warmth of his. He tugged her forward, his movements sure despite the black cowl that surrounded them. The steps were wooden and seemed to bend under her weight. It reminded her of the warehouse and the trap Jasper had set. A trap that had very nearly killed her.

"Last step," Michael said after several minutes.

She tensed, but her feet hit rock, not wood. At least it wasn't likely to collapse underneath her...

"We have a choice of three tunnels," he continued. "Which one do we go down?"

They did? She frowned at the blackness. Why could she see so clearly before and not here in the tunnels? It made no sense. She wrapped her fingers around the watch again. "Straight ahead."

They continued on. The air was fresher here, stirred by a faint breeze. There had to be another opening somewhere, which was only logical. Whoever was behind the kidnappings wouldn't be able to risk using the entrance through the treatment room all the time.

Ahead in the darkness, something stirred. She bit her lip. It was nothing she could see or hear, just a whisper of evil that trailed across her senses.

Michael stopped so abruptly she ran nose-first into his back.

"I do wish you'd give me a warning before you do that," she muttered, rubbing her nose.

Nikki, hush.

The command ran through her mind, sharp with concern. Her stomach turned. *What's wrong?*

Vampires ahead.

That was the evil she'd sensed stirring. She licked suddenly dry lips. *How many?*

Two. He hesitated. Power tingled across her senses as he searched the night. *And two more behind.*

The door must have been alarmed. It was stupid, really, not to think it would have been. *So what do you want to do?*

We can try running, though I doubt it'll do much good.

Running sounds good to me. She'd rather be a running duck than a sitting one any day.

He squeezed her hand. Warmth pulsed through her, but did little to ease the chill of fear.

Follow me, then.

As if she would do anything else right now. He tugged her forward again, racing them through the darkness. Her footsteps echoed. Somewhere ahead, evil began a frenzied dance.

The strength of the breeze grew stronger and carried with

it the slight taint of balsam. She hoped it meant they were getting close to the second entrance. Hoped they'd get there before the vampires closed in.

The sense of evil swamped them. Should have known her luck had never been that good.

Michael slid to a stop then thrust her sideways. She hit the tunnel wall hard, her breath leaving in one gigantic whoosh of air. Stunned, she slid down the wall, blinking away tears and fighting the rush of unconsciousness.

The air above her stirred, the sense of evil so heavy she could almost taste it. Fear surged, along with energy. It burned through her body, then lashed at the darkness above her. Something solid hit a far wall and slid to the ground.

She scrambled to her feet. She could hear the scuff of movement, the smack of flesh against flesh, but she couldn't see a damn thing. She clenched her fists, wanting to help Michael, but not daring to get in his way.

Movement to her left. She jumped sideways, lashing out with her fist. Her hand was caught in a vice, her fingers crushed. Pain shot up her arm, surged like fire through her body. She yelped, dropping to her knees, blinking back tears. Energy surged again and sparks danced across her fist, momentarily illuminating the gaunt features of the young vampire who held her. Then the energy hit him, and he was flung away, crashing through the darkness.

Footsteps echoed through the blackness, moving away from them. Michael cursed, and she felt the breeze of him moving, going after the fleeing vampire. She waited tensely, her breath rapid gasps, and her heart pounding so loudly it seemed to reverberate through the tunnel. A certain lure if there were any more vampires nearby.

After a few minutes Michael returned, though it was more a wash of concern through the link that warned her than anything she heard or saw.

Are you okay? He touched her face gently.

I think one of them broke every finger on my hand, but other than that, yeah, I'm fine. You?

They were only fledglings. No match, I'm afraid.

What do we do now? They couldn't leave the young vamps here, or whoever had turned them would know for certain that someone had been down here. Until they found Matthew, Rachel, and Rodeman, they really couldn't risk that.

The mere fact that they are missing will alert the person who turned them.

His mind voice was terse. She wondered why. *True. But it might also give us a little more time.* He was the one who'd told her the newly turned were unstable. Maybe their maker would just think they were off hunting somewhere. *We have no other option, Michael.*

No. He hesitated. *Let's see how far away the other entrance is. Though it is nearing dusk, there's still enough strength left in the sun to destroy these youngsters.*

He ran his hand down her arm and captured her fingers. She followed him through the darkness again. After a few minutes, the blanket began to rise, revealing the rough brown stone of the walls and floor. The air became fresher, rich with flowery scents. They turned a corner, and the wall opened up. She'd never been more relieved to see blue sky in her life.

The meadow below them was a sea of colorful wildflowers that swayed lightly in the breeze. To their left, a path curled around the rock face and disappeared. To their right, a drop of about forty feet to the meadow. She looked over the edge. Only rocks to cushion a fall. The ledge crumbled a little under her weight, showering the rocks below with dust.

"Not too near the edge," Michael warned, tugging her away.

She glanced at him. His expression was grim, and he had a cut just above his left eye. Blood trickled down his cheek.

"You're hurt." She dug a handkerchief from her pocket and dabbed carefully at the wound.

"I'm fine." He brushed her hand away almost impatiently.

She raised her eyebrows at his tone. There was a bleak light in his eyes, and tension flowed through the color of his thoughts. Fear stirred anew. "What's wrong?"

"Nothing." His voice was flat, devoid of emotion. A sure sign there was a problem. "Stay here while I go fetch the bodies."

He disappeared into the tunnel. She crossed her arms and glared at his back. Something had happened in there, something beyond the vamps attacking them, and it was obvious he had no intention of telling her what.

Damn, he could be frustrating sometimes. She snorted softly. Most of the time, really. If she didn't love him so much, she'd probably kill him.

Sighing slightly, she rested her back against the rock face. The sun trailed warmth across her skin, and she closed her eyes, raising her face in appreciation. Why would anyone give this up for eternal darkness? Even Michael, who was over three hundred and sixty years old, couldn't stand the touch of the sun the entire day.

Yet at least he could walk in sunlight. How long had it taken him? And was there ever a point where a vampire could walk in the noonday sun and survive?

Michael reappeared, carrying the bodies of the two young vampires. They began to smoke the minute the sunshine hit them. She closed her eyes, not wanting to see any more. But it was hard to ignore the smell of burning flesh. Harder still to ignore the images of another time, another teenager, burned to death by the warmth of the waning afternoon sun.

He returned a few minutes later with the remaining two bodies. Smoke plumed skyward, tainting the clear skies.

"People will investigate that," she said. Yet even as she watched, the breeze dissipated the smoke so that it was little more than a yellow stain.

"By the time anyone of importance gets here, there will be nothing to find. The rocks will not hold a pyre's stain like earth will. Ready to go back?"

"We're not continuing our search for Matthew?" she asked in surprise.

"We can't take the risk now that we've sprung that alarm." His voice was absent, his attention on the path.

What fascinated him so? Did he sense someone coming? She bit her lip, searching the rocks above them. She could hear distant laughter, and the high pitched squeal of a child, so the hotel wasn't that far away. Yet she could hear or sense nothing close.

He began moving up the path. She scooted after him, but found it difficult to keep up.

"You seem in an awful hurry to get somewhere," she muttered between gasps for air. "Care to tell me what's going on?"

"We should not be seen on this trail, just in case someone does come looking for the fledglings."

A perfectly good answer, but not the real reason behind his haste. Besides, he hadn't even looked at her. His gaze was focused on the hotel, now visible above them. As if he was looking for someone.

"We going to eat when we get back?" she asked. "Maybe make out? Do the wild thing in the pool in front of all the other guests?"

"You should eat."

She snorted softly. Yeah, he was really paying attention to what she was saying. They reached the plateau, but still he didn't slow. She paused, hands on her knees, and took several deep breaths. Her heart was a freight train racing in her chest, and sweat trickled down her face. Michael kept walking. Either he hadn't noticed she'd stopped, or he didn't care. She swallowed to ease the sudden dryness in her throat—a dryness that had nothing to do with her exertion and everything to do with fear.

Once her breathing had eased a little, she ran after him again. She had no intention of missing whatever it was that had caught his attention so completely.

Meadow grass and wildflowers gave way to the hotel's manicured lawn. He made his way through the gardens and around to the back of the hotel. In the shadows of a large pine he stopped and studied the pool area below them.

There were several people lounging in chairs near the water, and two children splashed in the spa. But it was the woman in the pool, the woman in an itsy-bitsy red bathing suit that he stared at.

Fear stepped fully into Nikki's heart, squeezing it tight. Whoever this woman was, she represented danger—and in more ways than one. That was obvious from Michael's haste to get here.

"Who is she?" she said, her voice little more than a strangled whisper.

"That," he said softly. "Is the woman I gave up life for."

Thirteen

Nikki stared at him. The tone of his voice told her how much he'd once cared for the woman below. How much he still cared. Which didn't make sense if this woman was responsible for turning him.

"I loved her, Nikki. I willingly crossed the line."

Oh God. Just the sort of competition she needed right now, when everything was still so uncertain between them. But at least she finally understood the look on his face, the disappointment in his thoughts, when she'd asked all those months ago why on Earth anyone in their right mind would want to become a vampire. He'd made the choice, just like Monica. They'd both given up life to be with someone they loved.

She stared at the woman below. How in the hell could she fight someone with that sort of hold on him? "What are you going to do?"

"Talk to her." His voice was still absent, but there was a smile in his eyes, as if he were reliving old times.

Nikki clenched her fists against a rush of anger. Railing against fate wasn't going to get her anywhere. "Then?"

He shrugged. "What happens then depends very much on her answers."

"The vampires in the tunnel," she said in sudden understanding. "They were hers?"

He nodded.

"Why didn't you tell me? You brought me here to help you, Michael. But, damn it, how can I do that if you won't tell me anything?"

He finally looked at her, but his eyes were as distant as his thoughts. He was still lost in past memories. "I had to be sure before I said anything. It's been a long time since we've seen each other, and I might have mistaken her scent."

"But if she's responsible for the vamps in the tunnel, then she might be involved with the kidnappings."

"Elizabeth likes young men, and she likes her harems, but

she's not evil."

She clenched her fists again and barely resisted the impulse to hit him. "How can you know something like that? How long has it been since you've seen her?"

His gaze drifted back to the woman in the pool. "Two hundred years."

Two hundred years, and still he carried a torch for her. Nikki's throat felt so dry it ached. "Two hundred years is a long time, Michael. Anything could have happened in that time."

"She's close to eight hundred years old. If she was going to change, she would have done so long before I met her."

Eight hundred years old? Nikki stared in astonishment at the woman. She barely looked twenty. You'd think that after all that time of undead life there'd be some damn sign of aging. "Ginger mentioned a woman helping the man that binds them— a woman who is a vampire. And it was a woman who kidnapped Matthew and hurt Jake, too. A little bit of a coincidence, don't you think?"

His irritation seared the link. "Don't jump to conclusions, Nikki. It's dangerous."

She snorted. "And so is getting so lost in the past's afterglow that you can't smell the shit that's under your nose."

He glanced at her, his expression so angry she took a hasty step back. "Do not speak of her that way," he warned softly.

Energy danced across her fingertips. She held her weapon in check and glared at him. "Then don't ignore me or brush aside my suspicious just because you hold fond memories of that woman. People change, regardless of what you seem to think. Don't let the past color your judgement of the present."

"I'm not."

"Aren't you? You haven't even talked to her, and yet you're saying she can't be involved with the kidnappings or Jake's stabbing."

He thrust a hand through his hair. Anger still whisked through the link, but it was muted by a hint of confusion. And guilt. "You never saw the woman in the warehouse, and there's more than one female vampire on this Earth."

But *this* particular female vampire was the only one who

could totally destroy whatever feelings Michael might have for *her*. Nikki rubbed her arms, suddenly chilled. "Are you going down to talk to her?"

He sighed. It was a sound full of regret. "No. Not yet. Seline is expecting a report this evening, and we should be seen in the restaurant to keep our cover intact."

If this woman was involved in the kidnappings, then their cover might be well and truly blown. If Michael had sensed her presence then why wouldn't she, as his creator, know he was here? Jasper had always seemed to know where Monica was.

"When *do* you plan to talk to her, then?"

"After dinner. If she keeps to past patterns, she'll be in the bar, on the hunt for someone new to seduce."

She had a sudden vision of a black widow spider, and a chill raced across her skin. Did this particular widow follow tradition and devour its mates? And if so, how had Michael escaped her net?

He tucked his fingers around her elbow and propelled her away from the pool. He seemed in an awful hurry again. Annoyance flashed through her, but she held her tongue. Anger wasn't going to get her anywhere. That much was obvious.

They changed in their room and headed down to the restaurant. Dinner was a silent affair. *If we're here to protect our cover,* she thought, *then we're making a damn mess of it.* He barely said two words during her entire meal. But given her quickly-fading bruise, maybe people would think they'd been fighting.

After an hour of silence—an hour in which he'd either contemplated his untouched soup or stared thoughtfully out the window—she took the napkin off her lap and threw it on the table. "I gather you don't want my company when you meet the ex-." Her voice was tart, but she didn't really care. She grabbed her purse and stood up. "So I'll just head on up to our room."

His gaze jumped to hers. There was both understanding and annoyance in his eyes. "She's no threat, Nikki."

"No threat because there's no chance of a relationship between you and me, or no threat because you don't love her anymore?"

He didn't answer, and her anger stirred again. He was so pigheaded he'd probably turn to this damn woman just to get *her* out of his life. And all because of some vague, almost chivalrous concept that he had to protect her from the darkness of his life. As if she couldn't find enough darkness in her own life!

"Just don't forget what you came here to do," she continued. "Listen to what she says with your mind, not your heart." *And remember what we shared. What we could still share, if only you'd give us a chance.*

Not giving him the chance to reply and maybe break her heart, she made a hasty retreat from the room.

Michael scrubbed a hand across his jaw. The urge to run after Nikki, to hold her close and soothe away the hurt in her warm amber eyes, was so strong he actually half-stood. He sat back down, then grabbed his glass and downed the remainder of his wine.

He'd acted like a fool today. Acted like the young man he'd once been back in Dublin when he'd first set eyes on Elizabeth. And he wasn't even sure why. Hell, it had been a very long time indeed since Elizabeth had held any real grip on his thoughts or emotions.

Maybe it was simply the shock of feeling her here in America, the one place he'd always thought he would be free of her memory.

But Nikki was right. Two hundred years was a long time, and people could change. He had. He was no longer the young fool so rapturously in love with the dark-haired, doe-eyed Englishwoman that he'd willingly sacrificed life and all he had ever known to be by her side. No longer the man who had visited for a day of laughter in Paris two hundred years ago and ended up staying for more than a month. A month in which his resolution not to drink human blood, and maybe even his sanity, had been sorely tested.

There was a lot of darkness in Elizabeth, even if during his brief time with her he had never actually witnessed any real atrocities. He certainly couldn't deny she was capable of it, though.

She was his maker, and part of his heart would always belong to her. That was inevitable, and maybe even the reason he had acted as he had today. But his lifestyle had given him a strength she would never have, a strength that muted, if not cut, the ties that bound them.

It was probably the only reason he still lived to laugh and remember the good times with her. Most of her fledglings died young in her embrace.

He sighed softly, then rose. He'd better get this meeting over with. Given the furious state in which she'd left, he wouldn't put it past Nikki to go hunting Matthew or MacEwan's niece alone. She did stupid things like that when she was angry.

He was tempted to reach out through the link and tell her he was sorry for the thoughtless way in which he'd acted. But maybe it was better to wait until he could tell her in person. She deserved that much, at least. Besides, the more he opened the link, the harder it would be to keep it closed.

He made his way across the lobby and into the stylish bar. It was crowded with men and women dressed to the nines. Those who weren't sitting at the bar or around the scattered tables were slow dancing to the strains of a waltz being played on the piano.

He scanned the crowd and saw her sitting at the bar, watching a young man in the far corner. That the young man had a woman with him wouldn't have mattered to Elizabeth had she decided she wanted him.

As if she'd felt his stare, she turned around. There was no surprise in her dark, honey-colored gaze, only a welcoming warmth. Michael smiled. She must have sensed his presence near the pool earlier.

She stood as he approached, a smile touching her ruby lips. Like Nikki, she was short, the top of her head barely reaching his shoulders. Her dark hair had been pulled into the bun she favored for evening wear, and seemed to make her features look severe, almost gaunt. Or maybe they'd always been that way, and he'd never really noticed before.

"Michael," she said, her voice melodious, soothing. "So nice to see you again."

"And you." He kissed her cheeks and sat on the barstool next to her. "Didn't think I'd ever see you in this part of the world."

She grimaced prettily. "I still prefer Paris, darling. So much more civilized." She hesitated, generous lips curving into the smile he had once ached to see. "Do you remember Paris? We had such fun."

"Yes, we did." Until she had tried—and very nearly succeeded—in bringing back his bloodlust. He ordered them both drinks from the bartender then touched her face, running his hand down the silk of her pale cheek. Her skin was hot—hotter than what was normal for a vampire. "Do you still own that apartment?"

Her smile deepened. Heat flared deep in her eyes, echoing through him, though it was little more than the natural heat of a fledgling for his master. This time, it held no true passion.

Because of Nikki, he realized suddenly. Because of what she meant to him. Because he'd found with her what he'd been unable to find with Elizabeth.

"I go back there every year. You've never visited, Michael."

He smiled. "Life keeps me busy." Truth was, he'd never dared, even if in times of utter loneliness he had sometimes dreamt of doing so. Not for the sex, which he could get anywhere, but for the warmth and the laughter and the close companionship only a true lover could provide.

Longings that had disappeared since he'd met Nikki.

"So why are you here?" She regarded him over the top of her wineglass, her heated gaze touched by wariness.

He shrugged. "Work."

She raised an eyebrow. Wine glistened on her lips and looked like blood. His hunger stirred, as it always did when he was in her company. Her lust for blood, like her lust for life itself, was strong and always overran those not powerful enough to stand against it. As it had overrun him for more years than he cared to remember.

"The word is that you're working for some charitable organization now—that true?"

He nodded and wondered if she'd been checking up on him. Though surely Seline or the Circle itself would have warned him had there been any computer searches. "Yes. I hunt down missing people, stuff like that."

"And that's why you're here?"

"Partially." It was no good lying to her—she would sense it the minute he tried. And if she *was* involved in the disappearances, it would only make matters worse.

"And you're not here alone."

It was a statement rather than a question, and unease slithered through his gut. Elizabeth knew about Nikki. How? Had she checked the hotel register when she'd felt his presence this afternoon, or had she known all along that Nikki was here with him?

Their chance meeting might not owe so much to chance as to planning. "She's not a companion. She's a thrall."

It might have been dangerous telling Elizabeth that, but it was just as dangerous not telling her. Even if she wasn't involved in whatever was happening here at the resort, he wouldn't put it past her to seek Nikki out and play a few games with her. He'd seen her do it to lovers of her other fledglings too often in the past. And Elizabeth's games always ended with bloodshed. But if she thought Nikki no more than a thrall, a servant to his wishes and desires, she might leave her alone.

Elizabeth raised an eyebrow again. "I remember telling you about thralls. You swore at the time you could never do it to another."

"I've sworn a lot of things over the years." He shrugged again. "But I found I just needed the company."

"You always did. It was one of your failings as a vampire. You'd rather talk to your prey than eat them."

He smiled slightly. "Still do."

She sighed softly. "Where did I go wrong?"

"You didn't."

He touched her hand, briefly wrapping his fingers around hers. Her palm was heavily blistered, which could have only happened if she'd grabbed something silver. Perhaps a silver knife—just like the one that had stabbed Jake.

Her pulse was slow but steady. She wasn't worried by his appearance here. Maybe she thought he presented no real threat. "So tell me," he asked after a moment. "Why are you here?"

"Why am I anywhere?" Her gaze met his, challenging him. *Ask what you came here to ask*, it said. *Don't play games with me.*

He let go of her hand and picked up his wine, taking a drink. "Are you here to hunt?"

"I hunt every day, Michael, no matter where I am."

True. But it wasn't so much the sweet strength of human blood she was addicted to, but the rush of her victim's fear and loathing, the sense of power and utter domination such a killing gave her. And while there had been a spate of disappearances from the hotel, all but three of those had returned. If Elizabeth was hunting, she wasn't doing it here or in nearby Jackson Hole.

"What happened to Vance Hutton?"

A slow smile spread across her face. "What do you think happened to him?"

He studied her for a moment. Hutton was dead, consumed by Elizabeth—that much was obvious from the amused light in her eyes. He would have been too tasty a morsel for her to resist. Michael wondered where she'd dumped the body. "Are you involved in the disappearances?"

Excitement began to overtake the amusement in her eyes. She'd always liked a challenge. "Maybe." She paused. "Are you here to stop me?"

He met her gaze steadily. "Maybe."

"Interesting. What if I say I am not in this alone?"

"Then I would ask who else is."

"And if I said that it was a person more powerful than you and me put together? That if you valued your life you would leave the hotel and not come back?"

It wasn't a warning, and it wasn't threat. It was merely a statement of fact. Yet fear echoed in the recesses of her eyes. Whoever this man was, she hated him, even if she worked with him. "Then I would ask why do you not take your own advice."

She touched his knee, the warmth of her fingers pressing heat clear through to his bones. He frowned slightly. Nikki's touch had contained the same sort of fire when the flame imps had taken possession of her. "I have never run from anything in my life, Michael, but you have. I think you should continue to do so."

Her words reminded him of Nikki. She, too, refused to run in the face of most dangers. In some ways, she and Elizabeth had the same sort of strength, the same sort of courage. "I have work to do here, Elizabeth. I'm not leaving."

She took her hand away and sighed. "Then I may be forced to stop you."

"You can try."

She met his gaze. After several seconds, she nodded. The lines had been drawn. If he stepped over her mark, she would kill him. Or try to.

She smiled slightly and motioned to the dance floor behind them. "One more waltz, for old times sake?"

It was her way of saying good-bye, of closing the door on everything they had once shared. Her way of saying the next time they met, there would be no history between them, only the present.

He held out his hand. "In memory of the laughter and the good times we once shared," he said and led her to the dance floor.

Fourteen

Nikki leaned against the patio railing and stared moodily at the distant mountains. Half an hour had passed since she'd left Michael, half an hour that had stretched like eternity. She so desperately wanted to go down there, to meet the woman he'd loved enough to give up life for. Yet she couldn't. If she was to have any hope of holding his affections, holding him, she had to trust him. Even if it meant she risked losing him.

He loved *her*. He might not want her in his life, but he loved her. Of that much she was certain. And she was certain, too, that under normal circumstances, he was not the type of man who gave his heart then roamed once he had.

But did normal rules apply when the woman in question was the vampire who had turned him? How much of a hold did this Elizabeth still have on his mind, his affections?

She bit her lip, then pushed away from the railing and went back inside the room. She couldn't stay here any longer. The same questions had been going around and around in her brain and were driving her crazy. She needed to do something, anything, to get her mind off what might be happening in the bar below.

Looking for Matthew was out. There was no way on this Earth she was going down into those tunnels alone—not at night, anyway. And if Rodeman was a captive down there as well, then he too would just have to wait.

She headed to her bag and dug out the bra belonging to MacEwan's niece. She'd had no real sense of direction from the few readings she'd taken, but maybe, if she concentrated enough, she might be able to get some hint of Rachel's location. And if it was down in those tunnels with the other two, then she might just raid the minibar and get plastered. Better that than sitting here letting her imagination go crazy.

She sat down on the plush leather sofa and opened the plastic bag. Holding the silken wisp of material in her hand, she closed her eyes and reached deep.

Images came, muted flashes of color and sound. She

frowned, trying to focus on the *where* rather than the *what*. The images had a slight sense of distance—Rachel wasn't in the hotel, or the tunnels, but she was still somewhere nearby. Music swam around her, country music, alive with the sound of thumping feet. *Boot scooting*, she thought. Laughter mingled with the twang of guitars, accompanied by the melody of many voices. She reached deeper...and suddenly she was with Rachel, becoming one with her thoughts and her actions...

The room was crowded, and the air a putrid mix of sweat and beer and lust. The scents rolled over her, churning her already agitated stomach. The heat was intense, washing in waves across her skin, as intoxicating as the echoing sound of a hundred hearts, all beating a rhythm only she could hear.

Her canines lengthened in anticipation. She kept to the shadows lining the edges of the room, looking for someone solitary, someone who wouldn't be missed.

He had taught her that much, at least.

Fear trembled across her skin. *He* wouldn't be happy that she was here. She rubbed her arms. She needed to eat so badly it was an ache burning through her stomach. She couldn't survive on his meagre rations any longer. She needed more.

In the deeper shadows near the band she saw a man watching the crowd and drinking a beer. There was loneliness in his thoughts and his eyes. His heartbeat was rich and strong, a siren's song that made her mouth water. Perfect.

She walked up to him. His pulse rate increased, and excitement lit his thoughts. She led him onto the dance floor, ignoring the ache, the need. Waiting heightened the thrill, the anticipation of the kill.

They danced. She tasted the sweat glistening on his neck, felt the rapid beat of his pulse under her tongue. Could feel his excitement pressing against her stomach as he pulled them together. Time, she thought, time.

She let him lead her outside. He took her to a truck and touched her, kissed her, loved her. Excitement thrummed. She waited, holding back, until he was deep inside, the waves of release shuddering through him. Then she took him, tasting his blood, draining his life, and relishing his shock and the realization of death, letting it wash over her until her own body shuddered in glorious release, and he was nothing more than a lifeless corpse beneath her.

But the hunger still stirred, as yet unsated. It had been too long. She adjusted her dress and walked back to the bar. Where there was one, there would be more...

...Nikki dropped the bra and scrambled to her feet, running for the bathroom. The next few minutes she spent hanging over the toilet, throwing up what little dinner she'd managed to eat.

When there was no more to lose, she slid down the wall, leaning her head back and closing her eyes. God, what was that? How was it possible that she could suddenly immerse herself so completely in another's mind that she felt every damn sick craving and desire as if it were hers? Her stomach churned, threatening to rise again. She wished she had something to wash the bitter taste from her mouth, yet still felt too weak to get up and get some water.

"Nikki?"

Michael's voice rose out of the silence, soft yet filled with concern. *Wishful thinking*, she thought. Surely he was still in the bar, with *her*.

"Nikki?" he repeated, voice and concern sharper.

Suddenly he was beside her, his fingers pressing warmth into her cheeks as he held her face. "What's wrong?"

She opened her eyes. He knelt next to her, eyes rich with worry. She touched his lips with her fingertips, trailing them down his chin and neck and pressing them against his chest. His heart beat a rhythm that could only be described as erratic for a vampire. He was definitely real, not some ghost her fevered imagination had brought into being.

"Damn it, woman, will you answer me?"

Her gaze jumped to his. The concern is his eyes was so strong she might have named it fear in anyone else. "I'm okay. I just need a drink."

He fetched a glass of water and sat beside her on the floor. His arm brushed against hers, and warmth pulsed through her body, erasing the chill.

"What happened?" he asked.

She rinsed her mouth with the water and spat it out in the toilet. "I tried tracing the whereabouts of MacEwan's niece."

"And?"

He didn't sound surprised. Maybe she was becoming predictable. "And I not only found her, but became a part of her." She shuddered and took a hasty gulp of water, half wishing it was something stronger. "She's hunting, Michael. I was with her when she fed."

He wrapped an arm around her shoulders and drew her toward him. She rested her cheek against his chest, listening to the steadying beat of his heart. She felt so safe, it was almost scary.

"You should have pulled out sooner." He brushed a kiss across the top of her head. "If you don't, you run the danger of losing yourself in the other person's desires."

She glanced up at him. There was a smudge of red on his cheek. Lipstick, from a kiss. This close, she could smell the other woman's perfume, a sickly-sweet scent reminiscent of orange and honey. But he was here, not with *her*, and for now, that was all that mattered.

"But why is this happening now? Is it some sort of fallout from you sharing your life force?"

"No. It's an ability you've always had." He brushed the hair from her eyes, tucking it gently behind her ears.

Her skin tingled from his touch, and her heart began to accelerate. Deep inside, a familiar ache began. One she had no choice but to ignore. They didn't have the time. Or rather, Rachel's next victim didn't. "But it's something I've never been able to do until recently."

He raised an eyebrow. "Think about what you do. Psychometry is the ability to pull images of past events from certain objects, is it not?"

She nodded.

"But that is not what you do, is it? You use the objects to pull images from the present, to see where the owners are or what they are doing. Not strictly psychometry, more a light mind-meld, using the object in hand as a link."

Put like that, he was right. She'd never thought about it before. "But why is it showing up now?"

"It's probably a result of the mind-meld we did to find Jake. Up until then, you hadn't realized the full extent of your capabilities."

Another shudder ran through her. Touching someone's mind so intimately that she felt their needs and desires wasn't a capability she wanted. "We have to stop Rachel. And we have to stop her tonight, before she kills anyone else. But we can't kill her. Something strange is going on with her."

He rose, then pulled her up as well. "We may have no option." He tugged her so close their bodies molded against each other, then wrapped his arms around her waist. "Have I ever mentioned the fact that you smell delicious?"

She grinned. "Even when I've been throwing my guts up in the toilet?"

"Even then," he said and brushed a kiss across her lips. "Let's go capture this vampire of yours."

Right then, with her lips still tingling from his brief kiss and his arms around her waist so tight it felt as if he would never let her go, moving was the last thing she wanted to do. But move she had to if she wanted to stop Rachel killing again.

She sighed. "We'll have to rent a car. She's in Jackson Hole."

"The hotel has cars available for guests. It shouldn't be a problem getting one." He released her waist and caught her hand, wrapping his fingers around hers. "But just remember, we may have no choice but to kill her. She's newly turned and probably not what you'd call rational."

Nikki grabbed the bra as they headed out of the room, stuffing it quickly into her pocket. "But that's it," she said. "Rachel wasn't acting like Monica. She hungered, but not insatiably so. She took the time to seduce this guy, let him make love to her, and didn't eat until he'd finished." And had become orgasmic while doing so.

A chill raced across her skin. Maybe it was too late to save Rachel—if saving her had ever been an option.

He frowned. "Not the normal behavior of a fledgling."

"If Monica was a sample of normal behavior, then no."

They reached the concierge and made arrangements to rent a car. Five minutes later they were cruising toward Jackson Hole in a small sedan.

"Where to?" Michael asked as they approached the welcoming warmth of lights.

She wrapped her hand around the bra. Images teased her mind, lust and hunger mingled with rising excitement. Rachel had found her next victim.

She licked her lips. "Take the next left, then cruise down the street until you see a bar with lots of pickup trucks parked out the front."

He turned left and slowed. The bar was halfway along the street. He parked, and they both climbed out. The breeze tugged at her hair, whipping strands across her face. She pushed them back, studying the building across the road. It looked like a leftover from the eighteen hundreds, a big, old, ramshackle construction that should have had horses lined up out front rather than trucks. Music and laughter ran across the night, and the breeze was heavy with the scents of alcohol and cigarette smoke.

Michael glanced at her. "Ready?"

Ready to maybe kill another human being? No, she thought. *Never.* She took a deep breath. Rachel wasn't human anymore, and the longer she stood here hesitating, the more chance there was that people would die.

"You can stay in the car, Nikki. You don't have to do this."

She grimaced slightly. "I owe this much to MacEwan." Because he would want to know the truth of what happened, and would sense a lie.

Michael nodded and held out his hand. She wrapped her fingers in the heat of his, yet felt no safer for it. A chill crept down her back, spreading ice through her veins. The night air seemed suddenly heavy, thick with the scent of evil.

The same evil she'd sensed out in the field before the flame imps had attacked her.

"Something's here."

His gaze searched the darkness around them. "Yes. Come

on, let's get inside and find Rachel."

He hurried her across the street and into the bar. Heat and smoke hit them the minute they opened the door, so thick they could almost carve it. Music thumped, and people stomped in time, the noise so loud it seemed to vibrate through her entire being. She coughed, her eyes watering as she looked around. The place was crowded, and it was hard to move without brushing against someone. It wasn't going to be easy finding Rachel.

"Maybe we should split up." She glanced up at Michael. He was frowning, staring at the darkness that hovered near the band. Fear thrust through her. "What's wrong?"

He looked at her, his eyes midnight pools that held no emotion. *Michael at his most dangerous.* She rubbed her arms briskly, but the chill in her bones had seeped into her soul. It felt as if she'd never be warm again.

"There's a man cloaking himself with magic in the far corner of the room." He squeezed her fingers, then let her go. "Stay here while I investigate."

"But what about——" She stopped. He had become one with the smoky darkness, and she was talking to nothing more than air. Cursing softly, she thrust a hand in her pocket and walked down the steps. Rachel was here somewhere. Someone had to stop her, and it might as well be her. A vampire who was little more than a fledgling she could cope with—hopefully.

The heat and noise seemed more intense on the dance floor. She pushed her way through the sweating mass of people, ignoring the curses or snide remarks, absently swiping away the hands that pinched or touched her.

In the middle of it all she saw a woman with strawberry blonde hair dancing with a tall, gangly young man. Rachel and her next victim. She was rubbing her pelvis against his, licking his neck and tasting his sweat, as she had with her last victim. Nikki's stomach turned. Death was a shadow grinning in anticipation over the young man's shoulder.

A hand grabbed hers, spinning her away. Nikki yelped and lashed out kinetically. A cowboy went flying, a surprised looked on his face.

"Hey, he only wanted to dance," a woman wearing a floral shirt said. "You could have just said no."

"He could have asked first," she muttered and spun around, looking for Rachel. The man was leading her toward a side exit.

She cursed and pushed through the dancers. *Michael?* He didn't respond. Maybe the link didn't work when he was little more than a shadow. She continued anyway, just in case he was listening but not answering. *Rachel's heading out the side exit with her next victim. I'm going after her.*

Silence shimmered down the line. Frowning and wondering what he was doing, she bounded up the steps and out the side door.

Rachel and her next meal were heading around the back of the building. Nikki closed the door, then hurried after them. The wind slapped against her as she came out of the building's protection. She hesitated, scanning the darkness, until she found them. The young man was fiddling with his keys, trying to open the door of a white van. *No time*, she thought and broke into a run.

Her footsteps echoed across the night. Rachel spun. Moonlight gleamed off her canines as she snarled. Nikki slid to a stop, energy dancing across her fingertips.

"Let him go, Rachel. You've had all you're going to get tonight, I'm afraid."

Rachel looked her up and down, a slight sneer touching her blood red-lips. "Who do you think you are, telling us what we can do? We can break you as easily as a twig."

"I think you're overestimating your vampire abilities." Nikki glanced at the gangly young man. His eyes were wide, his gaze flicking between the two of them, as if trying to decide whether he should be scared or not. "Run, while you still can."

"Crazy. Both of you." He backed away several steps then turned and ran.

Rachel leapt after him. Nikki hit her with kinetic energy, holding her still. She screamed in frustration, twisting and kicking in an effort to be free. Sweat trickled down Nikki's forehead, but her net held.

Finally, Rachel stopped moving and contented herself with glaring. "You will pay for this."

Nikki crossed her arms, trying to ward off a deepening chill. The scent of evil was beginning to saturate the night breeze again. It was coming here. Coming for Rachel. "No. You will. MacEwan sent me here, Rachel."

Surprise ran briefly through the other woman's eyes. "How did he know we were here?"

"That doesn't matter. What does is the fact he knows what you are. He knows what you are capable of. He will kill you if you continue down this path."

"He will never find us." She shrugged. "And you will be dead the minute you release me."

Nikki frowned. Surely such confidence was out of place in a vampire only a few months old. Something was wrong. "Who is the man you refer to as *he* in your thoughts?"

Fear touched Rachel's expression, darkening her blue eyes. She licked her lips. "How do you know about him?"

"He's here, Rachel. Looking for you."

It was only a guess, but terror replaced the fear, contorting the young vampire's face.

"You have to let us go. Please. We can't stay with him. He makes us do things." She wrung her hands, shifting from one foot to the other, her whole body quivering with the need to run.

Nikki bit her lip, battling for the strength to keep the leash intact. An all too familiar ache began in her brain. Sweat trickled faster down her face. "Tell me about him, then."

"We can't."

She frowned. Why was Rachel continually referring to herself as *we* rather than *I*? It was odd—especially given Ginger spoke in much the same manner... Nikki stared at the young vampire in sudden realization. When she'd searched earlier this afternoon for Rachel, she felt heat, sorrow, and chains made of words. A flame imp had been bound in the young vampire's body. She shivered. What sort of monster cared so little for life that he destroyed two at a time?

"Then we wait for the man who comes," Nikki warned, though it was the last thing she really wanted to do. Still, Rachel didn't know that.

"He's evil," Rachel said, her voice little more than a desperate hiss.

"But does he have a name? What does he look like?"

"He is called Randolf Cordell. He is tall, with blonde hair and green eyes. Now let us go."

It sounded like the man she'd seen in those first visions, the man who had turned Rachel. Was their magician also a vampire? "Why is he using the flame imps? Why is he forcing them into the bodies of others?"

Rachel spat. "We don't know, do we?"

The sense of evil was a blanket threatening to smother her. Across the silence, she heard a door open. He was coming their way.

She couldn't stay here, nor could she let Rachel go. And she couldn't hold the kinetic net for much longer. Nikki bit her lip, knowing there was only one real option. Gathering what was left of her energy, she thrust Rachel back, smashing her skull against the car. The vampire slumped, her weight tearing at the net. Pain shot through Nikki's head. Blinking against the sting of tears, she released the kinetic cage and ran forward. Though unconscious, Rachel's pulse was as steady and as strong as a vampire's ever got. She hadn't really hurt her then. Good.

She rose and scanned the parking lot. There was a Dumpster near the back fence. Perhaps she could find something there to restrain Rachel—at least until Michael got here to help her.

She grabbed the young vampire's hands and began dragging her. The wind chilled the sweat dripping down her cheeks and back, and the sense of evil was so thick she could barely breathe.

It seemed to take hours to reach the bin. Her arm, leg and back muscles were all protesting fiercely by the time she got there. She leaned Rachel against some boxes that had fallen from the bin, then thrust a hand through her sweat-tangled hair and scanned the night. No sound, no movement. The sense of evil was unmoving, as if he too stood listening.

The flame imp in Rachel, she thought suddenly. They'd told her that he couldn't see them, that he could only sense their power. *That's* what he'd been following. When she'd knocked out Rachel, she'd also knocked out the flame imp, and the man Rachel had called Randolf Cordell had lost all sense of them.

But if he was a vampire, he only had to come around the corner, and he'd find them. Her heart was a rapid drumbeat that would call him toward them.

She stepped over Rachel and peeked inside the Dumpster. Luck was with her. The bin was not only filled with boxes but used packing tape as well. She grabbed as much of it as she could reach, then quickly wrapped it around Rachel's feet and hands. For good measure, she wound some around the vampire's mouth.

Then she squatted next to her, listening to the wind moan through the trees behind them. The sense of evil was still stationary, still centered on the left-hand alley. Why didn't he move? What was going on?

Pain hit her then, pain so fierce it burned through her brain and knocked her sideways. She gasped, holding her chest, feeling as if she'd just been hit by truck.

Only it wasn't her pain.

It was Michael's.

Fifteen

Nikki scrambled to her feet. Michael was hurt. She didn't know how or why, but she had to find him. Help him.

She reached for the link. Pain pulsed, a red-hot glow that burned through her. She bit her lip, gaze sweeping the night. He was in the left-hand alley—right where the evil was.

She ran. Her footsteps echoed across the night, a rhythm oddly in tune with the thumping beat of the music coming from the bar. She rounded the corner of the building and slid to a stop.

A pair of hands hovered above the ground, seemingly unattached to anything but the night. Lightning arced from them, leaping across the darkness, a ragged, blue-white streak of energy that hit Michael in the chest and threw him backwards. He hit the wall with a crunch and slid down to the ground.

He didn't move.

She couldn't tell if he was alive or not. *No*, Nikki thought wildly. *No*. Energy surged, burning through her, crackling at her fingertips, sparkling like fire through the night as she hit the shadows that hid Randolf Cordell with everything she had. The hands disappeared into night and something heavy hit the trash cans, scattering them.

Pain seared through her brain, almost blinding in its intensity. She bit her lip so hard she tasted blood. Energy still tingled across her fingers despite the fire lances in her brain. She watched the shadows and waited. The hands appeared again, ghostlike in the night. She hit them kinetically, flinging him away.

For an instant, a figure appeared, sprawled across the sidewalk—a long, lanky body above which a flame imp rotated. It looked washed out, gray, as if every ounce of energy had been sucked from it. Maybe it had. Maybe that was where the lightning originated.

The shadows closed in again, concealing Cordell. She clenched her fists and waited for an attack, be it physical or magical. Nothing happened. The sense of evil that was Cordell dissipated, and the night became friendly once more.

He'd gone. She heaved a sigh of relief and ran to Michael. Kneeling by his side, she touched his face, his neck. His color was abysmal, even for a vampire, but his pulse was steady and strong. Relief surged so fiercely that tears stung her eyes, blurring her vision

"Michael?" She brushed the midnight strands of hair from his closed eyes. "Michael? Can you hear me? Are you okay?"

She felt his thoughts stir. Pain bloomed, followed quickly by anger. "Did you get the number of that truck?" he muttered, holding his chest and wincing slightly.

"What happened? Why did you show yourself to him?" She quickly undid his shirt, noticing with a slight smile that he was still wearing her cross around his neck.

"I didn't. He obviously sensed I was there because I came out the door, and he was waiting for me. Must have had some sort of magical wards set in place to warn him if someone follows him."

"And maybe he sensed you because he's also a vampire." It was certainly more believable than magical wards—whatever the hell they were. She pulled his shirt to one side. His skin was an angry red and already blistering. "We have to get something cold on these burns."

"What do you mean, he's a vampire?" He brushed away her hands almost angrily. "I'll be all right, damn it."

She glared at him. "Just because you're feeling like an idiot, don't go taking your anger out on me. And you'll do as you're damn well told. Now, stay here while I go get some ice."

"Nikki—"

She ignored him and disappeared inside the bar. When she got back five minutes later with ice wrapped in a cloth, he reached out and gently thumbed the moisture from her cheek. Heat slithered through her, as warm as the caring in his dark eyes.

"You really are the most irritating and bossy woman at times, you know that?"

"And it's taken you this long to realize it? Damn, you're slow."

She placed the ice on his chest. He winced slightly, then leaned back and briefly closed his eyes.

"Thank you," he said, after a moment. "I think you may have saved my life."

"Twice more and you're mine," she said lightly, echoing the words he had said to her when they'd first met.

In his gaze she saw amusement and longing. He might admit what he felt, but he wasn't yet ready to admit they needed each other—that they needed to be in each other's life.

"What did you mean when you said he was a vampire?" he said after a moment.

Coward, she thought, and felt his amusement shimmer though the link. "Just that. He's a vampire. His name, by the way, is Randolf Cordell."

He raised an eyebrow. "And just how do you know that?"

"Rachel—who's currently hog-tied in the back parking lot and waiting for us to pick her up."

He snorted softly and shook his head. "Maybe I should just leave this case to you. You seem to be doing a hell of a lot better at unpicking the pieces than I am."

She grinned. "That's because I attract trouble better than most. You able to stand?"

"I'm burned, not disabled. Of course I can stand."

Her grin widened. "Just as well vampires don't get sick. You'd be a horrible damn patient."

"And you'd be the most annoying nurse." He stood, then pulled her towards him, crushing the ice pack between them. If it was cold, she didn't feel it. He smiled slightly. "But I wouldn't mind seeing you in a nice little nurse's uniform."

"Oh yeah? That some sort of fetish I should know about?"

"Maybe," he murmured. He bent and kissed her so hard and so long it snatched her breath and left her dizzy.

"Damn," she muttered when she was able to breathe again. "Maybe you should get mugged more often."

"If you stayed—" He hesitated then stepped away, catching the ice pack as it fell. "You want to lead the way to Rachel?"

If you stayed. The unfinished sentence echoed through the link, through her soul. She smiled slightly. At least he was thinking about it, even if he wasn't yet ready to take that risk.

"This way," she said, and led the way to the back parking lot and Rachel.

Michael squatted beside the prone vampire and lightly touched her cheek. She was hot, burning hot. Like Nikki had been when the flame imps were in her. Like Elizabeth was this evening.

He met Nikki's gaze. "She has an imp in her?"

She nodded and crossed her arms, as if to ward off a chill. "Yes. And I think its controlling her fledgling desires, at least to some extent. It's given her control."

"And yet she still desires to eat." It meant the vampire urges were strong—maybe too strong to save her. He glanced down at the young vampire. Rachel was awake, her blue eyes dark with fury. *Do you want to live?*

He filled the thought with cold anger. She blinked, and fear stirred in her thoughts. She nodded. *We want to live.*

He wasn't sure if it was the imp replying, or Rachel, or maybe even both. It didn't really matter, as long as they obeyed. *If I release you, you will do as you're told? You will not try to escape?*

Again she nodded.

Because if you do try... He left the thought hanging. Rachel knew what would happen if she tried. He could see the knowledge of death hovering in her mind. He took the car keys out of his pocket and handed them to Nikki. "Bring the car around. I'll contact Seline and see what we can arrange."

She spun away, her footsteps echoing across the night. He scanned the parking lot, then reached out with his mind.

About damn time, came Seline's grumble. *I was beginning to worry.*

If she were truly worried, she would have sent someone else out here to see what was going on. *Got several problems for you, Seline. First up, is there anyone near Jackson Hole who could come and collect a package?*

Package? Human or other?

Other. A young vampire who may be hosting another entity in her body. Nikki believes both can be saved. He didn't think so himself—not if the hunger in Rachel's mind was anything to go by.

Doyle's flying in from Utah. I can get him to divert immediately. Silence filled the line for several seconds. *A friend of his owns the Triple T ranch off Moose-Wilson Road. Apparently it has a private air strip. As long as he can get the proper clearances, he'll be there in twenty minutes. What's this other entity? Anything dangerous?*

Nikki drove up. Michael began unwrapping the young vampire's feet. *They apparently call themselves flame imps. They're some sort of fire creatures. I haven't seen them, but Nikki has. They can inhabit the bodies of others, controlling them.*

Did Elizabeth have one in her? Was this magician's control over the imp in her the reason she couldn't leave?

Surprise whisked down the line. *Flame imps? Haven't heard of them for ages. I didn't think there were any here in America.*

Nikki climbed out of the car and walked toward them. She had a distracted look in her eyes, as if she were listening to something. Maybe she was, he thought, and snapped the link closed between them. She blinked, then glared at him. He smiled slightly and rose, pulling Rachel roughly to her feet.

Then you've heard of them?

There's mention of them dotted throughout ancient texts. So what are they, exactly?

Michael thrust Rachel into the back seat then climbed in beside her. She might have promised to behave, but he wasn't about to trust her. Not with Nikki in the car with them. "Head toward Moose-Wilson Road," he said, as Nikki climbed back into the driver's seat. "We're looking for the Triple T ranch."

She nodded and didn't ask the questions he could sense in her mind.

Seline's shrug shimmered down the line. *The imps are energy spirits, basically. They're generally only seen during the lunar cycle's new moon phases. It is said they can find human form during that time, and that no human male who sees them can resist them.*

If they can find human form, why were they being forced into people like Rachel—and maybe Elizabeth? *So they're some sort of energy siren?*

Partially—they do not devour their prey, just suck the energy from them, leaving them drained but alive. And only during their mating cycles. I've never heard of them actually cohabiting within another's body.

It's something they appear to have no choice in. The man behind the kidnappings is apparently using magic to force them into the bodies of others—generally vampires, from what I've seen.

Probably because a vampire is the only being capable of withstanding the heat of the imp for any length of time. Humans would literally melt.

Nikki hadn't, but then, they weren't really in her that long. But the vampire at the airport *had* melted. Maybe there were limits, even then.

I take it that you've encountered the man behind all this?

Yes. He's a vampire named Randolf Cordell. He's using a magic-induced shield to cover his appearance. Which should not have been necessary if the man was a vampire. Walking in shadows should have been cover enough.

I'll do a search and see what I come up with. In the meantime, be careful. Do not trust her, Michael.

Anger surged again. *You could have told me Elizabeth was here, Seline. I didn't need to discover that myself.* Particularly when Nikki had been there to witness it.

You needed the shock of her appearance to see her as she is, not as she lives in your memory. It worked, did it not?

Yes. Or maybe it hadn't been the shock of seeing Elizabeth, but rather the shock of seeing the hurt and anger in Nikki's eyes and suddenly realizing she meant a hell of a lot more to him than Elizabeth *ever* had. He might have given up life for Elizabeth, but he would give up eternity for Nikki.

Amusement shimmered down the line. *Always knew you had the makings of a romantic somewhere in that dark heart of yours.*

And you, witch, know better than to intrude on my thoughts like that.

She chuckled. *We ran that check on Lucas and Ginger Rodeman and came up with some interesting results.*

He raised an eyebrow at the wisp of excitement in her mental tones. It usually meant she was on the verge of cracking a big case, and that certainly wasn't happening here. Not that his was the only case the Circle had on their plate. Hell, Doyle had been in Utah sorting out some disaster there, and they had close to twenty other agents currently scattered throughout America and Europe.

What did you find?

For a start, that image you gave me came up as a match for three separate people—Michelle Hannerman, reported missing by her husband some three months ago. Frances Baker, reported missing some two months ago by her husband, and Mary Gordon, who's car was found smashed into a tree some eight months ago.

Hannerman and Baker were two of the fifteen men who had been lost, then found, at the resort. Ginger had told Nikki she was a lure, and she obviously hadn't just meant Rodeman. *Is Mary Gordon still missing?* If she was, then maybe they'd found Ginger's true identity.

Yes, and police suspect foul play, as there was blood all over the car.

It wouldn't have taken a bright mind to reach *that* conclusion. *There would be, if she'd just had a car accident.*

Yes, but there was more blood than the accident would account for.

What about Ginger Rodeman? Any chance that she's really Mary Gordon?

According to the marriage license, Ginger's maiden name is Holemont. So far, we haven't been able to find her in any records. What we have discovered is that in recent months there's been some unusual cash transactions in all the abductee's accounts.

He's stealing their money? It was hard to believe someone

would set up such an elaborate plot just to steal a few dollars.

It's not just a few dollars, Michael. These men are all incredibly rich, and we're talking millions from each. But it's heading to a charity that appears perfectly legitimate.

Appearing legitimate didn't actually make it legitimate. *You're checking it out, I gather?* He glanced out the side window. A sign indicated they were nearing Moose-Wilson Road.

Yes. I'll get back to you as soon as I have anything. In the meantime, as I said, be careful.

If she was repeating her warning, she had to be seeing some bad shit headed his way. *I will. Thanks.*

The link closed. He glanced up and met Nikki's gaze in the rearview mirror. Her eyes sparkled with gold fire in the darkness and were filled with an odd mix of anger and understanding.

"All sorted?" she asked.

"Yes. Turn right at the intersection. The Triple T, from memory, is only a mile or two down on the left." He'd heard Doyle talking about it a couple of times and just had to hope he'd heard the directions right. What they didn't need right now was to be wandering up and down the road looking for a damn ranch.

She nodded. He ripped the tape from Rachel's mouth. She hissed, but otherwise managed to control the fury he perceived in her mind. "We're giving you both the chance to live."

Rachel snorted. "We do not want your charity. We do not want your help."

He leaned back, regarding her steadily. "So you're happy to continue doing Cordell's bidding until you literally melt away? Which, from what we've seen, is only a matter of months away."

Rachel stared at him for several seconds, then licked her lips. "What do you mean, melt? We are not melting."

"It happened to the chauffeur at the airport," Nikki said, watching Rachel through the rearview mirror rather than watching the road. "And it killed both the imp and his vampire host."

"No. It's not possible. He told us there would be no danger."

Nikki raised her eyebrows. "And you believe a man who

has already killed eight of your number?"

Michael leaned forward, tapping her on the shoulder, redirecting her attention to the road and the sign she was about to sideswipe. She straightened the car and flashed him a grin that burned his soul.

"Who told you this?" Rachel asked, crossing her arms and glaring at the back of Nikki's neck.

Lust rushed in heat waves through her mind, and the look in her blue eyes changed to hunger as her canine's lengthened.

Michael grabbed her face, squeezing her cheeks hard enough to fracture bone. "Don't even think about it," he warned flatly, forcing her to look him in the eye. "You touch one hair and you're dead, understand?"

With most fledglings, the threat would have been useless. They were too caught up with their cravings, too consumed by the need to explore who they were and what they had become, to understand threat. But Rachel nodded and gulped. Maybe it was the imp in her, giving her the sanity it took most fledglings years to attain.

Nikki slowed and turned into a driveway. There was a man at the gate. She opened her window and spoke to him for several minutes. Michael touched the man's thoughts, erasing all memory of Rachel—just in case Cordell came looking for them. "Runway's lit and ready," she said, driving on.

"Park nearby and wait." He turned his attention back to Rachel. "What else can you tell us about Cordell?"

"Nothing. We know nothing."

"How did you meet him, then?" he asked.

Rachel crossed her arms, her look petulant. "We met him on the Internet."

He glanced at Nikki. *Didn't Matthew meet his abductor via the Net?* He didn't mention Elizabeth, though her name hung in Nikki's thoughts. Elizabeth hadn't exactly admitted to being involved—hadn't denied it, either—and her burned hand was an ominous sign. But he wasn't ready to accuse her when they had no definite proof. He owed her that much, at least.

Yes. Nikki's annoyance was a black cloud that stung his mind. *And isn't it odd that the link seems to open every time you have a question that can't be asked out loud. You wouldn't happen to be blocking it, would you?*

Now is not the time for this, Nikki. He slammed the link closed again, but nevertheless felt the surge of her anger. Ignoring it and her, he looked back to Rachel. "And you became lovers?"

"We were before he turned me."

Meaning, obviously, they were no longer. Why? Did Cordell lose the taste for them once he had turned them? "He must have told you something about himself in the time you were lovers. Where did he live?"

"He had an apartment in The Heights."

"A plane is coming," Nikki said. She stopped and craned her head out the window.

Michael saw the lights beginning to descend. He glanced back at Rachel. "If he could afford to live in The Heights, why is he kidnapping these millionaires?"

She shrugged. "He hates them. He thinks they owe him."

He frowned. "Why would he think they owe him?"

"We don't really know, do we? Probably something to do with his accident."

"Accident? What type—"

"Michael," Nikki interjected. She was staring out the rear window, and there was fear in her tone, her face, and her thoughts. "He's here. He's somewhere behind us."

"Where, exactly?" He twisted around, searching the night. Light flared behind them, a jagged blue-white beam that cut through the night, heading straight toward them. Fear tightened his gut. "Get out!" He reached across Rachel and thrust open the door. "Get out now!"

He pushed Rachel toward the door, saw Nikki dive out, then flung open his door and rolled out.

He'd barely hit the ground when the night, and the car, exploded into flame around him.

Sixteen

Nikki huddled against the ground, nose first in the dirt, her hands over her head and heat searing her back. Chunks thudded into the soil around her, bits and pieces of red-glowing metal, all that remained of the car. The air sizzled, thick with smoke and burning her lungs with every intake of breath.

Michael? She twisted around quickly, scanning the fire-drenched night behind her.

Here. I'm okay. You?

Relief swept through her. *Fine.* Even if her ears were ringing so loudly the roaring flames were little more than a whisper of sound. On hands and knees, she crawled farther away from the car and the heat, then sat down and stuck a finger in her ear. It didn't seem to help. *I think I've gone deaf, though.*

Can you see Rachel?

She looked around again and saw the young vampire sprawled ten feet away. A jagged piece of metal poked out of her back. She staggered across to her and felt for a pulse on Rachel's neck.

She's injured but alive.

A warning tingled across her skin. She glanced up. Michael stood opposite her, though the shadows were wrapped tightly around him. He was little more than a slight shimmer in the darkness. Fear surged anew. "What's wrong?"

Nothing. Can you sense Cordell any more?

She studied the night for several seconds. Out on the main road, coming from the right, lights approached—the flashing lights of emergency vehicles. How had they gotten there so fast? The ranch owner had obviously called the fire department.

I can't sense him anywhere near. Why aren't you showing yourself?

We have to get Rachel away from here. She's too dangerous, and we won't be able to keep her restrained once the cops get here. Cordell obviously wants her dead, so we have no choice but to save her.

The man at the gate saw her in the car with us—won't

he think it a little suspicious... She hesitated, suddenly remembering the slight wash of power she'd felt before. *You erased his memory, didn't you?*

It's safer that way—for him and for us. I'll wrap Rachel in shadows and take her over to Doyle. You wait here.

She glanced over her shoulder and saw the small plane taxiing to a halt at the far end of the runway. *Will Seline be able to help her?*

His shrug was something she felt rather than saw. *Probably not. But it's Rachel's only chance.*

And killing Cordell might be the flame imps' only chance. She shivered and rubbed her arms. *Don't be long.*

I won't. Night crawled across Rachel's form, stealing her from sight. Nikki sat back down on the ground, picking bits of grass from her hair and watching the approach of the emergency vehicles.

Five minutes passed. The plane lifted off again as the firemen clambered out of their truck and put the fire out. The police began to make noises about sending someone after Michael—at which point, he reappeared, running towards her, his face a mask of fear. He knelt beside her, frantically touching her, kissing her, as if they were true newlyweds and he was assuring himself she was all right.

You should have been a damn actor. She wrapped her arms around his neck and hugged him close. Not for the sake of the watching police, but because she simply wanted to hold him.

"I was." His breath brushed warmth past her ear as he whispered, "Remind me to show you the posters one day. I was a Broadway sensation for all of, oh, two weeks."

She buried her face against his neck to hide her grin. *Rachel?*

Safe with Doyle. He'll take her back to Seline and see what can be done.

One of the police officers cleared his throat, and the questions began again. It was another twenty minutes before they were able to order a cab and leave.

They headed straight back to the hotel. After explaining

what had happened to the rental car—and horrifying the concierge in the process—they headed up to their room.

She grabbed her cell phone and called Mary. Jake was still in intensive care, but he was stronger. The doctors were hopeful. Relief coursed through her. She hung up, then flopped back onto the bed and closed her eyes.

"Jake's okay?" Michael asked from near the bar.

"Getting better." Only time would tell for certain. "Are we safe here, now? If Cordell is behind the kidnappings, he'd have to know we're staying here."

The bed dipped slightly as Michael sat next to her. She opened her eyes and accepted the drink he held out.

"We have no other choice. We can't get on the hotel grounds unless we're guests." He took a drink, dark eyes thoughtful. "I doubt he'd make a direct assault, not here in the hotel, anyway. But he's forewarned now, and that will make it more dangerous when we head into the caverns."

"He might even leave." She raised up on one elbow and sipped the drink. She grimaced. Too much bourbon for her taste buds.

"He has a very nice setup here, and I doubt he'd leave unless he thought it was absolutely necessary. As yet, we haven't provided much of a threat."

True. And he had the safety of numbers on his side as well. "What are we going to do, then?"

He leaned forward and picked grass from her hair. "Do you feel up to entering the caverns tonight?"

She licked her lips. After witnessing what Cordell was capable of, she sure as hell didn't want to go anywhere *near* him. "What about your burns? Shouldn't you rest?"

His smile made her heart do strange things again. "You have to stop thinking of me in human terms."

He undid his shirt and showed her. The blisters had already disappeared, and his skin was only slightly pink.

"Amazing," she said, running her fingers lightly across his chest. "You're not even going to scar."

"No. One of the few advantages of being a vampire." He caught her hand and brushed a kiss across her fingers. "I can go into the caverns alone, if you wish."

"It'll take you too long to pinpoint Matthew." Besides, his ex- was prowling around down there somewhere. Alone was the one thing he was *not* going to be the next time he met her. Trusting him was one thing, trusting *her* was another matter entirely. "But won't Cordell be expecting such a move?"

"I doubt whether he'd expect it so soon. If we wait, we give him the chance to fortify his defenses."

"I wish I had my knives with me." She might be able to protect herself with kinetic energy, but she still felt a whole lot safer with the weight of a knife in her hand. Which was no doubt a hang-up from her days on the streets, when the obvious protection of a knife did more for her safety than the unseen threat of energy. She gulped down the rest of the bourbon and shuddered. "Ready when you are."

He rose from the bed and offered his hand. She accepted his help and found herself pulled into his embrace. "You will do as I ask down there, won't you?" His expression was a mix of amusement and worry. "You're not going to wander off alone, are you?"

She grinned. "I always do what I'm told. You know that."

"That's exactly why I'm asking." His voice was dry.

Grin widening, she raised on her toes and wrapped her hands around his neck. His eyes were dark jewels that sparkled with caring, his mouth a breath away, warm and inviting. Too inviting to resist—so she didn't. His arms tightened around her waist, and the kiss deepened, sending ripples of pleasure pulsating through her until her need for him became an ache so fierce she wanted to scream.

But her timing, as ever, was wrong.

He pulled away, his breath ragged, brushing heat across her skin. "If I wasn't what I am," he said softly. "If I didn't do what I do for a living—"

He didn't finish the sentence. He didn't need to. "If you weren't a vampire and hadn't come to Lyndhurst, I would be dead. But you saved my life and made me a part of you forever." She cupped a hand against his cheek, staring into the dark eyes that she loved. "I want to share your life, Michael, and I'm not going to give up the hope that one day I will. No matter what you say or do."

He sighed, his thoughts as troubled as his expression. "Nikki-"

She pressed a finger against his lips. "Just think about it. That's all I'm asking."

"I have spent the last six months thinking about *nothing* else."

"Then think about the fact that my life is also filled with danger and death. Think about Jake, lying in the hospital, and how easily it could have been me. The woman in the warehouse sensed your life force in me and, no doubt, knew how to kill me. The danger in my life won't stop just because you're not a part of it."

"Maybe," he murmured. He brushed the hair from her eyes then kissed her forehead and stepped away. "But I know for a certainty it *will* increase should you become a part of my world. You mean too much to me to take such a risk."

Then they were at an impasse—again. Yet the flame of hope flared brighter in her soul. The more they talked about it, the more she could make him see she knew and accepted the risks that were such a major part of his life.

She walked over to her bag and dug out the small flashlight she'd packed, then picked up Matthew's watch. Images teased the outer reaches of her mind, flashes of color and emotions that sent chills running down her spine. There was something very wrong in the taste of those images—something dark and deadly. She licked her lips and glanced at Michael. "Ready when you are."

"Keep close," he warned again, and offered his hand.

Right now, she had no intention of doing anything else. She wrapped her fingers in the safety of his and followed him from the room.

***

They entered the tunnels from the ledge entrance they'd discovered earlier. Nikki eyed the darkness warily, fear stirring in the pit of her stomach. With no sunlight to warm or guide them, and the heat of the day still seeping from the rocks, they might have been entering hell itself.

And she couldn't shake the sudden feeling that hell was what would greet them further in.

Michael squeezed her hand. The link flared to life, and warmth wrapped around her, a cocoon of strength and courage.

Why? she asked. Why block her, and why open it now?

I cannot sense anyone near, but we dare not make much sound. Better to use the link than talk.

That wasn't what I asked.

No. His sigh was a cool breeze that tempered the warmth in the link. *The link strengthens every time we use it.*

That might be true, but she suspected the real reason he kept the link blocked most of the time was because, with the link open, he could not hide behind words. She could see the truth in the color of the emotions flowing from his thoughts to hers.

Meaning, the more you use it, the less you'll be able to block me?

He hesitated, then answered almost reluctantly. *Yes.*

She grinned. *At least I now know where the next line of assault should be.*

You're incorrigible. His amusement shimmered around her.

I'm also headstrong and stubborn and very bad-tempered in the mornings before I get my coffee. And I'm in love with the most muleheaded man I have ever met in my entire life.

And he loves you, even if he doesn't want you in his life.

She stopped dead, pulling him to a halt as well. *That's the first time you've actually said you loved me.* Why couldn't he have said it while they were in their room, when she could see him, see his eyes?

You don't need to see my eyes, Nikki. You never have. His smile danced through her heart. He touched her face, cupping her cheek. *You knew what I felt. You have always known.*

Maybe. But it's nice to hear it said occasionally. She turned her face into his hand and kissed his palm. *As much as*

I would love to discuss this matter further, I think we'd better keep moving.

Yes. He pulled his hand away and continued on. The darkness closed in around them, and the air was still, stale smelling. They were headed downward, and the chill gradually increased. She shivered and wished she'd put on a sweater. But at least there was no sense of evil. Maybe Cordell wasn't back yet.

She touched the watch in her pocket. Sensations vibrated through her. Hunger and need, similar to a vampire's and yet not. Nikki frowned, unsure what that meant exactly.

We're coming up to that three-way split in the tunnel, Michael said. *Do we go left or straight on?*

She studied the darkness for several seconds, even though the answer throbbed clearly through her fingers. The air felt heavy and the silence intense. There was still no indication that Cordell or any of his cohorts were here, but something felt wrong.

Can you sense anyone?

Power shimmered bright enough to burn should she attempt to grasp it. Michael, searching the night, looking for the dangers she could feel.

Nothing, he said eventually. *You?*

Not a person...just something. Maybe it's just nerves.

Maybe. Doubt filtered through the link. *Which way?*

Left. I don't think Matthew's far.

He tugged her on. The path became uneven. Stones scooted away from her feet, rattling across the silence. She bit her lip but resisted the urge to turn on the flashlight. Cordell might not be near, but something was. Turning on the light might only force into action whatever stood out there in the darkness watching them.

They made their way slowly through the blanket of night. The closer they got to Matthew, the stronger the pulsing in the watch became. Images flicked brightly through her mind, recalling moments of sweat and sex and loathing. Matthew and Elizabeth had been intimate, if the visions were anything to go by.

At least one wish had come true for the teenager, and she hoped the price he'd had to pay wasn't too high—though she had a bad feeling this wasn't the case.

Goose bumps chased their way across her skin. She rubbed her arm with her free hand and uneasily studied the cloak of darkness past Michael's shoulders. It was still there, still watching them—whatever *it* was. Would it do anything more than watch? She couldn't say, and that worried her.

I can sense only Matthew, Nikki. He's alone, just ahead.

No sign of Rodeman?

Not in this section of tunnels.

Damn. That meant they'd have to come back once they got Matthew out. It was a prospect she didn't look forward to. Michael stopped. Her vision flared, seeming to expand again. Suddenly a door appeared in the darkness, its metal hinges and latch glowing with icy brightness. Her stomach churned. Her night sight had never been like this—at least not until Michael had shared his life force with her.

I can see a door.

Amusement shimmered around her. *So can I.*

No, I mean I can see it so well it's almost glowing. And yet I can barely see you, and I certainly can't see the damn walls. Even though they were so close she could reach out and touch them.

You've always had good night vision—you told me that not long ago.

But not like this. Never like this.

I'm not sure what's happening, then. His concern ran down the link. *It may have something to do with me sharing my life force, and it may not. Seline's doing a check on thralls. I'll know more when she gets back to me.*

Thralls? What the hell is a thrall?

He hesitated. *Technical term for what you now are.*

Why didn't she like the sound of that? Another chill ran through her. Maybe because if there was a term, there were sure to be problems and disadvantages.

He squeezed her hand then stopped. *The door has a lock on it.*

So I can see.

Think you can break it without making much noise?

Do pigs have wings?

Try, Nikki. Impatience edged his mental tones.

She grinned and held the lock. Energy danced from her fingertips to the metal, making it glow briefly before it shattered. It was little more than a scuff of sound against the silence around them.

He pushed open the door. Shapes glowed in the heavy darkness cloaking the room beyond—a chair, table and a rough-looking bed. It looked like a cell—and probably was, if what she'd seen when she'd joined Matthew's mind was anything to go by.

She couldn't see the teenager. She wrapped her fingers around the watch again, watching the flow of images, listening to their intensity. He was there, somewhere, watching them. He wasn't afraid—wasn't anything, she realized. Beyond the rush of his memories, she felt little emotion. It was if he were a slate wiped clean and waiting to be filled.

Energy flowed across her senses. Michael, searching the darkness, trying to find the dangers they both sensed were there but couldn't see.

I do not like the feel of this.

Neither do I. Why was Matthew merely sitting there? Why didn't he *do* something? She licked her lips. There had to be a trap of some kind. Had to be. *We can't just stand here.* Nor could they run, though every instinct was telling her to do just that.

No. You wait while I check out the cell and the teenager.

Separating us may be the whole idea. And she didn't want to be left alone in this darkness.

We can't stand here like fools, either.

The warmth of his hand left hers. She bit her lip. He stepped into the cell then hesitated. Nothing happened. He stepped forward again. There was a soft click, as if a button had been pushed somewhere. He froze, his tension flowing like fire through the link. Her stomach churned, and her breath was caught somewhere in her throat. For several seconds nothing happened. Then with an almost silent sigh, the ground gave way and plunged her into a deep pit of darkness.

Michael spun and dove forward, his stomach scraping against rock as he grabbed her hand and hung on tight. The sudden shock of her weight slid him forward several inches, and his straining arm muscles burned a protest through his body. He grunted, trying not to crush her fingers in the force of his grip. She hung in the darkness, staring up at him, eyes amber fire.

Don't drop me, don't drop me... Her litany ran through him, her fear so sharp he could taste it in the back of his throat.

Metal creaked, a sound as sharp as a gunshot in the silence. He glanced up, saw the glimmer of metal spikes hurtling toward him. He only had two choices. One of them was dropping Nikki and rolling into the safety of the cell.

He took the other option and dove into the pit with her.

Seventeen

He plunged into water, sinking deep. Like the night itself, the water was dark and cold, and it was hard to know which way was up. He drifted for several seconds, trying to get orientated, then kicked toward the surface.

He broke it with a gasp and looked around. "Nikki?" There was no response, and the water around him was still, silent. Fear clubbed him. She couldn't swim. *Nikki!*

He thrust the link wide open but was met with silence. He took a deep breath and dove under the water, kicking deep into the murky depths. She'd been close to him when they'd fallen. Surely she couldn't be too far away.

Hair floated against his fingers. An instant later he touched her neck, her shoulders. She wasn't moving. He couldn't tell if she was holding her breath or simply not breathing. *She can't die,* he reminded himself fiercely. *Not like this, anyway.* But repeating those words over and over didn't help the sick sensation churning his gut.

He grabbed her shirt, then kicked back to the surface, pulling her with him. Holding her head above the water, he looked around quickly, seeing nothing but darkness. He blinked and switched to the infrared benefits of his vampire vision. Walls became visible, then a rocky shelf, and beyond that, a path that disappeared into the darkness. He glanced at Nikki, saw the rich glow of blood welling from a wound on the side of her head.

Fear slammed past any reaction his vampire instincts might have made. He swam quickly toward the ledge, thrusting her onto her it before climbing up beside her.

"Nikki?" Still no response. He pulled her onto her side, then opened her mouth and checked for obstructions. She wasn't breathing.

She couldn't die. He knew that. But seeing her like this, so pale and unresponsive, terrified him. What if he was wrong? What if his life force wasn't enough to keep her alive through most injuries?

Cursing fate and his own lack of knowledge, he began resuscitation. Fear was a knife digging deep into his heart. He didn't want to lose her—not now, not like this. Not ever.

For several long minutes nothing happened. He continued resuscitation and hung on to hope. Then she shuddered and coughed, and water spewed from her mouth. Relief surged through him so strongly it left him trembling. He thrust her onto her side, holding her while she vomited the rest of the water from her stomach.

"Oh God," she murmured. "Did you get the number of that truck?"

Her voice was weak and shaky, but never had he heard a sweeter sound. He smiled and pushed the wet strands of hair from her eyes. "Do you remember what happened?"

"After the truck? Not a thing." She hesitated. "I'm wet. So are you."

"We fell into water." She sounded stronger, but her skin was cold, and she was still shaking. It might have been shock or the cold or a combination of both. Either way, they had to get back to their room before she caught a chill. "Are you able to get up?"

"To echo the grouchy words of someone else, of course I can. I'm just wet, not an invalid."

Oh yeah, she was definitely feeling better. Smiling slightly, he rose and helped her to her feet.

"Where are we?" She clutched his arm, hanging on tight, as if afraid she was going to fall.

Maybe she *wasn't* feeling as well as she was making out. He opened the link again, felt the knot of pain and weakness in her thoughts. He glanced at her head and saw the glimmer of blood. But the tide had slowed to a trickle, and she wasn't in any danger of bleeding to death.

"I don't know where we are. Are you able to walk?"

"Yes." She teetered forward a few steps. "What exactly happened?"

He wrapped an arm around her waist, holding her close as they walked, trying to keep her warm. "You don't remember?"

She shook her head, frowning slightly. "I remember falling

and cracking my head on something, then nothing."

"You must have hit your head when we fell. We'll head back to the room and—"

"No," she said, stopping abruptly. "We've got to get Matthew out of here."

"Nikki," he said, as patiently as he could. "You're wet, and shaking and—"

"I said no, and I meant it." She glared up him, fists clenched and eyes sparkling with anger. She'd never looked more beautiful. "We may not get another chance at this."

He rubbed a hand across his eyes. What she said made perfectly good sense, but he just wasn't willing to risk her life again.

"It's my life to risk, Michael."

She was back to reading his thoughts. As he'd feared, the barriers he'd raised to stop her were beginning to fade.

She touched his cheek, her fingers cool against his skin. Her thoughts spun around him, through him, tender and persuasive. "A chill is not going to kill me," she said softly. "But any delay might mean the difference between life and death for Matthew."

She cared more for her client's safety than she did her own. Always had. And no matter what he said or did, she wasn't going to be swayed. "Stubborn wench," he muttered and pulled her close, kissing her cold lips.

A shiver ran through her, but he knew it had nothing to do with being cold. He could feel her need as heavily as he did his own. It was an ache growing steadily stronger by the hour. But if he gave in to desire and made love to her as he so desperately wanted to do, he knew he wouldn't have the strength to leave her again. And he had to leave. He couldn't face seeing her cold and lifeless again. Twice was more than enough for his heart to take.

He stepped away, though it was the last thing in the world he wanted to do right now. "Let's go find a way back up to Matthew, then."

A knowing smile touched her lips. "You won't win this battle, you know. Fate is on my side."

His shrug was noncommittal. He had to at least go down fighting. He held out his hand, and she slipped her fingers into his. Once more he led the way through the caverns, his pace slow at first, then gradually speeding up as she recovered and regained her strength.

They wound their way through the darkness, heading steadily upwards. The air was damp and stale, and it felt as if it hadn't been breathed for many years. Cordell and his cohorts obviously didn't come down here much. If they had, the air would have caught their scents and left them lingering.

The path flattened out. In the distance, like a far-off drum, he could hear the beat of a single heart, guiding him on even as it called to the darkness in him—a darkness he was increasingly able to ignore.

We're getting close to Matthew's cell again.

Her thoughts were touched by fear. He scanned the night, wondering what she felt. He could find nothing, taste nothing in the stillness of the night. Only Matthew. *What can you sense?*

Something is watching us again. I can feel its presence.

That he couldn't see or feel anything meant little. In some areas, her psychic abilities far outweighed his, and he'd learned to trust her instincts. *Is it dangerous?*

I don't know.

He scanned the night again. Still nothing. *Tell me if it moves.*

I will. Her tension was a lump sitting heavily in the link.

He squeezed her hand lightly and continued on until they reached Matthew's cell. The door was still open, the teenager still sitting on his bed. He didn't even look as if he'd moved.

Something's wrong, she said. *No teenager in recorded history has ever sat still for so long.*

Maybe he's just scared. Yet he could feel no emotion, taste no fear. Frowning, he touched the teenager's thoughts— and found nothing more than memories. All self-awareness had been wiped away, leaving only the desire to please.

He clenched his fist against the surge of anger. He'd seen this done before, though thankfully only rarely. Matthew had, in some sense, become a thrall, but not one like Nikki. In Matthew's case, his mind and his will had been sucked from his body, leaving him little more than a robot, waiting to fulfill the wishes of his master. It took a vampire with exceptional telepathic abilities to achieve such a thrall. He could never have done it, despite the fact his gifts were very strong. But Elizabeth could.

Michael, what's wrong with him?

His mind has been wiped. His anger surged through the link.

He felt her wince, then her growing horror. *What do you mean, wiped?*

Just that. Let's go in for a closer look.

She regarded him doubtfully. *Do you think it's safe?*

Yes. The trap door had already been sprung, and there was no feel of magic in the air. Cordell was either extremely confident no one would find their way through this darkness, or he was a fool. Maybe even both.

He helped Nikki step over the hole, then guided her past the metal spikes that had threatened to skewer him, and the loose stone that had opened the trapdoor. No sense in hitting it a second time, just in case Cordell wasn't a fool and he did indeed have a second trap waiting.

"Matthew?" Nikki let go of Michael's hand and walked across to the teenager. There was no response from him, no spark of life. It was if she were facing a robot. A chill ran through her. She squatted down beside him and gently pinched his cheek. "Matthew?"

Michael stopped behind her and crossed his arms. His anger was a storm crowding the link. He knew who was behind this, even if he wasn't saying. Not that it took great intelligence to guess that it was probably Elizabeth.

The teenager didn't respond to either Nikki's touch or her words. She glanced up. Michael's face looked as grim as she felt. *Why would someone do this? He's only a kid, for God's sake. They could have just asked him to do what they wanted. They didn't have to do this.*

No, they didn't.

She bit her lip, studying Matthew again. *What are our options now?*

He is little more than a robot. He has no future like this.

What he was really saying was that they had no option but to kill him. She closed her eyes and took a deep breath. *I know. But you can't. Not yet. Maybe whoever did this to him could undo it.*

No one can replace what has been wiped.

She bit her lip. *Can you touch what remains? We need to know why they kidnapped him. If we can't save him, we have to at least try to stop this from happening again.*

Nothing remains in him, Nikki. Nothing but memories, and the need to obey.

Memories? Michael might not be able to access memories, but *she* could. She dug a hand into her pocket. Matthew's watch had survived the dunking, but Michael grabbed her wrist before she could wrap her fingers around it.

Damn it, don't be a fool. His mind voice was as fierce as his grip. *You risk losing yourself in his thoughts.*

Then be my anchor and pull me out if you feel it's dangerous. He'd done it before when Jasper had kidnapped Jake. *We have to try this, Michael. It's our only chance.*

He sighed. That was one of the things she loved about this man. He was willing to admit when she was right, and he didn't go on arguing endlessly.

Get comfortable on the bed. I'll open the link fully and keep watch. The minute I feel your thoughts begin to blur into his, I'm pulling you out.

Though she wasn't entirely sure what he meant, she nodded and sat down on the bed beside Matthew. The teenager didn't move, didn't react in any way.

The link opened fully, and Michael's mind ran beside hers, a field filled with the brilliant color of his thoughts and emotions.

Ready when you are.

His thought was a breeze of wariness. He might be helping her, but he still wasn't happy about it. She could feel his fear, see it in the unhappy tinge of gray that swirled through the link, through her.

She licked her lips and curled her fingers around the watch. While he hadn't worn it for a few days, the images still came thick and fast, thudding through her mind.

Control it, Nikki!

She frowned, concentrating on the images, sorting through them quickly. Found the ones she wanted and dived deep—so deep that she become one with them...

***

...Matthew scrubbed the back of his hand across his nose. He hated the darkness, hated the cold, and hated the fact he was so damn scared he was almost pissing his pants.

He *had* pissed his pants when Lizzie jumped him. She'd laughed and later brought him back a fresh pair but, he could still smell the stink on his skin.

He touched his neck. It was swollen and sore and he had no idea why she'd bitten him. Sucked him. It hadn't really hurt at the time, though. Just scared the piss out of him.

Next time it would be better, she'd promised. Next time, you might just get lucky. He didn't want there to be a next time, even if it did mean staying a virgin. He just wanted to go home.

Footsteps echoed across the silence. He edged back against the wall. The door opened and light filled the room, making him blink. The squat stranger was back. Behind him stood Lizzie. Her eyes looked weird, bright yellow and somehow intense. Like a cat's, he thought, just before it pounces on a mouse.

He swallowed heavily. He didn't want to be her mouse. "What do you want with me?" He sounded like a girl, his voice all high and shrill.

"The time has come to prove your worth, young man." The stranger's voice was as dead as the smell in the air. "Elizabeth, bring him along."

She walked into the room, a smile touching her lips. Lips that were the color of blood. His blood, maybe. He gulped, squeaking in fright when she grabbed him. But she didn't bite him, just dragged him one-handed to his feet and pushed him toward the door.

The stranger was ahead of them, wheeling down the corridor at a rate of knots. A weird little light rotated above his head, sending flickers of red and green up the walls.

They reached some stairs and stopped. The light above the stranger's head pulsated, fading in and out of color. The stranger levitated in the air, scooting forward. Matthew gulped. Lizzie chuckled and dug her nails into his back, propelling him up the stairs.

They came to a doorway, then a small room. It hadn't been used for a while and was filled with dust. *Mom would have had a fit.* They didn't stop, heading into a warm, well-lit corridor.

"One wrong word, and you're dead meat," Lizzie whispered, then licked his ear.

It felt like she was tasting him. He shuddered and sidled away. She chuckled again.

A woman stood at a counter, serving a couple of men decked out in shorts and sweatshirts. The stranger greeted her. She smiled and waved and didn't even look at him and Lizzie. It was like she didn't even know they were there.

They went down the hall and into an office. Computers lined the wall. Lizzie locked the door, and the stranger stopped in the middle of the room, then swung around to face him.

"You once boasted you could get into any computer you liked, even government ones."

He'd said many things he hadn't meant. "Yeah? So?"

The stranger smiled. He had teeth like Lizzie's, long and sharp. "What about bank computers?"

"Oh yeah, that's easy." Banks thought they were clever but they weren't. They'd never picked up any of the cash he'd transferred.

"Could you transfer money from one account to another, then on to another, creating a trail of money so confusing the authorities will never sort it out?"

"I suppose." He frowned. "These your accounts? I don't want to be involved in anything illegal." Not *too* illegal, at any rate. Stealing a few extra dollars was one thing. Stealing thousands was another. He didn't want to end up in jail.

The stranger's smile turned nasty. "You will do as we ask, one way or another." His gaze slid past him. "Elizabeth? I think another session is called for. He's not quite pliable enough."

A hand grabbed him. He tried to scream, but it lodged somewhere in his throat. He felt her hands, felt her teeth, felt her thoughts in his mind. But his scream became silence, just endless silence...

***

...Nikki's silent scream reverberated through Michael's soul. He wrenched her free from Matthew's memories, and caught her as she slumped forward. Her whole body was trembling, her mind a tangled mess of Matthew's memories and her own.

"Well, well, well, what have we here?" a dry voice said behind him.

He froze for a second and silently cursed his luck. Elizabeth was the one person he *didn't* need right now. He must have been so caught up in watching Nikki that he hadn't even sensed her nearness. He pushed Nikki back against the wall, holding her upright with one hand, then turned to face his maker.

She leaned casually against the door frame, a smile touching her ruby lips and ice in her eyes. He wondered briefly what he'd ever seen in her.

"There was no need to destroy the teenager's mind, Elizabeth. We both know you could have achieved control without going to this extreme."

Her shrug was grace itself. "You know I have a taste for virgins. Sometimes excitement gets the better of my control."

If she'd wanted to control her instincts, she would have. But she liked destruction just as much as she liked the fresh taste of an unwoken mind. Or body. Matthew had no doubt provided her with a double dose of pleasure.

"What brings you here? There's nothing left of the boy to play with." He glanced briefly at Nikki. She still looked out of it, but awareness stirred through the link.

Elizabeth raised a dark eyebrow. "I might ask you the same question, only I guess the answer is somewhat obvious. You always did fancy yourself mankind's savior."

"Not a savior. Just a protector."

She waved an elegant hand. "Same thing. When will you learn they are not worth it?"

Never, if it meant joining the likes of Jasper. And maybe even Elizabeth. "Why are you doing all this? You certainly don't need the money."

"It was just a game at first." She hesitated, shrugging. "Now I have little real choice in the matter."

He frowned, not understanding why. Elizabeth was nearly eight hundred years old. There weren't many vampires left alive who had the strength of mind to overpower hers. And the brief glimpses he'd had of Cordell certainly hadn't led him to believe *he* could. So why did she have no choice? Why couldn't she leave, as she seemed to want to do?

Then he remembered the heat in her touch. "Cordell put an imp in you."

"You always were quick." Amusement glimmered in her eyes. "Yes, one of the energy creatures now shares my body, and through his control over it, Cordell governs most of my actions."

Most, but not all. Maybe because of her age, she'd retained a degree of control over the imp that Rachel and the other vampires had not.

"It will kill you, you know."

"It cannot. It merely resides within me, controlling me when I'm within Cordell's boundaries."

If her actions now—or lack of them—were anything to go by, then she was currently well outside those boundaries.

"The imp killed the young vampire who was supposed to meet us at the airport, Elizabeth. His body could no longer contain the imp's heat, and he literally melted. Ginger has already told us her form will not long contain her. What makes you think your fate will be any different?"

A frown flickered across her face. "You lie."

"You would taste it if I did."

"Yes." She hesitated, then shrugged and glanced at Nikki. "Is this your thrall? Does she taste as pretty as she looks?"

"Keep away from her, or I promise you, I'll tear your cold heart out of your chest." He kept his voice flat, devoid of any emotion. But anger rose in him, as well as fear. Elizabeth was a bigger danger to Nikki than she had ever been to him.

She raised her eyebrows again. "Touchy. One might be inclined to think you cared for her."

He shrugged. "She suits my current needs, and I have no

wish to make another."

A red cloud of annoyance flashed through the link. Nikki was awake. And listening.

"I'm sure she does," Elizabeth murmured. "She looks... athletic. Boringly so."

The annoyance became a cloud of indignant anger, and he had to bite down on his amusement. Boring was one word he would never use to describe his and Nikki's lovemaking—what little there had been of it so far.

"However," Elizabeth continued, pushing away from the door frame,"I did not come here to discuss your thrall. Your presence has presented me with something of a quandary."

Tension knotted his gut. He watched her carefully, knowing from the past that she would give no warning if she chose to attack. "You cannot take the teenager."

"Don't be tedious, Michael. I must. What I don't want to do right now is have to kill you. "

"Presuming you could."

Her smile was that of a mother indulging a child. "What is the point of protecting him? Without me, he is nothing. An empty shell."

"I don't mean to protect him, Elizabeth."

"Ah. Well. I can't let you kill him. Not yet."

Her canines were beginning to show. She was anticipating the fight, even if she wasn't yet ready to actually fight him. "Then we are, as you say, at an impasse."

"Not really," Nikki muttered and flung out her hand. Energy seared through his mind and across his skin. Elizabeth's eyes widened in surprise, and she jerked backwards, tumbling down into the well. After several seconds there was a splash, then silence again.

"That witch deserved a good dunking. Boring indeed!"

He grinned, even though he knew the sudden swim would only make Elizabeth angrier—make her more inclined to go after Nikki.

He grabbed her hand and pulled her to her feet. "I take it you've recovered from the trip through Matthew's memories?"

The amusement fled from her face. "Yes." She shuddered.

"It was awful, though. God, I felt her suck his thoughts dry. It felt like she was sucking mine..."

He wrapped his arms around her, holding her close, comforting her even though he knew they had to get going. Elizabeth wouldn't hesitate to attack a second time—not if she found them still in this room.

"We only have one choice, Nikki. We can't leave him like this. They'll only continue to use him, and when they've finished, they'll kill him anyway."

"I know." She hesitated, then pulled out of his arms. "Make it quick."

Hands clenched and back rigid, she walked to the door, her back to the room. He turned to the teenager and gently closed the kid's unseeing eyes.

I hope you find peace in death, Matthew.

The words echoed through the emptiness that was the teenager's mind. Anger tore through him. Elizabeth had no right to do this. Not to a mere boy like Matthew. Not to anyone.

He wrapped an arm around the teenager's neck, grabbed his head with the other, and twisted sharply, just the once. Human life was all too fragile, so easily taken. He laid Matthew gently on the bed and joined Nikki by the door.

She glanced up at him. There were tears in her eyes and her thoughts. "How could you love someone capable of doing something like that?"

"I don't love her." It was the truth. He hadn't loved Elizabeth for a very long time—if he'd ever truly loved her. It had just taken him a long time to realize it.

"But you did love her once."

"Perhaps." He touched her back, feeling the chill in her skin through the dampness of her clothes. She needed warmth, not darkness and death. He guided her past the traps. "Let's move, before she gets back."

She shivered, but he wasn't sure if it was the cold or the thought of Elizabeth returning.

"Will she come after us in revenge for Matthew?"

He doubted very much whether Elizabeth would really even care about the boy. She'd had her fun, and it was Cordell who'd wanted the teenager's help, not her. Besides, if she had really wanted them dead, she would have attacked right away, when she'd had the upper hand.

"I think it's Cordell we have to worry about, not Elizabeth."

Doubt ran through the link, as bright as fire. "Don't trust her, Michael. The darkness in her heart is stronger than you think."

Seline had said much the same thing, and he wasn't about to take either warning lightly. "It's Cordell who's pulling everyone's strings, Elizabeth's included." And it was about time he did something about it.

But not before he got Nikki out of this resort and back home to safety.

Eighteen

Nikki flopped on the bed and closed her eyes. Images ran past her eyelids—visions of fear intermixed with pleasure. Elizabeth had sucked Matthew's mind dry even as she made love to him. And it had all happened in that office, with Cordell watching avidly.

Sick. They were all sick. She swallowed heavily. They might be sick, but they were also very dangerous. Michael had locked all the doors to their room, but she couldn't escape the notion that if Cordell wanted to get in here, he could do so without using the doors. Easily.

From the bathroom came the sound of running water. Michael preparing the hot tub for a bath she didn't want. She didn't care about the need to get warm. She just wanted Michael to take her in his arms and hold her. She had a very strong suspicion time was running out for them.

She knew, too, that he intended to ask her to go home. But he had a snowball's chance in hell of making *that* happen. He was going to need her help to survive the battle that loomed, and she had no intention of going anywhere.

"You're not getting undressed."

She opened her eyes. He leaned against the bathroom door frame, dark hair tousled and a warm light in his eyes. "I don't have the energy."

"If you don't get up and undressed, I'll throw you in, clothes and all."

"If I go in, you're going in, buddy."

His sudden grin was almost boyish, and he looked so damn sexy she just wanted to grab him and kiss him and make love to him. How could he treat her with such warmth and tenderness and expect to keep her at arm's length?

She couldn't. Wouldn't. Not this time.

"Up, woman. You need to get clean, and you need to get warm. I will not take no for an answer."

She smiled slightly. Neither would she. She kicked off her shoes then stopped. "Sorry. Too much effort involved."

"You're going to make me pick you up, aren't you?"

"Uh huh." She closed her eyes and waited.

His hands slipped under her, trailing heat through her body. He lifted her, holding her close, his grip gentle and his body warm against hers.

"Now, this I can handle." Grinning, she wrapped her arms around his neck and lightly kissed his chin. "I'll warm up in no time if you just keep your arms around me like this."

"But it won't wash the dirt from your skin," he said dryly as he carried her into the bathroom and stopped beside the hot tub. "And I may have a vampire's strength, but even my arms would protest after the first hour or so of holding you."

She raised an eyebrow. "Are you calling me a dead weight?"

He glanced down at her, dark eyes suddenly intense. "Never that," he said softly. Then the boyish grin hit her again, warming her senses to overload. "In you go."

"Don't," she yelped, only to have the words snatched away as she went under the water.

She came up spluttering. The bubbling water was frothy and hot. The mild perfume, a mix of jasmine and rose, caught her nose and made her sneeze. Foam flew, covering her face and hair. Michael watched, a silly grin on his face.

"Think it's funny, do you?" she muttered, and hit him with kinetic energy.

A second later, he was spluttering in the hot tub beside her. "Told you," she continued, voice all innocence. "I go in, you go in."

"Witch." He grabbed her shirt and tugged her toward him. "Whatever am I going to do with you?"

She kissed his wet lips. "Washing me would be a good start."

He raised an eyebrow. "Too weak, are we?"

"No." She smiled sweetly. "I just want your hands on me."

"Well," he said, sounding as put out as all hell—an image somewhat destroyed by the amused anticipation in his eyes, "for the sake of sleeping in clean sheets, I guess I shall have to help."

He undid her shirt and slid it from her shoulders, his hands skimming her skin and caressing heat through her body. Her jeans and undergarments quickly followed and were tossed wetly on the tiles beside her shirt.

"Hair first." He grabbed the shampoo, then tucked her between his legs and began washing her hair. She closed her eyes and simply enjoyed.

"Rinse time." He reached back, grabbing the flexible hand shower, stretching it to capacity as he turned on the taps. He rinsed her hair clean, then turned off the water and grabbed the conditioner.

He massaged it through her scalp, sending ripples of pleasure reverberating down to her toes.

"You're awfully good at this," she murmured. "Don't tell me—you were a hairdresser at one time, too."

"Three hundred years is a long time to stay in one job, you know. And people tend to get a little suspicious when you show no sign of aging."

"A problem," she agreed. She leaned against his chest, listening to the thunder of his heart.

"I can't massage the back of your head like that."

She smiled. "I don't really care. I'm comfortable."

"Oh really?" He cupped his hands around her breasts, then gently tugged at her nipples, teasing them to full bloom. A shudder ran through her, and deep inside the ache began. "How comfortable is that?"

"Probably as comfortable as you are in those wet jeans." She shifted position and closed her eyes. Energy shimmered, and his clothes joined hers on the floor. She moved back between his legs.

Michael grabbed the bar of soap and began washing her arms and chest. He took his time, working his way down her stomach, every now and again reaching back up to cup her breasts and tease her nipples. Eventually, he slipped his hand between her legs, stroking her gently at first, then faster when the tremors began. Her hips surged, thrusting against his hand for several seconds before she went lax and still against him. But ripples of pleasure ran heat through the link, and her sigh was a sound that reverberated though his soul.

"I hope you didn't treat all your customers this well," she murmured.

"Baths weren't really big enough to share with any comfort way back then," he said, reaching for the soap again. "And they were generally only taken on a weekly basis anyway."

She sighed. "This is so much more civilized."

Amusement mixed with love ran through the link, shimmering around him, through him. He knew he should leave the spa, knew that he was risking his resolve to keep her out of his life—but right then, he didn't care. He needed her—emotionally as much as physically—and just this once, he was giving in to that need.

He began washing her again. The last time they'd made love it had been too quick, too rushed—too full of uncertainty and desperation. This time, while they still had time left to them, he would pleasure her more fully.

"Turn around and face me," he said, dropping the soap.

She did. He took her left foot in his hands, gently massaging her toes. Gradually, he worked his way up her leg, watching her amber eyes dilate with anticipation. When he touched her again, she sucked in her breath, squirming against his hand. He slid his fingers inside her, caressing her, feeling her heat, bringing her close to the brink again before pulling away.

Her need filled his mind, his body, and almost shot his control to hell. He slammed the link closed, not ready yet for this to end.

"Tease," she muttered, her breathing hot and hard.

He smiled and made his way down her right leg, then raised her foot and gently sucked on each of her toes. Her moan of pleasure ran like fire across his senses. He lowered her foot and tugged her closer. She ran a hand down his chest and stomach, and every inch of him trembled in response. He stopped her, raising her fingers to his lips and kissing them. "This night is for you and about you," he said softly. "Just let me love you as you deserve to be loved."

Tears glimmered in her eyes. She blinked them away, but her smile remained tremulous. "I only want to give you the same."

"I take pleasure in your pleasure. I could stay here forever and just watch you, Nikki. Let me do this."

She sighed. "I'm enjoying this way too much to say no right now."

"Good."

He began his gentle exploration again. Ran his hands down the full length of her lean body, caressed her small breasts, sucking her nipples until she was panting with need, then claimed her mouth, greedy for the taste of her.

Their minds entwined, wildfire ready to explode.

He cupped her again, slid his fingers inside her, bringing her to her climax hot and fast, until the shudders racked her body and left her limp in the water.

"Again," he said, pulling her closer. "This time with me."

"I can't," she moaned. "It's impossible."

"It's not." Nothing was impossible between them. He savaged her mouth, drowning in the heat and urgency of her kiss. Got lost in the wonder of her body, until the ache in his was a fire that burned through the link, wrapping them in heat and passion and love. *I could make love to this woman every day for eternity and never tire of her.* And he knew with certainty that that's exactly what he had to do. Somehow, he had to find a way to hold her away from the danger of his work and yet keep her a part of his life. He couldn't walk away. Didn't want to walk away. He'd been a fool to even think he could.

He caught her hair, pulling her head back, kissing the long line of her neck, working his way back up to her mouth. Her breath was hot and quick against his lips. "Say it, Nikki."

"I love you." She moaned and wrapped her arms tight around his neck. "Oh God, I love you."

He plunged himself inside her, then thrust her back against the spa, plunging deep again. "Say it again."

"I love you, I love you." Her softness encased him, muscles contracting against him. He had to grit his teeth to keep from exploding.

"Again," he demanded, thrusting hard, wanting, needing,

every ounce from her.

Her litany ran over him, through him, exploding glorious heat through their minds. "And I," he vowed, "will love you for eternity and never leave you."

Her climax sent him spiralling beyond control and into bliss.

***

"I," she said, sometime later, "have no energy to move. I think I'll sleep right here in these bubbles."

"Your skin will wrinkle like a prune. Not a good look, let me assure you." He climbed out of the spa and quickly dried himself. "Up, woman. Bed is where you belong right now."

"My legs have no bones."

He grinned. "Good loving can do that to you."

"That wasn't good. That was *amazing*. I've never..." she hesitated and licked her lips. For an instant, she looked like a teenager just discovering the wonders of sex. "Let's just say that it has never been that good for me."

"Then it was a first for us both." He wrapped the towel around his waist, then leaned over the side of the hot tub and grabbed her lax arm, tugging her toward the edge.

She raised her eyebrows and made no move to get out. "I find that hard to believe. In three hundred and eighty years you must have had *some* good sex."

He forced a note of severity into his voice. "Three hundred and sixty, not three hundred and eighty, thank you very much."

Her grin widened. "What's twenty years when you're that old? And you didn't answer my question."

"I have had good sex. But I've never had sex that could so completely blow my mind as well as my body. Amazing, as you said."

She studied him for a second, her eyes amber slits of contentment. "What about Elizabeth?"

If she at all worried that Elizabeth might yet usurp her position in his heart, then it didn't show—in her voice or her thoughts. Still, he owed her the truth.

He sat down on the edge of the spa and tucked the wet strands of her hair behind her ear. "I gave up life to follow Elizabeth. She was my world—all I wanted at the time, and all

I thought I would ever want." Nikki frowned and looked away. He caught her chin, gently forcing her to look at him again. "But she never was, and could never be, what you are to me. You complete me, Nikki. She never could."

Her smile filled his heart and mind and stirred to life the embers of passion. "I really *do* love you."

He leaned forward, kissing her sweet lips. "Good. Now get your ass out of that water."

She sighed and struggled upright. He helped her out, then towelled her dry. Ignoring the rising desire to touch her more fully, he guided her into the bedroom and tucked her into bed.

"Wouldn't like to join me?" she murmured, patting the sheets next to her.

He would have liked nothing more, but there were things he had to do first. Like contact Seline. "I thought you had no bones? I can't make love to a boneless woman."

Her gaze flicked down his body and she grinned. "Parts of your body are refuting that statement."

"Parts of my body have a will of their own. Sleep Nikki. I have to contact Seline and see if she has found any information on Cordell."

"Which reminds me—I thought you said vampires could heal just about any wound inflicted on them?"

He frowned slightly. "We can. Why?"

"Cordell's in a wheelchair. I saw it when I was in Matthew's memories."

"That doesn't make much sense." Even if Cordell had broken his back at some stage, his vampire healing capacity should have fixed the wound within weeks. Unless...it must have happened *before* he became a vampire. As you were in life, you are in *un*life. If Cordell was crippled in some way before he became a vampire, he would have remained that way.

She shrugged. "I'm just reporting what I saw. Cordell was using Matthew to set up a series of electronic cash transactions."

"He's getting ready to pull out."

"It sounds like it. Though I can't understand why he'd bother transferring all this money to a charity organization in the first place if all he wanted to do was steal it himself. Why not just transfer it straight into is own accounts?"

He shrugged. "Seline said the charity looked legit. Maybe he needed to keep it that way until he'd hit all his targets and was ready to flee." He bent down and kissed her forehead. "You sleep. I have work to do."

"Don't be long," she murmured, closing her eyes.

She was asleep by the time he'd settled on the day bed. Smiling, he relaxed his mind and opened the lines of communication. Contact was instant. Seline had obviously been waiting for him.

Found lots of information on your Randolf Cordell, she said. *He's not a very pleasant type.*

If he was, we probably wouldn't be hunting him, would we?

Well, no, I guess not. Her smile ran down the line. *His parents died when he was eight. Cordell was shuffled between in-laws, none of whom really wanted him. The streets became his home. By the time he was thirteen he'd been up before the courts on several counts of assaults and robbery. When he was seventeen, he got involved in a car stealing racket but during one theft was involved in an accident, and the injury left him a paraplegic. He sued the driver for damages but lost the case. He then attempted to kill the driver, but was caught and charged, and spent the next ten years behind bars. Apparently, he was not a model prisoner.*

A charmer, all right. It was odd how differently people coped with their situations. Nikki had also made the streets her home after her parents had died. Yet she'd managed to escape with both her integrity and her humanity relatively intact. *Let me guess. The man who hit him was one of his first kidnap victims.*

Clever boy. William Parnell was actually one of the four major investors in a high-flying brokerage company. The other three men provided alibis for Parnell in the court case.

Victims two, three and four?

Yes. I would guess that by the time Cordell got around to penalizing the fourth man, Robert Carson, he'd gained quite a taste for kidnapping and easy money.

He frowned. *Cordell doesn't seem the type to be happy with siphoning money from their accounts. Especially as a means of revenge.*

These four are the types who think money is all-conquering. Cordell never had a hope in the court case, given his record and the fact· the car he was driving was stolen, but he never saw it that way. What he saw was big fancy lawyers and lots of cash burying the truth. I'm guessing he wanted that power, and that he wanted to take it away from them.

Do we know when he was turned?

Not exactly. He disappeared for several years after his ten-year stint in jail. The next mention I found was in a journal of an old witch—you remember a woman called Ladonna doing the fairground circuit some ten years back?

Vaguely. He wasn't into fairground mysticism—it was one of the few things he hadn't done through the years. *She was a shyster, wasn't she?*

No, she was very much the real thing, even though her act stunk to high heaven.

He smiled. *The sort of thing that gives witches a bad name, huh?*

Exactly. She sniffed. *Anyway, Cordell apparently joined her act, and they became quite a team. In her journal, Ladonna states that she had apprenticed Cordell and intended teaching him the art.*

Seline's tone told him she wasn't impressed. *I gather Ladonna followed the dark path?*

Yes. I warned her many years ago it would lead to her death, but power was all she could see, all she was interested in. Fool.

I think you've lost me. Why would teaching Cordell have cost Ladonna her life? Beside the fact that Cordell is a murderous creep, that is.

The only way those apprenticed in the dark ways can

gain complete mastery over the dark powers is by killing their master and absorbing their talents. Ladonna had failed to do this, which was why she was such an abysmal practitioner and no real threat to us. I haven't found a record of her death, but I have no doubt Cordell did kill her if he is now using the full powers of dark magic.

Could he use that magic to restore his ability to walk? He couldn't imagine women like Ginger and Rachel falling for a grimy little cripple like Cordell—not unless he was using some sort of glamour to hide the truth.

Maybe, if it was for short periods of time. That sort of magic sucks a lot of strength from the user, though.

Cordell is skin and bone.

Then he has used the magic often. It will make him weaker, but perversely, won't make him an easier target. Especially if he has found a way to siphon the energy of the flame imps.

Well, that solved the mystery of the imps' role in all of this. *What about the charity these funds are going into? Have you done a background check yet?* Cordell didn't seem the over generous type. The charity had to be a cover.

Yes. Cordell is listed as one of the directors and is being paid a huge salary. Three other directors are listed, but I cannot find more than postal addresses for them.

Surprise, surprise. *Then they are probably no more than names on paper.*

More than likely. But the charity is legit, insofar as it has all the proper registrations and has spent considerable monies providing hostels and shelters for street kids. On the other hand, considering the amounts donated, it is but a sneeze.

Why would he be kidnapping these men and risking possible exposure, if all he wished to do was siphon their millions? It doesn't make sense.

I would suspect that Cordell has the sort of personality that enjoys inflicting pain. He probably doesn't have to kidnap the men to make his scheme work, but he prefers to watch them suffer.

Then why use the imps?

She sniffed. *If he is a practitioner of the black arts, and as thin as you say, he probably needs their energy now to work his magic.*

Then that's why he's pulling out. According to Nikki, he has all but killed the imps off in this area. Though I still don't understand why he is forcing them into vampires like Rachel and Ginger. If they are his fledglings, they would do as he ordered, anyway.

But they would not have enough control of their bloodlust to seduce and coax these men into Cordell's arms. The imps probably give them that strength

Up to a point, anyway. Rachel's bloodlust had overcome the control of the imp inside her. Or had that simply happened because the bonding was still new? *Has Doyle arrived with our parcel yet?*

Yes, and what a parcel she is. I think your Nikki is being optimistic in thinking she can be saved, but we'll see.

Can you tell anything about the methods Cordell is using to bind the imp?

It will be a spell of binding, for certain. What type of spell I can't say, but you will need protection against it. I've already couriered two charms for you and Nikki. They should actually be there by now. Go down and check with the desk the minute we finish.

Nikki won't need it. She's heading home in the morning.

Seline's amusement filled the line. *If you say so. Give her the charm as a going away present, then. And make sure you wear yours.*

I will. Controlling the darkness inside him was hard enough. What he didn't need right now was a battle over control with an imp forced into his body. *What did you find out about thralls?*

Nothing much, although there was one suggestion it was better not to use those with psychic gifts. It didn't say why. Has she exhibited any other signs of emerging powers?

Her night sight has improved immensely, and the powers

she has have definitely strengthened.

You sound worried.

That's because I am. Elizabeth had created several thralls over the years, and never once had she mentioned anything like this happening. But then, maybe she'd never shared her life force with anyone who was psychic. Maybe she knew the risks and had just never mentioned it. He wished fleetingly he could go down and talk to her—but he didn't trust her. Not when it came to Nikki's safety.

I'll keep researching. In the meantime, go down to the desk and see if the parcel has arrived.

I will. Stop nagging.

Her laughter filled his thoughts, and the line went dead. He stretched and rose. The darkness shifted outside the window, shimmering briefly. He frowned. For an instant, a familiar taste ran across his senses, only to be whisked away before he could fully identify it.

He moved past the day bed and opened the door. The night was crisp and clear and touched with the faint scent of orange blossom. Elizabeth's scent.

Had she been watching him? For what reason? Did she merely wait for him to leave so she could attack Nikki?

Probably.

She'd enjoy robbing him of his thrall, especially after the dunking Nikki had given her.

He closed and locked the door. He wasn't about to go anywhere when there was a vampire hell bent on a good bloodletting roaming around outside their room. Seline's charms would have to wait until the morning, when the rise of the hotel's other guests forced Elizabeth away.

Nineteen

The sound of the suite door clicking shut woke Nikki. She peeked out from under the comforter, watching Michael carry a tray of croissants, fruit and coffee over to the table. He'd pulled on some jeans but wore no shirt, and the warm morning light played lovingly across his well-muscled chest and stomach. He had good skin color, considering how little he saw of the sun.

"Are you getting up?" He flipped the cups right-side up and poured two coffees.

She yawned and stretched. She felt like a cat, all warm and contented and full. But that didn't mean she couldn't do with more. Especially when the meal in question was standing a few yards away, looking mighty sexy in tight-fitting jeans. "That depends."

"On what?" He watched her over the rim of his steaming coffee mug, a smile crinkling the corners of his eyes.

"On whether you're intending to bring that coffee over to me." Not that she intended to drink the coffee once he'd bought it over. What she wanted was him in bed with her.

"Not a chance." Grin widening, he sat down. "You need to get out of bed, because we need to talk."

"That sounds ominous."

"It is. The coffee is delicious, by the way, and getting colder by the minute."

"Never tease someone who hasn't yet had their first morning cup. It could get ugly."

"I can handle ugly."

But he hadn't yet seen her in a coffee deprived fit. Even Jake quailed. She thrust the covers aside and wandered over to the table. She didn't bother dressing. Their room was isolated enough, and it wasn't cold. And after last night, he probably knew her body better than *she* did. She smiled. Besides, there was something deliciously wanton, almost erotic, about parading around without any clothes on—especially when his gaze all but devoured her.

He cleared his throat. "If you intend coming to breakfast dressed like that all the time, I'll definitely have to keep you around."

"Play your cards right, and I just might stay." She grinned and sat down next to him. "What do you want to talk about?"

His gaze ran over her, stirring heat where it touched. Her nipples hardened, aching for his caress. Whatever he wanted to talk about, he'd better make it quick, because she fully intended to do for him what he'd done for her last night—and she didn't think she had the strength to hold off touching him for much longer.

She picked up her coffee and sipped it. It felt cold when compared to the heat already burning through her body. She glanced sideways at him, a teasing smile on her lips. "You did say you wanted to talk, didn't you?"

He cleared his throat again. "Well, yes. Why don't you go put a robe on so I'm not so distracted?"

"Can't do that, because I'm enjoying distracting you. So say what you have to say." She already knew what it was, could tell by the cautious feel to the link. He was going to tell her to leave.

Only what he said first wasn't exactly what she'd expected.

"Elizabeth was outside our room last night. Watching us. Waiting for me to leave you alone."

Fear stirred her stomach. She took another sip of coffee. "Why?"

"To understand that, you must know a little about Elizabeth herself."

The last thing she wanted right now was a discussion about his ex. Talk about a mood killer. "I understand that she's a nut who likes little boys. What more do I need to know?" How old was Michael when she'd turned him? He hadn't been as young as Matthew, that much was for certain.

"I was twenty-seven, Nikki. An old man in my time."

She hesitated. "Married? Kids?"

He shook his head. "Neither. I worked my family's farm."

She raised her eyebrows in surprise. "Why?" From the little she knew of the sixteenth century, people married early and died young. It was rare for a man to be single at sixteen, let alone twenty. Twenty-seven was old-age material.

He smiled and trailed his fingers down her cheek, gently outlining her lips. "I never met anyone I truly loved and wanted to raise children with."

"So Elizabeth's hunger for virgins is what drove her to you?" She opened her mouth, gently sucking on his fingers.

Embers flared, breathing heat through the link.

"Yes," he said softly. "And I, mistaking lust for love, followed her into darkness."

"Can't be sad about that," she said. "Because that's what brought you here to me."

"True." He reached across to the tray and grabbed a croissant. Tearing it into pieces, he began feeding her. "And you, my love, are what I hungered to find all those years ago."

She sighed softly. He could say words like that forever, because she would certainly never tire of hearing them. Each time he fed her a piece of croissant, she ran her tongue across his fingertips or gently sucked them. The embers became a fire, and the heat burned them both. God, she wanted to touch him so badly she ached. But not yet. And even when she did, she would tease him as he had teased her last night.

"That doesn't explain why she was watching us," she said, once she'd eaten the final piece of croissant. "Neither of us are exactly virgins anymore."

"No." He paused, reaching for an apple and a knife. "What Elizabeth likes more than virgins is domination. She likes total control."

He peeled the apple and fed her a sliver. She sucked it slowly into her mouth, her gaze on his. Saw him swallow. Hard.

"What has domination got to do with you or-" She hesitated, fear washing through her. "She can't still dominate you, can she?"

God, wouldn't that be the mother of all ironies? To finally have Michael admit he needed her in his life, only to have it snatched away by the bitch who'd turned him.

She shoved the thought from her mind. Michael didn't seem too worried about that prospect, so neither should she.

He continued feeding her the apple. "Elizabeth and I have always had a somewhat uneasy relationship. She has never truly controlled me, and I think in many ways, she enjoyed the challenge I presented. I think that's probably why I survived my years under her care. I was a battlefield not yet won."

"Overconfidence goes before a fall, you know."

He smiled. "Yes. But as you are in life, so you are in *unlife*. I wasn't like most of her other fledglings. I was a quiet farmer, relatively content with my lot. Most of her other fledglings ran with danger in life and, therefore, enjoyed the harvest of death that turning provided. I did not, and that was something she could never change."

But she'd tried, if the edge in his voice was anything to go by. "What have her domination fantasies got to do with you and me?"

"It's nothing personal. Whenever a fledgling she had not yet grown tired of found pleasure in another woman's arms, she caught, tortured and killed that woman—and forced that fledgling to watch."

"A true charmer," Nikki murmured, chilled. "I gather then that she intends to try doing this with me."

"I'm still a challenge to her." He placed the knife and apple on the table and cupped a hand against her cheek, pressing warmth into her cheekbones. "But I promise you, she will never get near enough to hurt you."

She believed him. He'd made a similar promise with Jasper and had almost died keeping it. But she also knew part of that promise involved getting her to leave the resort—something she had no intention of doing.

Time for some extra distraction, perhaps. "Lift your hips."

He raised an eyebrow but did as she requested. She glanced down at his jeans and narrowed her gaze, concentrating. Power slid around her, around him. His zipper came down, and then she tugged his jeans from his body. She kinetically tossed them back toward the bed.

"I *am* trying to have a serious discussion here."

"Oh, I know." She straddled his lap. The hard length of him, still contained by the silk of his shorts, pressed against her.

She wrapped her arms around his neck and lightly kissed his lips. "By all means, do continue."

This close, she could hear the thunder of his heart, a rhythm that matched her own. She began to rock her hips back and forth, gently rubbing him. He jerked, then groaned.

"Even the Man of Steel would have trouble concentrating right now."

He touched her breasts, teasing her already aching nipples. She bit her lip then caught both his hands, placing them behind him.

"No touching. But do continue."

He swallowed heavily. "Now that Elizabeth knows what you mean to me, she will bide her time and attack when we least expect it. We cannot risk that, not with Cordell so close."

She leaned forward, pressing her breasts against his chest. Slowly, she ran her tongue up his neck and nibbled his ear. "It's going to take two of us to defeat Cordell, and you know it."

"Maybe." His breath was hot and quick against her cheek. "But I want you out of the firing line. I want you to leave."

She trailed tiny kisses across his cheeks. "No," she whispered against his lips. Then she kissed him deeply, giving him no time to respond.

They were both panting by the time she pulled away. She ached for him, ached so fiercely it was almost painful. He throbbed against her—so close, and yet so far. She continued to rock gently, teasing them both. Deep down, the quivering began.

"Oh, God, Nikki." He took a deep, shuddering breath. "If you stay here, she *will* come after you. Cordell is the important one. He's the one we have to stop."

She ran a hand down his stomach, then lifted her hips slightly. "You're wrong, Michael." She caught his boxers, pulling them out of the way and freeing him. "It was Elizabeth who took Matthew. It was Elizabeth who sucked his mind dry then spat him out. We have to stop them both."

He was trembling, his whole body hot with urgency. She didn't give him what he wanted—what she wanted—but continued rocking, covering him with her slickness.

"I made a promise, too, Michael. I told the flame imps I would try to stop Cordell. I don't intend to back away from that promise now."

"I'll fulfill your promise. This is what I do for a living. This is exactly what I don't *want* you involved in."

"I was involved in this case before you came to see me in the office. I have to see the end of it—for Jake, for Matthew, and for MacEwan."

The trembling was growing, becoming a tide threatening to overload her senses. She rubbed harder, heard his response— a quick, sharp gasp. Could feel him quivering and knew he was battling for control.

"Matthew's dead," he somehow ground out. "And Rachel's receiving the help she needs. Your part in this has ended. Go home. Be safe."

"I'm safe when you're safe, and I can't..." *hold off any more.* The tide washed over her. She gasped, grabbing his shoulders as the shuddering took hold. Needing him inside, she shifted, capturing him, thrusting him deep. Then she rode him fast and hard, until his tremors finally eased and they both were spent.

She leaned her cheek against his chest and sighed deeply. He wrapped his arms around her, holding her in place. Holding himself inside her. It felt good. Safe.

Which she knew they weren't.

After a while, he brushed a kiss across the top of her head. "Whatever am I going to do with you?"

"Make love to me like that every day, and you're halfway to making me a very happy woman."

His smile was something she felt deep inside. "And what would it take to make you wholly happy?"

"Coffee. Lots of it. Preferably fed intravenously."

His laughter rumbled through his chest, tickling her cheek. "For someone in such desperate need of coffee, you didn't seem to drink a lot of it this morning."

"I had other things on my mind." She pushed upwards far enough to see his face. "So what's our next move?"

He brushed the hair from her eyes, his face concerned.

"There's nothing I can say to make you go?"

She wrapped her arms around his neck and stared into his beautiful eyes. The sheer depth of love and understanding she saw there chased a shiver through her soul.

"No," she said softly. "And don't think you can force me— telepathically or physically. I'll fight you, with all my heart and all my energy. Neither of us can afford such a battle, with Cordell and Elizabeth so close."

"It wouldn't be wise," he agreed.

His hands cupped her rear, pulling her a little closer. Amazingly, she felt him stir deep inside. "Good lord, are you kidding? Does becoming a vampire also give you an amazing rate of recovery after sex?"

He kissed her, his mouth gently demanding. "No," he said, after a while. "The touch of a good woman does that."

"Smooth, real smooth," she said, laughing against his lips. "What about Cordell and Elizabeth?"

"We can't do anything until Cordell is asleep. He's not that old in vampire years, so he will have no choice but to slumber. If we wait until noon, we should at least be safe from him."

But not safe from Elizabeth, she suspected. Still, confronting them one at a time seemed a hell of a lot more sensible that confronting both of them together. "We really should try to find Rodeman, as well."

"Yes. Most of the other men who disappeared were gone a good week before they were found. Rodeman only disappeared yesterday. Hopefully, Cordell hasn't had the time to fully begin work on him."

"Sounds like a plan to me." She grinned slightly. "So what do you suggest we do in the meantime? Partake in a wildflower tour? Go see some wildlife?"

His reply was little more than a growl. "The only wildlife I'm currently interested in is the one sitting so snugly on my lap."

He pressed his hands more firmly against her rear, then rose. She gasped slightly and wrapped her legs around his waist.

"Besides," he added, his lustful look melting her insides. "We are supposed to be newlyweds. The staff will suspect something is wrong if we get up too early."

"Heaven forbid we do anything to destroy our cover," she murmured. Even though little more than ten minutes had passed, she so desperately wanted him to touch her again—something she had never thought possible so soon after such fulfillment. "I guess you'd better do the husbandly thing, then."

"I guess I'd better." He took her over to the bed and made her boneless again.

***

Nikki checked her flashlight. Water fogged the glass, but the light itself worked. Which was good. Something told her this time she would need it.

She slipped it into her pocket then walked over to the table. Michael was unwrapping a small parcel. "What's that?"

"Present from Seline." He tore open the box and held up two braided rope bracelets. "Charms to stop Cordell doing to us what he did to Rachel and Ginger."

He slipped one over her hand and pushed it up her arm so that even if she pushed up the sleeves of her cotton sweater, it wouldn't be seen. It felt like silk against her skin, despite the harsh look of the interwoven red, brown and gold cord. "How is rope supposed to stop him?"

He slid the second charm up his arm until it was hidden under the sleeve of his shirt, then shrugged. "I don't question her magic, I just let it protect me. And it always has."

"Cool." She'd have to meet this Seline one day. She sounded like an incredible woman. "Which entrance are we using into the caverns?"

"I think they'd be watching the one we used last night. We'll have to risk the office entrance."

She frowned. "But that's alarmed."

"Yes. I'll have to dismantle it first. But I also want to go past Cordell's office and act like we're going to break into it." He ushered her toward the door.

She frowned. "But his office is sure to be monitored."

"Exactly. And it'll provide a nice distraction if he *is* still up and around." He wrapped an arm around her shoulders, drawing her close as they strolled down the hall. "See those security cameras?"

She glanced up. Little black boxes were evenly spaced along the ceiling. She hadn't even noticed them until now. "What about them?"

"I want you to kinetically take out all the ones near Cordell's office."

She frowned. "Won't that bring security running?"

"Yes. When we get near his office, I want you to bust open his door. There'll be some sort of sensor in the frame—take that out, too."

She raised an eyebrow. "And maybe take out a computer or two as well? Give him something extra to worry about?"

He squeezed her shoulders. "The more worried he is, the better it is for us."

They were nearing Cordell's office. She looked up. Four cameras were trained on his door. The guy was definitely a nut case. Why would anyone in their right mind think they needed four cameras and an alarmed door? His office wasn't Fort Knox, for Christ's sake.

She shook her head and reached for kinetic energy. Glancing at the first camera, she ripped it sideways. Plaster flew in a cloud, raining down on a couple coming the other way. The woman screamed and jumped backwards, her eyes wide as she stared up at the ceiling. Nikki quickly repeated the process, until all four cameras swung limply from their wiring.

Now the door, Michael said.

She glanced at it sideways and pushed hard. The door flew off its hinges and smashed into two computers at the far end of the office. Sparks and glass flew everywhere. There was wiring running along one edge of the door frame. She ripped it free, tossing the strands back into the room with the door.

Men in blue suits came running from all directions. Power surged, burning her skin and spreading like a wave through the corridor. The other couple were grabbed by security, but no one came near them. It was as if they didn't exist.

She glanced at Michael. Maybe they didn't.

They walked on. There was a different woman manning the health center desk, but like the guards in the corridor, she gave no indication that she even saw them. They hurried past her. It was only when they were nearing the treatment rooms that the wash of energy slipped away.

Only to be replaced by the burning sensation of evil.

Something was wrong. Very wrong.

Her stomach tied itself into knots. She stopped, looking around. The corridor was quiet—still. The lighting had been dimmed in this section of the health center, and shadows haunted the far corners. But nothing lurked within them, waiting to attack. Whatever it was she sensed, it was coming from the treatment room. From the door itself.

The door Michael was reaching out to open.

"No!" She thrust him away kinetically. He hit the wall opposite with a grunt, then slid to an ungainly heap to the floor. She ran to help him.

"I gather you have a good reason for doing that," he said, rubbing a hip as he climbed to his feet. "But next time, try to give me a little more warning."

"Sorry. Something's wrong with the door handle." It was stupid, really, being so afraid of something as inane as a door handle, but she couldn't help it.

"Wrong how?" He stopped a foot or so away from the door and studied it intently.

"It's evil." She stopped beside him. This close, she could see the slight shimmer surrounding the doorknob.

She half expected him to laugh, but he didn't. "Magic," he murmured. "But what sort?"

"I don't know, and I don't care to find out. I think we'd be better off using the other entrance."

He squatted on his heels. "If they're using magic to guard this door, then the other will also have security. Go fetch me that chair, will you?"

He pointed vaguely down the corridor. She did as he asked. "What are you going to do?" She put the chair next to him.

"This." He rose and nudged the chair with his foot, pushing it toward the handle.

The back of the chair hit the doorknob. For an instant, nothing happened. Then something screamed, a high pitched wail that chased goose bumps across her flesh. Nothing living made a sound like that.

Steam began to pour from the metal, convulsing, condensing as it found form—found life. It became a flimsy, white-sheeted creature with rows of wickedly sharp teeth and soulless eyes.

Michael held her elbow, his grip tight enough to bruise— tight enough to hold her still and keep her from running. She licked dry lips. Energy tingled at her fingertips, but she didn't release her weapon. She wasn't even sure if kinetic energy would affect something that was little more than smoke.

The creature wrapped its flimsy gowns around the chair and screamed again. There was a sharp retort, like the backfire of a car, then the smoke and the chair were gone.

"What the hell was that?" Her throat was so tight with fear that her question came out hoarse.

"Devil spawn. They're a form of wraith. That one had obviously been set to destroy whatever touched the handle."

She shivered and rubbed her arms. "So if you'd touched that doorknob, you would now be wherever that chair is."

He glanced at her. "I wouldn't be anywhere. I'd be dead, consumed by the spawn. How does the door feel now?"

She looked at it. There was no sense of evil. Still... She thrust the pent-up energy toward the door, opening it. No alarm sounded. No sharp-teethed bits of smoke flew out to greet them.

The room was dark and still. She could sense nothing more than muskiness. Even so, she shivered. She had a feeling Cordell wouldn't stop at just the door. There would be other traps waiting for them in the darkness of the caverns.

"It's safe," she murmured, trying to ignore the churning in her stomach.

Michael tugged her into the room and closed the door. Furniture gleamed at her, ice bright in the darkness.

"What about the next door?" he said.

She glanced at the wall. "Safe. Maybe Cordell didn't expect anyone to get past that wraith."

"Maybe." There was doubt in his voice. "It takes a lot of power to dominate a spawn like that—and they usually work in pairs."

"So there's another one lurking around somewhere?"

He nodded, his face a mask of concentration as he probed the wall with his fingers. After a few seconds, he punched a hole into the plaster and pulled out some wiring. "Want to hunt around for scissors or something?"

She moved across to the drawers. Three were empty, but the fourth was a treasure chest—not only scissors, but several sharp knives, as well. She handed one knife to Michael, then grabbed the other. It was shiny and pointed, the sort of knife doctors used in surgery. It wasn't anywhere near as balanced as her throwing knives but it was better than nothing. She hunted around until she found some sticky tape, and attached the knife to her jeans. If she just shoved it in her pocket, the knife might well cut through everything—her jeans *and* her skin.

Michael sliced the wires then opened the door into the caverns. No alarm sounded—but it hadn't the first time, either. He offered her the second knife, and she taped it to her other leg. And felt just a little safer for it.

Once more, they entered the cavern and climbed down the stairs. The door slid shut behind them, and the darkness became complete.

Where to first? She shifted from one foot to the other, not wanting to stand here any longer than necessary. At least if they were moving they were harder targets to hit.

Though why she thought they would be targets merely standing here, she couldn't say. Maybe it was nerves. Maybe it was the sense of chilled expectation in the dank air.

Power shimmered around her again. Michael, searching the darkness, trying to find some sign of life in this blanket of night.

We'll try the left tunnel this time. There's a faint heartbeat coming from that direction.

She bit her lip, gaze searching the blackness. *Human or otherwise?*

Human. He led the way forward again. *It's too steady to be a vampire.*

Can you sense any vampires?

He squeezed her hand lightly. *Not yet. And I don't think*

it's vampires we'll have to worry about.

Oh great. She tried to ignore the goose bumps crawling across her skin. *So how do you kill a demon spawn?*

It's usually better to stay out of their way.

Cordell may not make that possible. Her sarcasm bit through the link but was swallowed swiftly by the warmth of his smile.

I guess not. Spawn are difficult to kill. They are creations of magic and fire, and as such are immune to both.

Well, considering neither of us have fire or magic at our disposal, it doesn't really matter, does it?

No. Water repels them. Silver can kill them. And we don't have those, either. Which is why I suggested we try to stay out of their way.

Let's just hope Cordell lets us.

Yes.

They continued on through the darkness. The air became almost dead, as if this section of the caverns wasn't used much. In the distance she could hear the gentle splash of water, a peaceful sound that somehow increased her edginess.

How much farther?

Not far.

The air stirred, whisking heat across her skin. She jumped sideways and bit down on her yelp. Fire leapt across her fingertips, lightning bright in the darkness.

Tension flowed through the link. *Nikki, what's wrong?*

Something touched me.

She stared into the darkness, seeing nothing, feeling nothing. Yet something had trailed across her skin—her cheek still burned with the heat of its touch.

I don't see anything.

Neither did she. But that didn't mean there wasn't something there. He tugged her forward again. She licked dry lips, gaze sweeping the darkness.

In the distance, light flared and became an incandescent jewel that gleamed brightly in the darkness.

Michael, a flame imp is here with us. Did it intend to help or hinder them? Had the flame imp meant to burn her, or was it merely catching her attention?

Where?

Ahead. Can't you see the pearl of light?

His frown slid down the link. *No, I can't.*

Ginger had warned her this would happen. She'd said that even Cordell couldn't see them—he could only feel their power. *It's about twenty feet in front of us.*

Its light glowed a gentle gold across the cavern walls, whisking brightness from wall to wall, gleaming brightly off the thin strand of wire stretched taut across the path.

She stopped and yanked Michael backwards. *Trip wire.* She pulled her flashlight from her pocket and shined the beam on the wire.

How in the hell did you see that? I couldn't, and I was using my vampire vision. He squatted, intently studying the wire, then the cracked cavern walls on either side.

The flame imp showed me.

So they're on our side?

She glanced at the pearl. It was hovering near a slight curve in the tunnel, its shade a green-tinged blue—colors that hinted at sadness. But why were the flame imps sad? Had another of their number died?

Cordell's killing them. We're their only hope.

He nodded absently, then reached over the wire and gently pressed his fingers against the ground on the other side. Something clicked. For a second, nothing happened, then there was a sigh of air and stakes stabbed in from either side of the wall. Michael fell backwards, barely avoiding having his arm skewered.

"Cordell's playing with us." He rose and dusted off his jeans. Though there was a touch of amusement in his voice, anger stirred through the link. "Those stakes were never meant to kill us."

They certainly *looked* deadly enough. She frowned at him. "What makes you think that?"

"Two things." He began snapping the stakes, creating a hole for them to walk through. "First off, the wire is attached to nothing more than rock. It was meant as a warning not a trigger. Second, the delay between pressing the real trigger and the stakes stabbing in was enough that we would have been safely past."

She rubbed her eyes. "But that doesn't make sense. Why would he do something like that? Why play games?"

"I don't know." He captured her hand again, his fingers so warm compared to hers. "Let's continue."

They stepped past the broken stakes and the pressure plate and continued down the tunnel. The flame imp kept its distance, hovering a good twenty feet away. Muted light fanned across the walls, enough to see but not clearly. She kept the flashlight's beam trained on the ground, just in case Cordell had more trip wires waiting.

The sound of water splashing became clearer. It seemed quite strong—a stream more than just water dripping off damp rocks. The cold was increasing, reaching icy fingers through her skin to chill her bones. She shivered, wishing she'd worn something warmer than a cotton sweater.

They rounded the curve in the tunnel. Ahead was a heavily padlocked wooden door. The flame imp hovered above it, but its color was still dark, and it was difficult to see.

Rodeman? She asked.

Behind the door. He stopped, eyeing it with a frown. *This is too easy.*

Maybe Cordell is simply overconfident. Even as she spoke the words, she knew they weren't true. Cordell wasn't a fool. Angry and somewhat demented, yes, but no fool. There would be traps waiting here somewhere.

Maybe. Wait here.

He released her hand. She bit her lip and fought the instinctive urge to reach for him again, to tell him not to leave her. Instead, she clenched her fingers and felt the tingle of energy flow across her skin. Tension rode his shoulders as he tested each step. But he reached the door without incident, and she sighed in relief.

Rodeman's inside. Drugged, by the feel of it. He skimmed his fingers across the door frame.

Anyone, or anything, else?

Not that I can see. You?

Nothing. And it didn't feel right. It had been far too easy to get this far. There had to be some sort of trap here somewhere. *Had to be.*

She again rubbed her arms. The chill air had settled deep inside, and her bones were beginning to ache.

Michael finished his inspection then reached for the door handle. Turning it quickly, he thrust his shoulder against the wood, shattering the lock and pushing the door open. Kinetic ability was somewhat superfluous when you had the strength of a vampire, she thought. He squatted on his heels, studying the ground.

She moved up behind him. The cell wasn't dark. A lone candle sat in one corner. In the wash of its flickering light she could see the end of a metal-framed bed and a foot encased in a shiny leather shoe. A rope was looped around his ankle and tied to the bed.

Rodeman. He hadn't moved, so he had to be either drugged or unconscious. She shivered, hoping that Elizabeth hadn't paid him a visit like she had Matthew.

Heat tingled across her skin. She glanced up. The flame imp hovered several feet above her, its color pulsing between blue and red. Did that mean that danger waited for them? She wasn't sure, and it worried her. She wished Ginger was here to translate.

Can you see anything?

I'm not sure. He hesitated. *There is magic here somewhere—I can feel the tingle of it across my skin. But I'm not sure where or what it is.*

He leaned sideways and scooped up a handful of stones, then tossed them one by one into the cell. Nothing happened.

Maybe the trigger needs something heavier.

Probably. I guess we have no other option, then. He rose and gave her a quick hard kiss. *Remember me if something happens.*

She glared at him. *That is not funny.*

Sorry. He shrugged, then brushed the hair from her eyes,

his fingers warm against her chilled skin. *Don't you move until I say it's okay—okay?*

She nodded. Whether she obeyed or not was another matter entirely. It depended on what happened.

He stepped into the cell, then stopped, looking around. She could see his tension in the set of his shoulders, feel it thundering through the link.

He took a second step. No sound, no soft click, no rush of evil to indicate something wicked was headed their way. But her hands were clenched so hard her knuckles were beginning to ache.

Rodeman has been drugged. His pulse has a sluggish feel.

And the magic you sensed?

Close by somewhere.

Be careful, please

Warmth flashed through the link. *Don't worry. I'm not that easy to get rid of.*

He took another step forward. It was one step too many. Without warning, the ground disappeared, and Michael dropped like a stone into the darkness.

Twenty

Michael! She lunged forward, dropping full length to the ground and peering over the hole's edge. It was so dark her flashlight barely penetrated more than a few feet. Wind rose steadily, a stream strong enough to blow her hair backwards.

Michael! Are you okay? Can you hear me?

Yes. He hesitated, and pain slithered through the link, through her. *It feels like I've twisted my damn ankle.*

His mind voice was distant. The hole was obviously very deep. *Where are you?*

God knows. I'm hip deep in water. It probably saved me from greater injury.

I'll lift you up kinetically.

No. His sharpness stung her mind. *I've seen what lifting the weight of a human can do to you. Get Rodeman and get out of the tunnels. I'll go after Cordell alone.*

Michael, you can't—

Damn it, we have no choice now. I haven't survived three hundred and sixty years without being careful. I'll be okay.

Elizabeth had been around a lot longer than that, and yet she was now under Cordell's control. What made Michael think he would fair any differently?

I'm still wearing Seline's charm, Nikki. I'll be okay. I'm more worried about leaving you alone up there.

Then forget Cordell and come back to me!

Cordell has to be my first priority. We have to stop him if we can.

I know, I know. But knowing didn't mean she had to accept it willingly. *Just make sure you come back alive.*

A little hard, considering I'm already dead.

She grinned. *You know what I mean.*

Yes.

The link flared to full life and his mind entwined hers, caressing her soul with such love and caring that tears stung her eyes. She blinked them away rapidly. She didn't want to lose him, and yet she had a feeling she might if he wasn't very careful. Damn it, she couldn't just leave him alone down there. Somehow, she had to find him and help him.

He sighed. *Don't. Look after Rodeman. I'll be okay.*

But—

No buts. Promise me you'll do as I ask. I need to know you're safe so I can concentrate wholly on Cordell.

Okay. I promise. Not to come after you until *after* I've made sure Rodeman is safe, she added silently.

Be careful. I'll see you later.

You'd better. She hesitated, biting her lip. *Love you.*

His smile shimmered through the link. *And I you. Be safe, Nikki.*

The link died. She rose and dusted the dirt from her shirt and jeans. Overhead, the flame imp hovered, its color still wavering between red and blue, deepening the shadows filling the cell's far corners.

"I wish you could damn well talk," she muttered. "I'd love to know what you know."

Gold flickered across the red, pulsating quickly. Maybe it could understand her, even if it couldn't talk. Stepping around the hole, she headed towards Rodeman. The millionaire lay stretched out on the bed, his hands tied to the headboard. His color was awful—his skin looked gray and sweat beaded his forehead.

She squatted next to him and felt for a pulse. Michael was right; it was sluggish. She frowned and touched his face. His skin burned. He's sick, she thought, and wondered if he'd had a stroke or something.

She pinched his cheek. "Mr. Rodeman? Can you hear me?"

He didn't stir. Didn't bat an eyelid. Great, she thought. What in the hell was she going to do now? The man had indulged in too much of the good life, and there was no way on this Earth she could lift his rotund figure.

She *could* lift him kinetically, but even then, she probably wouldn't get far. The pain would be incapacitating long before she reached the stairs.

First things first, she thought. She untied his hands then

moved down to the foot of the bed and untied his feet. The flame imp skimmed past her hand, its color bright red and movements suddenly frantic.

Fear surged. She looked around wildly. Nothing stirred the shadows, and yet a chill crawled across her skin. The flame imp skimmed past her hand again, then whisked toward the door. Almost as if it was telling her to get out.

Why? Did it want to lead her away from a trap or into one? She had no way of knowing if this flame imp was under Cordell's control or not.

Frowning, she half rose, then stopped, staring. In the far corner, yellow-tinged smoke billowed, curling through the darkness with unnatural heaviness.

Horror filled her. This wasn't fog or smoke or anything as simple as that.

This was the second devil spawn.

***

Michael limped through the shallows, following the strong breeze and hoping that it actually led somewhere. The darkness was veil-heavy and the air dank, rich with the smell of decay and things long dead. It was the sort of smell usually associated with city sewers, not a natural spring system like this.

Unless, of course, this is where Cordell and Elizabeth had been dumping the remains of their meals. Elizabeth wouldn't have worried about polluting the local streams. She'd never been particularly interested in environmental considerations.

Ahead, water dripped steadily, echoing through the silence. The lake around him had dropped from his hips to his knees and was steadily falling. Walking was at least easier. He just wished he knew where he was going.

He spun his senses through the darkness, searching for some hint, some sound, of life. No vampires nor humans anywhere in the near vicinity. Although that didn't mean there wasn't anything near. Cordell would have prepared for guests, of that much he was certain.

He splashed on. The mud under his feet gave way to rock, and the path began to climb upwards. Ahead, several mounds became visible, casting a palish-green light through the red of his vampire vision. Bodies, he thought with distaste, and wondered if perhaps he'd found the final resting place of Vance Hutton and the other missing abductees.

Their bloated, decaying smell hit him. He held his breath and hurried past. True death was never attractive at the best of times. When it had been left to rot like this, even the strongest stomach would revolt.

Just as well Nikki wasn't with him—she'd have lost her breakfast for sure. She might have lived on the streets and had a tougher life than some, but in many ways, she was still innocent when it came to the true horrors of life. Jasper had shown her some of that, but he was far from the worst.

He had to protect her from that. She was the one truly good thing that had happened to him since he'd turned. Somehow, he had to keep her from the horror that was such a major part of his life. And that was not going to be an easy thing to do.

The path continued to climb. In the distance, a heart thumped. Just a solitary beat, then silence. Vampire, he thought, flexing his fingers. Magic tingled across his skin, so close and sharp it burned. He stopped abruptly.

Heat of a different kind hit his senses. Vampires. Six of them, moving in fast from in front and behind, their bodies little more than red blurs in the night. Wind whistled. Swearing softly, he ducked. A baseball bat swished over his head. He clenched his fist and swung hard. His hand sank deep into flesh, and there was a cough of pain.

Movement behind him. He kicked backward, connecting with bone, then dodged sideways as one of the vamps lashed at him with a knife. Kicked out again and heard a thump as someone fell. Another blur of red heat, this time to his left. Metal gleamed, flashing downwards. Hands grabbed his arms, fingers digging deep into his flesh. Teeth tore at him. Fledglings, he thought. Fledglings desperate for someone, anyone, to eat. Which made *his* situation a whole lot more dangerous. Fledglings this hungry couldn't be reasoned with and wouldn't know fear like Rachel had.

He dropped, making them support his weight, and kicked away the descending knife. The fledgling didn't seem to notice, his hand hitting Michael's chest, his eyes wide and filled with desperation and blood lust. Michael head-butted him, knocking him away, then twisted, dislodging the two vampires holding his arms.

They fell like ninepins, scattering their companions. He leapt over the nearest vampire and ran back down the cavern. Past the bloated pile of bodies and into the water. There'd been a ledge around the last bend—a semicircular jutting of rock protected on two sides. An ideal place to make a stand.

The fledglings followed, their desperation reaching across the night and stirring the darkness within him. He knew the taste of that desperation only too well.

He climbed onto the ledge and backed against the wall. They swarmed after him and attacked. Hands grabbed him. Teeth tore at his clothes and his flesh. He punched one in the face then grabbed her hair, twisting her around and pulling her against him. Her companions tore at her instead, and the smell of blood stung the air. She mewed, fighting him, fighting them. Her distress was sharp and sweet and filled his soul with the need to taste her. His canines lengthened, and the darkness rose sharply, threatening to overwhelm his control.

He swallowed heavily, then shifted his hold and shattered the fledgling's neck. He thrust her away. Two of her companions followed, tearing at her like rabid dogs. At least she was dead. They would not be so kind to him.

Teeth tore into his arms, his legs. He punched in the face of the one on his arm, knocking him away. He then bent and picked up the two gnawing at his legs, knocking their heads together and thrusting them back into the water. Metal knifed into his side, and pain fired through his body. Heat flashed, followed sharply by a wash of cold sweat. He gritted his teeth against the agony and grabbed the hand holding the knife, squeezing hard. The fledgling screamed—a high pitched, prepubescent sound.

Kids, he thought in horror, *they were only damn kids*. Elizabeth's doing, surely. Anger rose swift and sharp, washing away the knife-edged pain. Nikki was right. Elizabeth had to be stopped.

He pulled the knife from his flesh then stabbed at the kid approaching from the right. The point went straight through the fledgling's eye and buried deep in his brain. He fell in a heap at Michael's feet and was immediately set upon by one of the other fledglings. Michael kicked her away, then turned back to the vamp whose arm he still held. He was kicking and screaming, his need for blood so intense Michael could almost taste it. Twisting him around, he wrapped an arm around his neck and gave him final release.

Three down, three to go. Better odds by far. Two fledglings attacked as one. He ducked under their blows, punching one in the balls and knifing the other through the gut. Both dropped. He finished them quickly, then turned to the fledgling still suckling on the body of one of her companions. Swallowing the rise of bile, he walked over and broke her neck. She fell backwards, her blue eyes wide, face still so young and pretty despite the ravages of turning. He felt like crying.

He dropped down on the ledge and rubbed a hand across his eyes. *God grant me the strength to kill Elizabeth, because this cannot go on.* She had to be stopped before she ruined more young lives.

Warmth ran down his side, and the metallic taste of blood stung the air. He tugged his shirt free and twisted around to look at the wound. Blood flowed freely, staining his jeans. The wound looked nasty, but it wasn't that deep. The fledgling must have stabbed at him while he was climbing up on the ledge, because the knife appeared to have nicked his jeans and gone off on an angle through his side rather than straight in. Luck had been smiling on him.

He leaned forward and grabbed one of the fledglings, dragging the body toward him. Removing the youngster's shirt, he tore it into strips and wrapped them tightly around his waist.

The rest he wrapped around the worst of his bite wounds— an open slash on his left calf. The remaining wounds were little more than nicks. He hadn't given his attackers enough time to do more damage. Thank the gods Nikki hadn't been with him. Her kinetic power had its limits and protecting her might have been the downfall of them both.

He rubbed his eyes wearily, then pushed up from the ledge. Time to get moving. He splashed through the shadows, ignoring the ache in his side and the red-hot needles that thrust through his leg muscles every time he put weight on his left leg.

Up the hill and past the bloated pile of humanity. Past the corner where the fledglings had sprung from their hideaways. The air became cleaner, fresher, and his footsteps began to echo. He glanced up. The tunnel was widening, the roof pitching upwards. He had to be approaching a cavern.

He slowed, casting his senses forward. There was no sound, no shimmer of life, and yet...something was there. He edged forward, back to the wall. The darkness of the tunnels opened into a cave of immense proportions. Stalactites hung from the ceiling, gleaming cold silver in the light of a single candle that sat on an outcropping of rock.

Beside that candle waited Elizabeth.

***

For several seconds, Nikki didn't move. Couldn't move. Her heart was lodged somewhere in her throat, and she couldn't even breathe. All she could do was watch in horror as the smoke creature found form.

The flame imp whisked past her, flashing heat across her face. She blinked. It had paused near the door again, pulsing a deep, distressed red, then flew out.

She swallowed, took one final look at the billowing smoke and the sharp teeth just forming, and ran after the flame imp.

The spawn screamed—a high-pitched sound not unlike a woman in distress. Fear spurted fresh energy into her legs. She flew down the tunnel, following the flame imp and hoping it was leading her to safety and not into some trap.

Suddenly it stopped then dropped to the floor. Horror rolled through her, and the sharp taste of evil filled every corner of her mind. She fell to the ground. Claws scraped her back, burning like fire, then the spawn was past her, billowing like a sail as it struggled to stop. She scrambled to her feet and hit it with everything she had.

It screamed and was flung backwards, splattering against a wall. Moisture dribbled from it, searing into the rock as if it were acid.

She shivered. The flame imp pulsed its warning. She ran after it, her footsteps as frantic as the beat of her heart. Warmth dribbled down her back. She knew she was bleeding, but she felt no pain. Terror had numbed her.

Ahead, the sound of running water was becoming stronger. Was that where the flame imp was leading her? She hoped so. Michael had said water repelled it, but what good would it really do? She couldn't stay in the water forever, and the spawn would have her the minute she stepped out of it.

The bitter taste of evil rushed through her again. Her stomach rose swiftly. Swallowing bile, she fell to the left. Her shoulder hit rock, bruising her. The spawn billowed past again, screaming in frustration. She hit it again, pushing it back against the wall. Glancing at the ceiling, she saw a fissure in the roof line and pulled. There was a sharp crack, and a huge chunk of ceiling fell, covering the smoky form with rocks and stones. Dust flew in the air, catching in her throat, making her cough.

The spawn screamed its fury. It was contained, but not for long. Tendrils of smoke were beginning to hiss from the gaps and solidify.

She ran on. The flame imp pulsated ahead, splashing red streams of color across the walls. Like blood, she thought. Her blood, if the spawn got hold of her.

Dread clutched her heart, squeezing tight. Energy tingled across her fingers in response, but the familiar ache was also beginning in her head. If she pushed too much further she'd lock her mind in pain, and the spawn would surely grab her.

She wished Michael were here, wished she could reach for the comfort of the link. But she couldn't. There wasn't anything he could do to help her, and opening the link so he could taste her terror would only panic him. If she wanted to be a full partner in his life, then she was going to have to cope with situations like this without his help.

Behind her, the spawn roared its fury. A chill chased across her skin. It was free. Ahead, the flame imp had stopped again. Color splashed across the walls—across the surface of a stream that cut through the tunnel.

If it's deep I'll drown, she thought, and dove toward the water anyway. Better death by water than being consumed by the smoke demon behind her.

Talons of smoke wrapped around her calf and fire burned up her leg. She yelped, swallowing water as she dove under. Stones grazed the side of her face then her head smashed into something solid. Stars danced briefly and panic surged. She thrust upwards, breaking the surface, coughing the water from her throat. Warmth trickled down the side of her face. She ignored it, twisting around frantically, searching for the spawn.

It was diving for her head. She screamed and battered it away kinetically. It splattered against the wall; rock hissed and bubbled as clear liquid spurted from it. It peeled itself away, then dove toward her again.

She ducked under the water. The spawn hovered above her, yellow smoke body pulsating, as if in frustration. Again, she lashed at it kinetically. Pain burned through her head. She rose, coughing and spluttering, gasping for breath and looking around frantically.

The flame imp whisked heat past her face again, then dove under the water. It rose, spinning frantically, then shot upwards, out of sight again. She frowned, wondering what...the burning sensation of evil filled her senses again. She twisted, saw the spawn coming in from behind. Grabbed it kinetically and thrust it under the water.

Steam rose, hissing through the darkness. The spawn became frenzied, twisting and surging against her hold. Pain shot through her brain, sharper than before. She wouldn't be able to hold it much longer.

The flame imp shot past her and hovered above a pile of rubble, its color washing between red and green. She reached kinetically, picking up the pile of rubble and dumping it on the twisting, screaming spawn. It didn't cover the creature completely. She bit her lip and reached again. Hot lances of fire burned through her brain. She blinked back tears and thrust a second load of rubble over the creature. This time it was covered. But just to be sure, she grabbed the remaining stones and dumped those over the creature as well.

She released her hold and scrambled backwards down the stream. The spawn's scream was a sound of combined fury and pain. But unlike the last time she'd buried the thing, there was no telltale leakage of smoke, nothing to indicate the creature was escaping. If water repelled it, maybe it could also contain it. Maybe that was what the flame imp had been trying to tell her.

She glanced up. The flame imp hovered several feet above her head, its color a muted green. It had saved her life. "Thank you."

As if in response, gold flicked through the green. She smiled and dragged herself from the water. Heat burned across her right calf, and her stomach churned. Biting her lip, she looked down. When the spawn had grabbed her leg, it had burned a hole through her jeans and seared her skin. In the muted green light provided by the flame imp, her calf looked scarlet with heat and was already beginning to blister.

But there was nothing she could do about it right now, except put up with the pain. She'd promised Michael she'd get Rodeman out of here, and that had to be her first priority. After that, she fully intended to go find Michael and provide whatever help she could. Maybe somewhere in between the two she could grab some pain killers and something to numb the burn.

How in hell was she going to get Rodeman out? She thrust a hand through her wet hair. She still wasn't sure, but there had to be some way. Maybe she'd just have to keep trying to wake him. He wouldn't stay under forever. Consciousness would eventually surface. Hopefully sooner rather than later.

She glanced up at the flame imp. "You want to lend me some light and maybe lead the way back to that cell?" Somewhere along the line, she'd dropped her flashlight.

The flame imp zipped past her, flashing gold across the walls. The color changed abruptly to red. Fear surged through her, but before she could react, hands grabbed her, covering her mouth and dragging her back into the water.

Twenty-One

Michael walked down the slight incline, his gaze not wavering from Elizabeth. She waited in the middle of the cavern, a smile touching her ruby lips. Stalagmites ringed the rock floor, forming a natural arena. An arena from which only one of them would walk free.

He stopped on the outer edges, watching the shadows cast across her face by the flickering flame. It made her look old—gaunt. "You don't have to do this, Elizabeth."

A bitter smile twisted her lips. "You're wrong. I do."

"Cordell?"

She nodded. "While he does not control me, he controls the flame imp who shares my body. I have no choice in this matter now."

"Cordell is near?" He couldn't sense him, but that didn't mean anything. The man might be using magic to cover his tracks.

"No." Her smile was brittle. "The fool thinks you raid his office files. He has gone up to check."

There had to be a third entrance to the caverns, because they certainly hadn't seen him on the way down. "But he left you here as guard."

"A guard he did not think would be necessary." She shrugged. "You should have left the resort while you still had the chance."

"You knew I wouldn't."

Her smile was almost sad. "Yes. And the pity of it is, you will not even provide a good fight. The fledglings have weakened you considerably."

As Cordell had no doubt planned. "Don't write me off just yet, dear Elizabeth."

"Determined to the end, as ever." She smiled, revealing gleaming canines. "I shall ensure the safety of your thrall in honor of your death."

"And I will kill Cordell in revenge for yours."

She inclined her head, an almost regal movement. The terms had been set and agreed. He flexed his shoulders, rolled his neck. Waited for her first move.

It came too quickly. One second she was twenty feet in front of him, the next beside him. Her first blow hit his chin but did little more than snap his head back. He blocked her second jab with his left forearm. She laughed and quickly backpedaled. He didn't bother following her. She was only teasing, and he wanted to save his strength for the main battle.

But it was already obvious he didn't have a hope of matching her speed or her strength. Not in his current condition. Which meant he'd have to lean heavily on psi abilities—abilities that were, in some respects, nowhere near as strong as Nikki's.

Elizabeth blurred, rushing in from the left. He faded to the right then twisted, sweeping with his injured leg. He caught her in the back and sent her flying.

Again her laughter rolled through the night. She reappeared on the far side of the arena. Amusement touched her eyes, making them gleam with golden fire. Just for an instant, he again saw the woman he'd given up life for.

I don't want to kill her, he thought. But he knew he had no other choice. He flexed his fingers and waited for her next move.

The shadows wrapped around her. He tracked her movements through the heat of her body, dodging to one side when she dove toward him. He saw the flash of silver in the gleam of the candlelight and reached kinetically, tearing the knife from her grasp. Then he smashed his fist into her mouth, felt her flesh give and her canines and jawbone shatter. When he saw the surprise in her eyes, he realized she hadn't thought he would really hurt her. She'd expected an easy kill, and he had to wonder why.

She twisted and stopped several feet away. Blood oozed from her broken mouth, smothering her chin. She wiped it with a finger then lightly sucked it. Hunger and need flared in her eyes. "You have improved since we last fought."

"And you have learned to cheat." He held up the silver knife. The hilt was wrapped in leather, but heat pulsed against the fingers nearest the blade. It had to be made of the purest silver to give such a reaction. If Elizabeth had managed to nick him, the wound would never have healed. "I can remember you scorning fledglings who dared fight with anything more than their fists or their wits."

She shrugged. "The knife was not my idea. I prefer an even fight. You know that."

He nodded. She'd been raised in the times of the Roman gladiators, and he had no doubt she still turned fledglings simply to watch them combat in her death arenas. "You could fight him, Elizabeth. You were never one to follow the desires of others."

Her bloody smile was resigned, almost sad. "No, I wasn't, and perhaps that is why I must now pay my dues. What goes around comes around. You once told me that."

He'd once told her many things. None of it had seemed to ever matter to her. "Fight him, Elizabeth. Don't let him do this to you. Never in my life have I ever met anyone as strong as you." Except, perhaps, Nikki.

She shrugged. "It matters not any more. Kill me if you can, my fledgling, for I have grown tired of this life."

He raised his eyebrows. He'd never thought he'd hear such an admission from her, but in a way, it explained her recent actions. Maybe draining Matthew and turning the children were a last, desperate measure to keep some excitement in her life. She'd never been one to enjoy the serenity of doing nothing.

He flexed his fingers, waiting for her to move. "Why didn't you attack Nikki in the warehouse?"

She smiled. "She had your taste, Michael. I thought she might bring you back to me."

In some respects, she had, but not in the way Elizabeth had hoped. "Then why take five fledglings with you? You've never needed help like that before."

She snorted softly. "I still don't. Cordell insisted. Perhaps he didn't trust me." Her sudden smile was full of maliciousness. "Perhaps in that he was right."

She wiped an arm across her bloody mouth, then let the shadows take her form and ran straight at him. He sidestepped at the last moment and slashed with the knife—not high, but low, cutting her tendons, wounding her as he had been wounded.

She screamed in fury and launched at him. He plunged the knife hilt-deep into her gut. Silver fire crackled across her abdomen, burning her flesh, burning him. There was no reaction from her. She tackled him, her weight knocking him down. The knife was still buried deep in her flesh, but she paid it no heed.

Her fingers were like talons, tearing at his face, his neck. The smell of her blood perfumed the night, and part of him wanted to taste her, feed from her, as she had fed from him so often in the past.

He ignored the need, ignored the hands tearing at him, and reached up to her neck. Anticipation gleamed in her eyes. She really *did* want this death. It hadn't been just talk. That was why she had toyed with him. That was why she had attacked as she had. Cordell might have forced her to fight, but he couldn't force her to win.

He wrapped his hands around her neck, then leaned forward and kissed her. "Good-bye Elizabeth," he whispered against her lips. "May you find in this death what you could never find in life."

Her smile was a mix of relief and sorrow. "Thank you, Michael. May the gods finally grant your heart's desire."

"They have. Her name is Nikki." With that, he twisted her neck sharply and felt bone shatter beneath his hands. Watched the life fade forever from her eyes.

He pushed her off him, then sat up and wiped the faint trace of her blood from his mouth. He shed no tears for her, and yet he knew if he'd had any other option, he would not have killed her.

He closed her eyes and removed the knife from her flesh. Then he crossed her arms and said a prayer for her, even though it had been more than a few centuries since Elizabeth had been near a church or a priest—except, that was, for the couple that had provided a quick lunch back in Paris two centuries before.

Her body began to steam, and he stepped away in surprise. He'd taken the knife from her flesh, so there was no reason for her flesh to be burning now. The tendrils of smoke began to condense above her body, forming a creature that resembled a ball of fire. The flame imp, he realized suddenly. Elizabeth's death had freed it.

It sparkled brightly in the darkness, its color flashing between green and gold. Why could he suddenly see them? Why now, rather than before?

When the last of the steam had left Elizabeth's body and become one with the fiery creature, the flame imp dipped slightly, as if bowing, then disappeared.

With the flame imp's life force gone, Elizabeth's body seemed to collapse and looked even older. The years since he'd last seen her had not been kind at all.

He picked up the knife and resolutely turned away. He'd given her the death she had craved. There was nothing more he could do, other than fulfil his promise to kill Cordell.

Of course, first he had to *find* Cordell. He continued on through the cavern then went back into the tunnel. Casting his senses forward, he searched the darkness for some clue to the vampire's whereabouts. Cordell would have felt Elizabeth's death and the flame imp being released from his control, but if he was moving anywhere nearby, Michael couldn't feel him.

He walked on. The air was stale and moisture seeped down the walls. Slime hung in strings from the ceiling, dripping down the walls like green tears. He wondered who they cried for— the flame imps, Elizabeth, or maybe even himself?

Cool air stirred his hair. He stopped abruptly, every sense alert. Something moved ahead in the tunnel, yet he could feel no life—human or otherwise.

He clenched the knife tightly, waiting. The wind got stronger, chilling his skin. Magic burned through the air, swirling around him, standing the small hairs along his arms on end. He backed against the wall. An attack was coming, but he wasn't sure from which direction.

Lights danced through the brightness, flashes of purple and blue in the night. The colors of a distressed flame imp, he thought, and wondered again why he could suddenly see them.

The wall to his left exploded, spraying deadly shards of rock through the night. He dove away, saw the red flash of the flame imp, felt the stir of wind against his cheek, and rolled to his right. A club materialized from the darkness, smashing into the ground where his head had been only moments before.

He leapt to his feet, slashing wildly with the knife. It connected against something solid, rebounding away and momentarily numbing his fingers. The bastard was using magic to protect himself.

The club appeared again. He dodged, and slashed again with the knife, this time aiming for the fingers holding the top of the club. The blade bit through wood and bone. Blood gushed as the club and several fingers dropped to the ground.

The night screamed. The air reverberated with the sound, and the wind became a cyclone, trapping him and preventing him from moving. The club rose from the ground, arrowing towards his head. Pinned by air, all he could do was watch. Pain exploded as the club hit, then darkness closed in, and he knew no more.

***

"Don't move," a voice whispered into her ear.

The hand against her mouth pressed heat into her skin. She could almost feel her lips burning.

"He comes."

Breath brushed past her ear, grazing her cheeks with the warmth of summer. But she suddenly recognized the voice, and her fear subsided a little. Whatever Ginger intended, Nikki doubted that she meant to harm her in any real way.

"Don't move," Ginger continued. "Or he will sense you."

She meant Cordell. Had he come this way to investigate the spawn's death, or was he just rolling by at the wrong time? Whatever the reason, she had no real wish to meet him without Michael by her side.

Sweat began to trickle down her back where her body was pressed against Ginger's, but her legs were so cold her toes were almost numb. But at least the burn on her calf had stopped aching.

A stone rattled in the tunnel beyond the small cave in which they stood. Tension ran through her and through Ginger's fingers which were pressed firmly against her mouth.

Wind sighed. More stones rattled. Then he was in front of them—an emaciated figure huddled in a wheelchair. He looked fifty or sixty at least, yet he had thick blonde hair that hung like a mane to his shoulders. He stopped the chair at the water's edge, and then he glanced around, looking straight at them.

"I can feel you, Ginger," he said, pointing a long, almost feminine finger their way. His voice grated, like nails down a blackboard. "Come out where I can see you."

Ginger released her and brushed past, oddly making no noise as she splashed up the stream.

"What do you wish?" she asked, stopping in the entrance.

"Get me over this stream."

Ginger raised her arms. Power crackled from her fingertips,

forking towards Cordell. The streams of energy looped around him then gently lifted his chair across the water, depositing him safely on the other side.

Ginger dropped her arms and slumped against the wall. Though Nikki could no longer see Cordell, his contempt lashed the air.

"I will need your strength in an hour for the ceremony. Be ready when I call."

"You kill us," Ginger murmured. "We cannot take much more."

"Then you will serve until you die. Just be there."

Ginger didn't reply. Cordell wheeled away, and silence returned. The color of the flame imp hovering above Nikki's head went from red to green. She splashed through the water and touched Ginger's shoulder. Almost instantly, she jerked her hand away. The heat was intense, burning her skin despite the briefness of her touch.

"You're burning up," she said.

Ginger sighed and turned around. "This form cannot hold us much longer. If it burns, we die."

She frowned. "Why? Wouldn't Ginger's death release you?"

"No, because this form was already dead when we were bound to it. It is our energy that gives it life. Yet it is our energy that kills it. Unlike the others, the spell that binds us can only be broken by *his* death."

Did this mean that the flame imp that had been bound to the vampire who'd melted at the airport had actually lived? She remembered the steam and hoped so. But if it *had* lived, why hadn't she been able to see it? "Then Ginger wasn't a vampire, like most of the others?"

"No. We were an experiment, the first test. We have lived longer than even the undead, but our time nears its end."

Nikki frowned. "If Cordell can bind the dead, why is he using vampires?"

"He did not turn this body. We are forced to let him use us, but he cannot control us as fully he does his undead ones."

So where did Elizabeth fit into the scheme of things? From the brief glimpses she'd seen of the woman, and from what Michael had said, Nikki couldn't imagine her willingly kowtowing to Cordell's wishes. Unless, of course, he'd somehow forced a flame imp into her, as well.

"What did Cordell mean when he said he wants you to be ready for the ceremony?"

Ginger shrugged. There was great sadness in her blue eyes. "He plans to bind one of us in his body."

She raised her eyebrows in surprise. "Why?" Surely he knew that such a course would inevitably lead to death.

"His body wastes. He will die soon. He hopes the ceremony will give him new strength."

"And will it?"

"Yes."

Then they definitely had to stop it. "What type of ceremony is it? What does it involve?" Not that she knew a damn thing about magic or ceremonies, but anything Ginger could tell her had to be of some help in the long run.

"It is a blood ceremony. You must take a life to save a life."

Rodeman, she thought with a chill. Maybe that was why he'd been so heavily drugged—to keep him passive until Cordell was ready to use him. They had to get him out of here. "We have to stop him."

"Yes."

The big question was how. Obviously, the first thing they had to do was get Rodeman to safety—something she couldn't achieve alone. But maybe Ginger could.

"Would you be able to lift Rodeman up?"

Ginger frowned. "We have done so, yes."

"Would you be able to take him from the cell back up to his room without raising much of a fuss?"

"Yes. His room has a hidden entrance. It is how we came down here." She hesitated. "Why do you wish this?"

"If Cordell plans a blood ceremony, then Rodeman is an all-too-handy sacrifice. If we remove him, then we delay his plans and give ourselves some time to find a way to kill him."

Ginger nodded. "We like this idea." She hesitated, her expression changing from sadness to great joy. "One of us is free."

Nikki frowned. "What do you mean?"

"*She* has died. The spell of binding has dissolved."

Elizabeth, Nikki thought. Was Michael responsible? Was

he okay? "How did this happen?"

"He who bears her taste killed her. We will trust him now. Help him, if we can."

Fear swirled through her. She reached for the link, only to be met by silence. Michael wasn't blocking her, but he wasn't answering, either. Why? "Is he okay?"

"He walks away."

She licked her lips. If he could walk, he wasn't seriously hurt. Hopefully. "Where is he headed?"

"Down to the cave of magic."

"This the same place Cordell's going to?"

Ginger nodded. "*He* goes to prepare for the binding."

They had to kill him before that happened. Cordell had already shown them how strong he was. If he succeeded in binding a flame imp within him, he might well be unstoppable. "Will you look after Rodeman for me?"

"Yes. You go to the cave?"

"Yeah." If Michael was headed there, then she was too. "Which way do I go?"

"Follow this stream. It is the quickest way down there."

She nodded and hoped the stream got no deeper than it currently was. If there was any swimming involved, she'd have to find another way down. "Thanks. You'll go look after Rodeman now?"

Ginger nodded. "We will be seeing you later." She climbed out of the stream and walked away.

Nikki glanced up. The flame imp still hovered above her, pulsing green light across the wet rocks surrounding them. "You leading the way?"

As if in answer, the imp darted forward, hovering near the small gap through which the stream disappeared. She'd have to get down on her hands and knees to get through it. *Great,* she thought. *Just what I need.*

The imp disappeared into the hole. Green light whirled at her from the other side. She sighed and got down on all fours. It was a tight squeeze. The rock dug into her hips as she scraped by and would have torn her pants had she been wearing anything but jeans.

The tunnel on the other side gave her no room to stand. The walls seemed to loom in on her, glistening black in the muted light of the flame imp. She shivered and wondered if it was just the water's chill or a premonition of trouble headed her way.

She crawled on. The water tore at her, chilling her flesh and numbing her hands and feet. Rocks cut into knees and hands, but she could barely even feel them. Her teeth chattered, a sound that echoed through the darkness, mocking her.

The imp drifted on. The tunnel began to slope downwards, and the rush of the water grew stronger, pulling her forward. She battled to remain upright as the churning water leapt in icy fingers across her back, soaking her completely. Ahead, the water roared, the sound almost deafening. Waterfall, she thought, and hoped it wasn't very large. Or very deep.

The rocks under the water became smoother, making it harder to gain any hold against the rushing torrent. She slipped, going under, gulping water as the current grabbed her and smashed her sideways.

Panic surged, and she thrust upward into a sitting position. She coughed so long she could barely breathe, her face hot and throat raw. The imp flashed past her, green tinged with red. A warning, but she wasn't sure of what.

She hugged her arms across her chest and tried to stop her teeth from chattering. She should have tried to stop the water from flowing instead. It would have been a damn sight easier. Lord, she felt so cold that her bones ached with it.

The flame imp ducked past her again. Heat rolled across her skin, a moment of warmth that was gone all too soon. It hovered several feet away, its muted light showing a sharp turn to the right in the tunnel. The roaring of the water was close. The waterfall couldn't be all that far away.

She sighed and began crawling forward again. The water surged past her, tugging at her cotton sweater, thrusting it up to her armpits. She ignored it, crawling on, knowing she had to get out of this water soon. It was becoming harder and harder to move.

She rounded the corner, and walls gave way to space. The roar of the water intensified, echoing in the darkness. The imp hovered again, light whirling green and red, highlighting the downward plunge of the stream.

Gripping a nearby rock to steady herself against the water's pull, she peered over the edge. It was a good twenty-foot drop. Not a great distance by any means, but long enough when there was no other way down and she couldn't swim. Nor was there any way of telling how deep the pool at the bottom was—or if it was even deep at all. She might jump and end up breaking a leg—or worse.

She bit her lip and looked at the flame imp. "I don't suppose there's another way down, is there?"

It whirled in place, color flashing to red. She took that as a no. "Damn," she muttered. She'd have to jump and hope for the best.

She pulled herself upright, standing close to the edge, staring down. She didn't want to do this. It was stupid to do this. If she broke any bones, she'd be no help to Michael. But what help was she standing here shivering?

She was watching the water splash and dance, unable to make that final leap, when the decision was taken from her hands. Pain hit her, blinding in its intensity. Michael's pain, so sharp, so heavy, that it knocked her sideways—over the edge of the waterfall and into space.

Twenty-two

Michael regained consciousness slowly, aware at first of only the pounding ache in his head. But gradually other sounds seeped through, registering in his mind. Flames crackled and danced somewhere close, washing warmth across his skin and filling the air with the pungent smell of pine. Beyond that, water bubbled and gurgled—a stream, rushing past quite strongly.

Between those two sounds came another—a low, guttural chanting. Cordell doing God knew what. Michael tried to open his eyes but couldn't. Something seemed to be gluing them shut. He sniffed, tasting the air. It smelled like dried blood—his blood, probably, if the ache in his head was anything to go by.

He tried to move his arms, but they wouldn't budge. He twisted his hands. Rope burned into his wrists, and there was very little leeway. He tried moving his feet and got the same result.

He twisted his head, trying to wipe the blood off his face and onto his shoulder. All he succeeded in doing was sending the madman in his head into a drumming frenzy. Red flames of pain shot through his brain and he groaned.

The chanting stopped. Wind sighed, moving toward him.

"So, the ex-lover awakens." Cordell's voice was low but sharp. He smelled diseased—decayed. He smelled as unpleasant as a room full of zombies.

"Even if you kill me, Cordell, you won't get very far." He began to twist his arms, trying to loosen the bindings around his wrists. "The Circle knows all about your activities here. They will hunt you down and kill you."

"Yeah, right." Cordell snorted. "That sounds a little like *Get Smart* syndrome to me—would you believe a hundred men? No? How about fifty? No? What about two men with a semiautomatic?"

The man was a nut—and who in the hell was *Get Smart?*

"Elizabeth's dead," he continued. "Her fledglings are dead, and the flame imps are all but extinct thanks to your abuse of them. Your empire crumbles around your ears, Cordell."

"My empire has only just begun. And you, my friend, will pay for chopping off two of my fingers and, in the process, help my quest for more power."

"Not a chance on this Earth." Water splashed into his face, rinsing the blood from his eyes. He blinked several times.

"Who said the choice was yours?"

Metal rattled against the ground, then Cordell rolled into his line of vision and stopped. His skin was so pale it almost looked blue. His cheeks were hollow, and his lips cracked and bloody. He looked like he smelled—death on four wheels.

"As you can see, this body of mine wastes away. Your blood will empower my magic and bind one of the flame imps within. Their energy will renew and revitalize me."

It would also kill him, but not soon enough. "How long have you been a vampire, Cordell?" And why was a disease still active within his body? Surely the crossover from life to death should have killed it?

"I became a vampire two years ago. It was Elizabeth who turned me, you know. We were lovers." He grinned, revealing heavily stained teeth. He'd obviously been a heavy smoker in life. And maybe still was in death. "Surprising, huh?"

"Not really." Elizabeth would have sensed the black magic in him and hungered for that power. The looks of the man holding that ability would not have mattered to her.

And in the end, it was her insatiable need for power that had trapped her.

Cordell looked disappointed, as if he'd expected more. Michael frowned. Cordell might be in his forties, but mentally, he was more like a teenager. Maybe that accident had taken a few brain cells along with his ability to walk.

"Why does your body waste away?"

Cordell raised his eyebrows. "And Elizabeth told me your were the brightest of all her fledglings. It is the magic, of course, that wastes me. All magic has its costs, but black magic draws its power from the wielder. Every time you use it, it sucks a little more from your system. I could walk once, you know."

"Even after the car accident?"

"You have done your research, haven't you?" He wheeled

around to the left. Michael twisted, trying to keep him in sight. "The doctors thought I was paraplegic, but a few months after my rehabilitation ended, I began getting feeling back in my legs and toes. They said my brain had 'rewired' itself somehow. It took me nearly a year to regain my strength and walk, you know."

The rope around Michael's left wrist felt a little looser. Though his skin was slick with blood, he kept twisting and pulling. "Then why destroy all that hard work by using black magic?"

Cordell snorted. "After spending so much time in Elizabeth's company, I'm surprised you even have to ask that question."

Elizabeth hungered for power, for control, but Cordell, he suspected, hungered for a hell of a lot more than that. Utter domination and humiliation seemed more his forte.

Cordell reappeared on his left side and picked up a knife lying on a table. Michael tensed and tugged harder on the ropes. Felt them give a little more. Time, he just needed more time.

Cordell didn't turn his way, didn't even look at him. Chanting softly, he rolled toward the fire pit, stopping so close to the edge that the flames licked and danced across his toes. He rolled up his sleeve, revealing a bony arm that was a mass of crisscrossed scars. He drew the knife across his skin, then held out his arm and let the blood drip into the fire. The flames seemed to shiver, then gradually changed color, becoming a bright, unnatural blue. Magic shimmered in the air and burned across Michael's skin.

Time was the one thing he didn't have much of.

There was another knife lying on the table. He gazed at it through slightly narrowed eyes, concentrating. The knife rose and arrowed towards him, the metal blade glinting molten in the fire-warmed darkness. He glanced at his left wrist, angled the knife in the air and began slicing at the rope. Sweat dripped down his forehead, and the madman in his head began a renewed assault on his brain.

His left wrist came free. He grabbed the knife and hacked at the rope holding his right wrist. He sat up and sawed at the rope holding his feet.

Then he heard a curse. Felt magic burn toward him. He didn't turn around, hacking desperately at the ropes. Sweat dripped from his chin, splashing onto the shiny black surface of the rock underneath him. It gleamed like blood. It *would* be his blood if he didn't hurry. The ropes snapped. He threw himself sideways off the rock and crashed to the ground with a grunt of pain.

Lightning split the darkness, forking above his head. He rolled upright, keeping to the cover offered by the rock, and scrambled forward.

Legs appeared. Female legs. He glanced up quickly.

"We are sorry," Ginger said softly and smashed a thick piece of wood down onto his skull.

He blacked out and knew no more.

***

Nikki came to slowly, aware at first of only the numbing coldness creeping through her body. Her head ached, but it was a distant pain, one not her own.

Michael, she thought with suddenly clarity. In trouble and in desperate need of help.

She forced her eyes open. Above her, water leapt and splashed, and spray rose like steam through the darkness. She was lying half in, half out of the water, shivering strongly enough that her teeth were aching. How she'd ended up here she wasn't entirely sure. She couldn't remember anything after the pain had hit and she'd fallen over the edge.

She dragged her legs out of the water then lay there for several minutes, too cold to think let alone move. Every inch of her ached. But at least she'd appeared to have come through the fall relatively unscathed. That in itself had to be a miracle.

The flame imp dove past her, washing warmth across her skin. Color throbbed through the night, red and gold flashes that spoke of urgency. It skimmed past her again. Heat flooded her system, and her clothes began to steam. It was drying her, she realized.

Pain flashed through her brain then was gone. Michael's. Urgency began to beat through her. The knowledge that he was in serious trouble was a weight so heavy it was beginning to suffocate her. She reached out to the link, but again there was nothing but blackness. Silence. Fear rippled through her.

Something had happened to him.

But as much as she wanted to hurry, she also knew it would be disastrous to move before her clothes had dried and she'd thawed out a little. Her only real hope of rescuing Michael might lie in silence, so Cordell wouldn't know she was there. Though that might be hard to achieve, given he was a vampire.

Her fingers and toes began to tingle as warmth flooded back into them. She bit her lip, trying to ignore the pain. Her clothes were still damp, but they no longer dripped and, thanks to the flame imp, were at least warm.

The imp flashed past her again, its color a brighter red. She took the hint and followed it along the stream bank. The water bubbled into the silence, a cheery sound at odds with the air's heaviness.

A chill crept over her—a chill that had nothing to do with any lingering iciness left in her limbs. The smell of evil fouled the night. Cordell was close.

She walked on. The water was beginning to roar again, indicating another waterfall. She hoped this one had a path near it. Another dunking was not something she wanted right now—she was only just beginning to thaw out properly.

The flame imp hesitated, flashing blue-green highlights across an arch through which the stream disappeared. The color of fear, she thought. Cordell had to be just beyond the archway.

"Stay here," she murmured. The imp flashed gold, then darted away into the darkness. She didn't blame it. She'd have done the same thing if she could have.

Back pressed against the damp rocks, she edged around the arch. Beyond it lay a second, smaller cavern. The stream leapt into space again, and a path curved around to her left. In the center of the cavern below, strangely colored flames danced and shimmered, casting blue streaks of light across the darkness. Nearby, Michael lay spread-eagled on a stone table, arms and legs tied. He wasn't moving. Blood pooled near his head, and the left side of what remained of his black shirt seemed horribly shiny—the sort of shine that came from a lot of blood.

Fear swelled thick and fast, and for a moment she couldn't

breathe. She thrust a fist into her mouth to stop her scream, then saw his chest move. One breath—all a vampire really needed. He was alive.

But for how much longer was anyone's guess.

She glanced around quickly for Cordell. He was on the far edge of a circle drawn around a fire pit and Michael, fiddling with something on a table. There was a bloody cloth wrapped around his left hand, but it didn't seem to hamper his movements. His low chant echoed across the darkness, surrounding her with the stink of evil and rising power. Ginger stood next to him, her face remote, lifeless.

Nikki bit her lip, her need to move and help Michael as quickly as she could warring with the need to be careful. Cordell was too dangerous for her to fight him alone—she'd caught him by surprise in the alleyway, but this time he'd know her weapon and be ready for her.

Somehow, she'd have to wake Michael, then free him. Back to the wall, she began to edge down the path.

Michael? She put as much force as could into her call. Deep down in the void, awareness stirred.

She crept a little farther down the path. *Michael? You have to wake up. You have to help me.*

Cordell turned, rolling toward the fire pit. She froze, barely daring to breathe. There was nothing else she could do, nowhere she could go. The nearest rock was several feet away, and she couldn't risk moving. If he looked up, he'd see her for sure.

She clenched her hands, trying to hold back the energy tingling through her body. Even sparks would be dangerous right now. Cordell leaned over the fire pit, throwing a jar into the flames. Dust rose in a cloud, and the flames shivered, turning a deeper blue. Cordell's chanting grew stronger.

She licked her lips. The sense of evil was thick, and her stomach churned at the stench. Magic shimmered across the darkness, a cloud of power she could almost touch. Time was running out. She had to hurry.

Cordell turned back to the table. She scooted quickly down the path, going as fast as she dared, watching Cordell and only half watching the path.

He turned again. She ducked behind the cover of a large boulder, then peered out. He was throwing more muck into the flames. This time they burned a rich purple. His chanting rose another notch, and energy crackled through the night, accompanied by a high keening cry.

A flame imp, she realized. The magic was casting its net. The binding spell couldn't be that far away.

Damn it, Michael, wake up! He knew magic—she didn't. Surely he'd know the best way to stop Cordell.

She tore one of the knives from her jeans and glanced across at him. Energy burned through her and into the knife, and the blade went scooting across the darkness. She kept it low to the ground, only half watching Cordell. When the knife reached the table, she quickly cut the ropes binding Michael's legs and right arm. The other arm she left, not wanting to risk Cordell spotting it before Michael actually woke.

Michael, can you hear me? You have to wake up. You have to help me.

Awareness again stirred, along with pain. Tears stung her eyes, and she blinked them back quickly. What in the hell had Cordell done to him?

Cordell cast something else into the flames. They leapt high, burning almost black. Energy crackled, raising the hairs along her arms and the back of her neck. The keening grew more frantic. Ginger's hands were clenched and tears tracked down her cheeks, glinting silver in the fire's strange light.

An imp was torn from the rocks, its color as purple as the flames, flashing frantic spears of light through the darkness. Fingers of fire leapt upwards, forming a cage around it.

Cordell picked up a knife, holding it high above his head. His chanting reached a crescendo as he moved toward Michael.

Cordell was going kill him, she suddenly realized. Michael's death would be the final step in the binding.

"No!" She jumped to her feet and tore the knife from Cordell's hands, thrusting it away into the darkness. Then she turned her energy toward the fire, scattering the flames as far as she could. The flame imp darted away into the darkness.

"Bitch!" Cordell's voice was high and filled with murderous

fury.

Lightning arced towards her. She dove to the right, hitting the stony ground with bruising force. The rock exploded, the sound almost deafening. Deadly shards of debris sliced through the air, through her skin. She yelped and covered her head with her hands, rolling away.

Magic burned a warning through the night. She glanced up quickly, saw another streak of lightning cutting towards her. Looking around wildly, she saw the boulder to her left. Scant cover, but all she had. She scrambled towards it. The air seemed to howl behind her and heat bubbled across her skin. She screamed and flung herself sideways.

The ground exploded, thrusting her into the air. She twisted as she fell, thrusting energy wildly at Cordell. She hit the ground with a grunt and, for a minute, saw nothing but stars. It hurt to breathe let alone move, but move she had to if she didn't want to be an easy target for the lightning. She thrust up, biting her lip against the scream of pain that tore up her throat, and staggered away.

She searched the cavern for Cordell. He was hovering in midair, legs and arms dangling like a broken puppet. His chair righted itself, then he was turned and set back down. Ginger, she thought, and wondered where the imp was.

Nikki?

Michael's thought was little more than an agonized whisper, but at least he was waking. *I'm here. I think I've stopped Cordell's ceremony for now, but I'm going to need your help to stop him completely.* She couldn't bring herself to say the word kill, even though she knew that was what they'd have to do. She didn't want to think of herself as a murderer, even when it came to ridding the world of someone as vile as Cordell.

He rolled several feet forward then stopped, glaring at her through red-rimmed, glassy eyes. "You will pay for what you have done here tonight. I will taste your soul, and I will make you my slave."

"That's been tried before, and by a vampire stronger than you'll ever be." She clenched her fists against the energy burning across her fingers. Right now, she had to give Michael time to regain consciousness. Had to keep Cordell talking.

There's a knife near your right hand, Michael. Use it to cut the remaining rope. To Cordell, she said. "Why don't you just give it up? Your game here is over."

He smiled, revealing yellow-stained canines. "The game is never over until the clock hits zero."

He flung out his right hand. Energy ripped towards her. She dove away, felt heat cut across her leg, burning deep. She hit the ground with a grunt then scrambled to her feet. Pain surged up her leg, a white-hot ache that churned her stomach. She swallowed against the rising bile, glancing down. The lightning had finished what the wraith had started—sheared off her jeans at the calf, and made a two-inch wide welt bloom around her leg.

Rock scuffed behind her. She spun and saw Ginger approaching, a club held high above her head. She saw the anguish in the other woman's blue eyes and knew Cordell was forcing this action on her. The club arced towards Nikki's head. She wrenched it away kinetically, then knocked Ginger back, thrusting her hard against a wall. She slumped to the ground and didn't move. Nikki turned to face Cordell.

Why in the hell wasn't Michael moving?

I think Cordell has broken my right arm. His thoughts skimmed hers, warm and reassuring but still very distant. Yet his pain throbbed through her, as did the concern he was desperately trying to hide. *I can't grab the knife, Nikki.*

Oh God. Maybe his legs were broken as well. Maybe she'd have to cope with Cordell alone...She tried to remain calm. If they'd combined their powers to beat Jasper, surely they could do the same to destroy Cordell.

But if Michael had any control over his kinetic abilities, wouldn't he have used them to lift the knife and free his arm?

She clenched her fists. She had to concentrate on one problem at a time. Any more would overwhelm her at the moment. *How about your legs?*

They're okay. I'm okay. It's just...my arm.

I'll try to free you.

No...Cordell's too dangerous.

Like she didn't already know that. The vampire in question rolled several feet towards her. She flexed her fingers, watching him warily. His skin was so pale it was almost transparent, giving his face a skeletal look. His lips were bleeding, and blood dribbled unheeded from the side of his mouth. She shivered. Give the man a black cape and a scythe, and he'd look like the Grim Reaper on wheels.

She grabbed the second knife, her knuckles almost white with the force of her grip. Somehow, she had to distract Cordell long enough to cut the remaining rope and free Michael.

Cordell snorted softly. "That little sticker you're holding won't do you much good, you know."

Tension rolled through her. Why wasn't he attacking her? What was he waiting for?

"Maybe it won't. But how well can you perform magic without eyes, huh?" Her stomach churned at the thought, but she battled to keep it from showing. If she revealed one ounce of weakness to Cordell, he would exploit it, of that she had no doubt.

Power began to burn through the night, an unseen force rising like a wind at her back. She bit her lip, wanting to turn around and see what was approaching, and yet she knew that was probably what Cordell wanted. Sweat began to trickle down her face, and her palm felt slick against the knife hilt. Energy burned through her, aching for release. She waited, watching Cordell. Saw the hunger growing in his eyes. Saw his canines beginning to lengthen.

She threw the knife. His eyes widened in shock, and he flung up an arm to protect his face. But she'd never intended to hit him. Instead, she grabbed the knife kinetically, directing it toward Michael, slashing the last rope holding him captive. Still he didn't move. She let the knife clatter to the ground.

Cordell laughed—a low, insane sound. "Not much of a threat with a knife, are you?"

She shrugged. Behind her, the force was growing. The sense of evil was so thick it was almost suffocating. Every breath burned, as if his scent was toxic.

Goose bumps chased a chill across her skin. She battled

the desire to attack Cordell, battled the need to run. She had to protect Michael until he'd fully regained consciousness.

Whether he'd be able to help her once he *was* conscious was another matter entirely—and one she just didn't want to think about right now.

The force behind her became the scream of wind. The sensation of danger tingled across her skin, so sharp it burned. She risked a quick look over her shoulder. Nothing stirred the darkness. Nothing was creeping up on her.

And it was nothing that wrapped cold fingers of air around her body, grabbing her, propelling her forward, toward a waiting Cordell. She planted her feet, trying to stop her movement, but it was useless.

Cordell's eyes were alight with anticipation. Her knees slammed into his, the unseen hands of energy bending her, forcing her face, her neck, toward his. His breath washed over her, a putrid mix of rotten meat and soured milk. She screamed, thrusting her arms between them, desperate to keep him from tasting her.

His teeth sank into her arms. Agony burned white-hot through her soul. Cordell watched her, his gaze mocking as he greedily sucked her blood. Energy rushed through her, exploding from her body, surrounding them both. She pushed him hard, rolling him back. The still wind wrapped around her, holding her close. She couldn't escape him.

A wave of dizziness washed through her. For a minute, she saw stars, dancing red through the night. She blinked and realized they were flame imps, swirling frantically near the waterfall.

She didn't understand why the imps wanted her near the waterfall, but she had no option but to trust them. Cordell was sucking her dry. If she didn't do something now she'd die. *But I can't die, can I...?*

She had no time to worry about that now. Besides, she'd be better off dead than Cordell's slave.

She flooded the night with energy, forcing Cordell backwards. The water's music flowed around them, overpowering the howl of the unseen force holding her close to him.

Cordell's grip on her arm suddenly loosened. Realization and fear ran through his gaze, but it was too late for him to do anything about it. Still locked together, they flew into the water and plunged deep into the icy depths.

***

Nikki's terror plunged through Michael's soul, shaking the last vestiges of unconsciousness from his mind. He jerked upright, only to have pain shoot through his brain—a white-hot agony that almost sent him back to the darkness.

Teeth gritted and his breath little more than a hiss, he turned, his gaze searching the cavern for her. There was no sign of her. No sign of Cordell. The flames no longer burned in the fire pit, but the darkness was heavy with the stench of magic.

He reached for the link. Her terror clubbed him, filling his mind with a rush of tangled, undecipherable thoughts.

He swung his legs off the table. Her thoughts were close— she had to be here somewhere. *Nikki? Where are you?*

He waited tensely for an answer, but nothing came. The link was a void washed with her horror and growing panic. *Damn it, woman, answer me!*

Still no response. He slipped off the table, but his legs refused to hold his weight and he fell to his knees. Cursing the weakness, urgency beating through his soul, he gripped the table with his good arm and forced himself upright again. Forced his legs to hold.

Moisture trickled down his face. He thrust at it impatiently, knowing by the smell it was blood. The gash on his head was a good three inches long and probably would have been dangerous had he been anything other than a vampire.

He expanded his senses, searching the night again. Pain beat though his head, an agony he had no choice but to ignore. The colors churning through the void were becoming more frantic. Wherever Nikki was, she needed his help fast.

There was no one in the cavern—not Nikki nor Cordell. He cursed, thrusting a hand through his blood-matted hair. This didn't make sense. She *was* here somewhere, regardless of what his senses were saying—her thoughts were too close, too strong, for her to be anywhere else.

Flame imps darted across the waterfall's pond, their color flashing red and gold. *Oh God, no...* Gut twisting, he hobbled forward. The imps' light washed red across the churning surface of the water, making it look slick with blood. Magic stung the night, and the air seemed to howl.

The churning in the water grew more agitated. Suddenly, Cordell's limp body surged free, shooting past Michael to land like a wet sack of rags near the fire pit. He didn't move, but he wasn't dead. Michael could still hear the tremulous beat of his heart.

Time to kill the fiend. He took a step toward Cordell, then stopped. Nikki hadn't surfaced, and the churning water had calmed.

He cursed and jumped into the pond. The water was icy, its touch numbing, snatching away the pain of moving his shattered limb.

It wasn't just the imp's light making the water look red. There *was* blood, and lots of it. Fear slammed through him. He reached for the link, but was met by silence. Her terror was gone, replaced by an odd sort of peace.

It was the same sort peace that he'd felt in her once before when the specter of death had almost claimed her life in the mine collapse Jasper had arranged.

She can't be dead. Surely he would know. She was part of his heart, part of his soul. All that mattered to him. Surely he would know if she had died.

He kicked his feet, twisting around, diving one-handed to the depths. The pond was deeper than it looked, the water as dark as hell itself. She could be anywhere. He didn't care. He'd search for an eternity if that's what it took to find her.

His hand brushed against cotton, then skin. He grabbed her hand, kicking upwards, dragging her back to the surface with him.

Cordell hadn't moved. Michael kicked toward the edge until he could stand and dragged Nikki out of the water, thrusting her onto her side. She coughed, water spewing from her mouth. He dropped beside her and touched her neck. Her skin was like ice, and she was shivering so hard that her teeth were clashing together violently. Her pulse was fragile and weak, but at least she was alive. The weight lifted from his chest, letting him breathe again.

Then he saw the slash in her sweater, the raw welts on her skin. Cordell had tasted her, fed off her. Fury washed through him. For that alone, the bastard would die.

He rose and hobbled towards Cordell. The fiend moved. Lightning split the night, arcing towards him. Michael dove away, landing with a grunt on his left side, jarring his broken arm. A sea of red swam before his eyes, and a scream tore up his throat. He gritted his teeth, and the scream became a hiss of pain. Sweat rolled down his forehead, stinging his eyes. He blinked it away and, supporting his right arm with his left, rolled back to his feet.

Cordell had propped himself up against a rock. His breathing was labored, his face little more than flesh stretched over a death mask. The magic was sapping his strength, taking him beyond the restorative powers of his vampire heritage. Maybe it was only the flame imps' energy that had kept him alive this long.

"You cannot defeat me, vampire. My magic will outlast your strength. When you collapse, I will feed off you. Then I will use the blood of your woman to complete my ceremony."

"I will see you in hell first, Cordell." He walked towards him, watching the fiend's eyes, waiting for the next attack. The more Cordell used his magic, the weaker he became. All *he* had to do was stay out of the path of the lightning and wait for Cordell's collapse.

Lightning split the air, weaker than before. Michael dodged, felt the sizzle of energy burn past his ear.

Cordell raised his hands. "Any farther, and I blast your girlfriend."

Michael clenched his fists but didn't stop. Cordell's last blast had been weak and wouldn't have held the strength to even reach Nikki, let alone hurt her. The man was bluffing.

Cordell's eyes widened in fear, but he wasn't staring at Michael but past him.

"Stop."

The voice was Nikki's and yet not. He stopped and turned. She stood near the waterfall, her skin glowing with heat, eyes afire. Two flame imps rotated above her head, their color a deep, dark red. The color of anger, he thought.

She looked ethereal, otherworldly. This wasn't his Nikki. The flame imps had taken over her body, using her now as they had used her once before. Quelling his fear, knowing there was little he could do anyway, he reached for the link. An inferno greeted him, but deeper than the flames he felt peace. Nikki wasn't afraid of the imps or their intentions.

He wasn't so certain of them. But they hadn't hurt her the first time, and he just had to hope they wouldn't hurt her now.

"Step away from him," she continued, her gaze not wavering from Cordell. "Move to the table. Use it as cover." Though her voice was flat, her amber eyes glowed with heat. Flames danced across her finger—real flames, not just the sparks of kinetic energy.

He stepped back to the cloth-covered table. Cordell made a strange sound in his throat and raised his hands. Lightning cut through the night, but its force was weak, fading long before it reached Nikki.

She didn't react. "In memory of those of who will no longer dance under the orb of life, we sentence you to death. In memory of the two legs that you have used, we sentence you to death. You will burn in the heat you seek to empty us of, and we will scatter your ashes on the wind so that you will never know peace."

Cordell whimpered and pushed away from the rock, dragging his half-dead body across the ground in a useless attempt to escape.

Nikki raised her hands. Fire leapt between her palms, pulsing brightly as it found form and became an orb that flamed as bright as the sun.

Michael threw up a hand to protect his face from the glare, but the growing ball raced heat across his flesh. Her words hit him—the heat of the sun was one of two things that could kill a vampire, and that was what the imps were attempting to create here now.

He ducked under the table and hoped the tablecloth was thick enough to protect him. Heat burned through the air, and Cordell screamed, a high-pitched sound of agony that quickly died. Flames crackled, and the smell of burning flesh rent the air.

The heat died. Michael climbed out from under the table. Cordell was little more than a patch of black soot. Even as he watched, a wind stirred his remains, spiraling them toward the roof and out of sight.

Nikki was still standing near the water, but her arms were by her sides, and the fire seemed to have left her flesh. Even the imps rotating above her head looked gray and lifeless. He hurried towards her.

She looked at him. Fire crackled through her amber gaze, but its touch was distant. "We thank you both for your help. You have released those who were bound, and now we are free to continue our dance. For that we rejoice. Tell this one good-bye. Tell her our flames will forever be a part of her."

The spark in her eyes died, and Nikki collapsed.

Twenty-three

Nikki woke slowly, but was aware almost instantly that things had changed—and changed for the better. She felt safe and warm, and the stink of evil no longer filled the air. In its place were the rich scents of coffee and cinnamon toast. Her stomach rumbled hungrily. She stirred and opened her eyes. Silk whispered against her skin, running down her arm.

Pajamas, she thought in surprise, then felt her legs. Pajama top, she amended with a grin. She flicked the sheet away from her face and looked around. What she expected was the luxurious surroundings of their room at the resort. What she discovered instead was the homey warmth of rough-hewn log walls and, to her right, French windows that opened out onto a balcony and a view filled with cottonwoods and pines. She raised her eyebrows in surprise. Where in the hell was she?

"In my home," Michael said from the doorway. He walked towards her, awkwardly balancing a tray in his left hand. His right arm was splinted and supported in a sling.

"Is your arm okay?" She grabbed the tray from him and placed it on the small table near the bed. "Are you okay?"

"I'm fine. Another day or so, and my arm will be fully healed and out of this damn cast." He sat down on the bed, his gaze searching hers. His hair was dishevelled, and there were dark circles under his eyes. He looked as if he hadn't slept in a week. "How are you?"

"Actually, I'm feeling a whole lot better than I should, considering what happened." Not that she was entirely sure what *had* happened once she'd tipped Cordell into the water, but she had a feeling both she and Michael had been lucky to escape with their lives. "How did I get here? What happened to Cordell? And what happened to the flame imps?"

"Cordell is dead. Burned to hell and beyond by the imps' flames."

She raised her eyebrows. "How? I was under the impression they couldn't defend themselves."

"They can't unless they have someone to focus their energy

through. You were that focus, Nikki."

"I can't remember it happening." She frowned, glancing at her hand. Warmth tingled across her fingers, a fire similar to and yet different from the heat raised by her kinetic energy. Perhaps the energy of the flame imps still lingered in her body.

"You wouldn't remember. You were unconscious." He caught her hand, entwining his fingers in hers. His touch was gentle, almost hesitant. If he felt the heat in her flesh, he made no mention of it. "You've been unconscious for nearly a week."

She stared at him in disbelief. "No. I couldn't have been."

"For a while, I was worried you might not wake at all."

Lord, no wonder there were such deep shadows under his eyes. She touched his cheek, ran her fingers down to his lips. "I'm sorry."

He pressed a kiss across her fingertips, then leaned forward and repeated the process with her lips. Longing shivered through her. Eternity could come and go, and still she would yearn for this man's touch.

"What about Rodeman?" she asked, after a while. "And Ginger?"

"Rodeman was taken to the hospital and, as far as I know, is still under observation. Ginger's body was found down in the caverns." He hesitated. "Her real name was Mary Gordon. She'd been dead for nearly eight months."

"Ginger basically told me as much." The person she felt sorry for was Rodeman—how would he cope with the knowledge that he'd loved and married a dead woman?

"He won't know. The police are putting her advanced state of decay down to the humidity and dampness in the caverns."

It some ways, it made better sense than the fact that an energy creature had inhabited Mary's body for eight months, keeping it alive. "What about that charity Cordell set up? Have you tracked down the money?"

"No need." He smiled. "Seline has had new directors installed, and they are currently going through the books and cleaning up Cordell's mess. The charity will be run properly from now on."

Obviously, this Seline was one powerful woman. Nikki

raised her eyebrows. "I thought Cordell had shifted all the money? Wasn't that the reason why he'd kidnapped Matthew?"

"It looks like Elizabeth took Matthew's mind before he could help Cordell with the transfers."

She remembered the feel of the teenager's mind, the emptiness of it, and shivered. She still had to face Matthew's mother and tell her he was dead. Still had to face MacEwan and tell him his niece was definitely a vampire. Neither was a task she particularly looked forward to.

Michael gently squeezed her fingers. "Seline's still working with Rachel. Even with the imp gone from her body, she shows a remarkable degree of control over her fledgling instincts. Seline's beginning to think that you were right—that she can be helped."

At least that was something—some hope she could hold out to MacEwan and his sister. "What about the other abductees? What happened to them?"

"When Cordell died, it seems whatever spell he placed on them dissolved. From the reports filtering in, most have no memory of events from the time they were kidnapped."

"He was controlling them?"

Michael nodded. "Through magic. They were basically on auto-control, making the motions of life but not experiencing any of it."

"Weird." She hesitated, looking down at their entwined fingers. "What now?"

"Now," he said, reaching for a mug of coffee and placing it in her hands. "You eat breakfast and regain your strength."

That wasn't what she meant, and he knew it. She wrapped her fingers around the mug, pressing the heat into her suddenly sweaty palms. "I meant about us."

"I know."

He met her gaze, and she almost drowned in the depths of love and understanding she saw there.

"If I've learned one thing in the last few days, it's that I definitely need you—want you—in my life. Whatever the risks to us both." He touched her face, his thumb trailing heat down her cheek then across her lips. "But I can't have you working with me, Nikki. That's one risk I won't take."

She smiled. Not the exact words she'd wanted to hear, perhaps, but close enough. He'd warned her not long ago that he couldn't change a lifetime's habits in just six months. Yet in a matter of days, he had gone from being determined to hold her at arm's length to admitting that he needed—wanted—her in his life. For now, that was enough.

Besides, eternity was on her side. She had time enough to change his mind.

She put her coffee cup back on the tray, then wrapped her arms around his neck. "Just how disabled are you with that arm?"

A grin twitched his lips. The link swirled to life, his thoughts caressing, filled with awakening fire. "Is that your way of saying you understand?"

"No. That's my way of saying I love you despite your pigheadedness."

Though a smile still touched his lips, his eyes were serious. "You won't change my mind, Nikki."

"I've heard you say that before."

"I mean it this time."

She raised her eyebrows. "You meant it last time, didn't you?"

"Yes." He stared at her for several seconds. "I just have one more question."

The sudden twinkle in his eyes made her cautious. "What?"

He ran a finger down her pajama top and slowly circled her nipple. "Who in the hell is *Get Smart*?"

"Not who, but what. It's a very funny old TV show. Why?"

He shrugged. His fingers were still circling, still teasing. "Nothing important. Just something Cordell said."

Ripples of pleasure were running through her. "You don't get much TV up here, do you?" she said, more than a little breathlessly.

"I don't get any. I haven't a TV."

"Then what do you do to pass the time?"

"Oh, this and that. Read. Watch the sunsets. Tend to the garden, make wine-"

It sounded idyllic. She grabbed his shirt and dragged him close. "Will you just shut up and kiss me?"

He grinned and proceeded to do just that.

And proved just how very capable a one-armed man could be.

But as she lay in his embrace in the warm aftermath of their lovemaking, she knew with certainly that the contentment she felt now would not last for long.

Trouble waited just around the corner.

For them, and for Jake.

Don't Miss the Next Chapter in
Nikki's and Michael's Story

CHASING THE SHADOWS
ISBN 1-893896-84-6

Four wealthy women kidnapped.
Three ransoms demanded and paid.
Two bodies returned, mutilated and drained of blood.
One man determined to avenge the wrongs of his past.

Nikki James is in San Francisco at the request of her partner and best friend, Jake. The wife of Jake's old friend is missing, and Jake intends to find her—whatever the cost. While the authorities believe the kidnapping's are the work of a sick mind, Nikki knows it's something much worse. Vampires. Six of them. And they know who she is, and why she's there.

Michael Kelly has just returned from a vampire-hunting expedition in his homeland and wants to spend some much needed relaxation time with Nikki. But when he discovers she's gone to San Francisco to pursue the vampire gang currently terrorizing the city, he has no choice but to follow. Not only to keep her safe from the gang, but because he fears the psychic talents she's beginning to develop. Abilities she should not have and cannot control.

The chase takes them through the sewers and tunnels of San Francisco. As the body count begins to rise, so, too, does the danger. Michael isn't the only one aware of Nikki's new abilities, and she becomes a target. But Nikki has no intention of obeying Michael's demands that she leave. She's tired of playing it safe and wants him to realize it's all or nothing. She's either a full partner in his life, or she's out.

But nothing prepares her for the price she has to pay for her stubbornness—the life of someone she loves.

Available Now

Don't Miss
Keri Arthur's
Acclaimed
"Damask Circle"
Series

Circle of Fire

ISBN: 1-893896-70-6

Circle of Death

ISBN: 1-893896-77-3

Circle of Desire

ISBN: 1-893896-92-7
(Coming in July 2003)

All Damask Circle books are
stand-alone romances and don't
need to be read in any specific order.

Available from
ImaJinn Books
www.imajinnbooks.com
or call toll free
877-625-3592

Don't Miss
Keri Arthur's
Acclaimed

BENEATH A RISING MOON
ISBN 1-893896-38-2

On the werewolf reservation of Ripple Creek, a killer is on the loose. Three women are dead, their bodies mutilated and faces slashed. A fourth, Neva Grant's twin, lies in the hospital, fighting for her life.

Psychically linked, Neva shared the horror of her twin attack and makes a silent vow by her sister's hospital bed. She'll hunt down the killer, if Savannah finds the strength to live.

The Rangers believe the killer is a member of the Sinclair pack, but Neva knows the Sinclairs will never talk to an outsider. To begin the hunt, she first has to seduce a Sinclair—and then she has to keep him interested long enough to find the killer. The only Sinclair not under suspicion is a wolf with a hard drinking, hard loving reputation. But has she got what it takes to attract a man with such experience? Neva doesn't know, but for her sister's sake, she has to try.

Duncan Sinclair has been called back home to find a killer, and he wants nothing more than to complete his task and get out of the town for which he has no love. Then he's approached by a wolf who obviously has more than seduction on her mind, and he finds himself ensnared in a growing web of desire and deceit.

As the murders continue and the killer's shadow draws ever closer, Duncan and Neva find themselves having to trust each other in order to survive. But can they trust the emotions flaring between them? Or will the lies of the present, the deeds of the past, and a killer's bloody intentions tear them apart?

Available Now

Printed in the United States
218956BV00004B/6/A